A JOSIE CORSINO MYSTERY

unnatural murder

A JOSIE CORSINO MYSTERY

unnatural murder

CONNIE DIAL

THE PERMANENT PRESS
Sag Harbor, NY 11963

For information, address:
    The Permanent Press
    4170 Noyac Road
    Sag Harbor, NY 11963
    www.thepermanentpress.com

Library of Congress Cataloging-in-Publication Data

Dial, Connie—
    Unnatural Murder : a Josie Corsino Mystery / Connie Dial.
        pages cm
    ISBN 978-1-57962-369-2
        1. Policewomen—Fiction. 2. Murder—Investigation—Fiction.
    3. Police—California—Los Angeles—Fiction. 4. Mystery fiction.
    I. Title.

PS3604.I126U56 2014
813'.6—dc23   2014023888

Printed in the United States of America.

To Michael and Mary Milazzo

ONE

The priest entered through the side door of St. Margaret Mary's church and stood in an alcove in front of the statue of the Virgin mother. This was his ritual before hearing confessions. The glow of a dozen votive candles at our Lady's feet cast a warm light onto her face. She was his perfect woman—a full sensuous face, gentle blue eyes, lovely mouth—the only woman who ever listened and understood him. Kneeling, he adjusted his uncomfortable cassock, said a quick prayer and was ready to face another Saturday night in hell.

When he realized the church pews were empty, he felt a sense of relief. This parish on the east end of Santa Monica Boulevard in Hollywood didn't have a real congregation. It was an erratic assembly of street boys, prostitutes, transients, and those immigrant families who were open-minded and poor enough to pray here.

This wasn't the life he'd anticipated when he found his vocation, but the church had abandoned him, and he would make the best of it even though dealing with the sordid details of these imperfect lives had begun to erode his mind and soul.

He started to snuff candles on the main altar when he noticed light coming from under the curtain in one of the confessionals. There was a moment of indecision when he wanted to walk away, pretend he hadn't noticed, and spend the next few hours at the rectory chapel in solitary prayer and meditation, but knew he couldn't do that. Instead, he would listen to more empty promises, give absolution and a meaningless penance while anticipating the sinner's willing decline into a life of decadence. The worst part was hearing the litany of sins every Saturday night, unimaginable desecrations of the human body that lately infected his dreams like a cancer.

Even the slightest noise echoed throughout the empty church, and he heard impatient coughing from behind the curtain. It sounded like a child's voice and it was late, so he hurried into the middle compartment and in the dark, slid open the small door as he made the sign of the cross. He was expecting to see one of the immigrant children, but in the dim light, he could make out the image of a large woman.

"Forgive me Father for I have sinned," she began in almost a whisper.

"I can barely hear you," he said impatiently. "You'll have to speak up."

"These are my sins," she said, slightly louder.

He leaned closer to the screened window, but could barely see the shadow sitting in the darkened confessional. Her voice seemed affected, a whispery imitation of Marilyn Monroe, he thought. It only took a few seconds to understand why.

"I was born a man but God made a mistake. I'm a woman in every way."

"God doesn't make mistakes," the priest said, coldly.

The man went on to explain his feelings, his impulses, describe his failed experiments and encounters living as a male knowing he was a woman. The priest folded his hands, resting them on the narrow ledge under the window and repeatedly tapped his forehead against his knuckles. His mind felt as if it would explode as the man rambled on about his fears, powerful evil men, something he had to do that was wrong but right too. He listened but stopped trying to make any sense of the words.

"Unless you reject this . . . sinful unnatural life . . . I cannot give you absolution," the priest said, interrupting him, stuttering in a nervous high pitched whisper he knew was too loud and impatient for the confessional, but he couldn't bear it any longer.

"Haven't you heard what I've said? What's the use . . . it's too late, anyway," the shadow said in a surprisingly deeper voice, then got up, pushed aside the curtain and was gone.

The priest could hear the sound of heels clicking on the tile floor; the heavy front door creaked open and closed . . . then silence. He had heard every word and sat there in the dark unable to move, knowing he'd given pain instead of comfort and understanding. After a few seconds, guilt overcame disgust, and he hurried from the church onto the street not knowing what he intended to do or to say if he found the man again.

Santa Monica Boulevard was as crowded as every other Saturday on a hot summer night, but the priest could see a big woman moving quickly, awkwardly on the sidewalk past gatherings of rowdy young men. He couldn't be certain that was his penitent but continued following until the woman stopped suddenly and went back where a group of neighborhood boys had mocked and teased her with sexual taunts. Thinking it was all pointless now, the priest turned and slowly walked back toward the church.

It was only a few short blocks to the church, but the wail of an approaching police siren caused him to glance over his shoulder as he climbed the steps of St. Marga-ret Mary's. A crowd had gathered where he'd last seen the woman. He hesitated, not wanting to go back, but was drawn to the commotion. By the time he reached the grow-ing crowd, several uniformed police officers were arriving, leaving skewed black-and-white cruisers abandoned on the street, sirens blaring in the background, red and blue emergency lights flashing, giving the moment a fractured otherworldly appearance.

Officers shoved everyone behind flimsy barriers of yellow police tape, but the priest pressed close enough to see a body sprawled on the sidewalk. He knew instantly this was the man who had wanted his absolution.

The victim was wearing high-heeled boots, a short skirt and tight blouse, the front saturated with so much blood. His wig had fallen off and lay on the ground near his clownish face—bright red lipstick smeared around his gaping mouth created a grotesque frown; black mascara tears tattooed his cheeks.

The priest turned away. Satan was mocking him again.

TWO

There wasn't a police officer in Los Angeles who worked the streets of Hollywood without losing innocence. All sections of this sprawling city had deviant elements but Hollywood was a magnet for the abnormal. Captain Josie Corsino had become an expert in recognizing the signs of overexposure and knew when it was time to pull out the transfer papers sending a young patrolman or woman back to the world of ordinary crime.

Older cops, like her homicide supervisor Detective · Red Behan, weren't affected by the external weirdness of this division but then he had his own problems.

She parked half a block away on Santa Monica Boulevard and walked to the inner perimeter of the homicide crime scene. This was the seedier part of Hollywood without the sparkling pink granite stars or celebrity impersonators. No tourists or paparazzi came here looking for the rich and famous. These sidewalks were broken concrete with weeds sprouting from endless cracks. The homeless runaways and addicts camped behind dumpsters and in vacant buildings leaving doorways and alleys reeking of human waste.

Shirtless young men and glassy-eyed girls sat on retaining walls and steps along the street, watching as Josie lifted the yellow tape and ducked under it. This was their world in the muggy early summer hours before dawn. They drank, used drugs, bought and sold sex until the sun came up and, then like vampires, disappeared again until night-fall leaving a trail of used condoms and bloody syringes.

The uniformed officers greeted her with the familiar "morning Cap' or morning boss." They were accustomed to seeing Captain Corsino in the middle of the night. No one noticed, or at least didn't comment on the fact she was still wearing the clothes she had on when she left the station late yesterday. Hollywood was a busy area. This was their third homicide in less than four weeks and the sweltering summer heat had just begun. They all knew it would most likely get worse, especially in this neighbor-hood where the high temperatures and cramped living spaces brought people outside to drink and fight over what little they had.

It wasn't standard practice to shut down any street, especially a major state thoroughfare, for a homicide that didn't have the body sprawled on asphalt between the curbs, but Red Behan never did anything without a good reason. All the police cars had been moved and were legally parked now, but she knew later this morning, even the light Sunday morning traffic would back up the rest of Hollywood's east/west streets as locals and tourists attempted to avoid driving through this area. She stopped worrying when she noticed a West Bureau traffic unit parked on the corner. Behan had remembered to notify them—a reassuring sign.

She found him talking to the coroner's investigator and his assistant while directing uniformed officers and the other detectives. Most of them, like her, believed he was the best homicide cop in the city, but she wondered how long it would be before she'd be forced to terminate his career. Josie's bureau commander had been badgering her to convince the tall redhead to retire. It wasn't a secret throughout the police department that her star detec-tive was an alcoholic. How could it be when in less than three years she'd ordered him into two different detox programs? But, drunk or sober, he was her friend, and she understood retirement would devastate him. His pension had to be divided among his five ex-wives not even leaving enough cash to buy cheap beer. His current wife, Victoria, was a very rich, much older woman who adored him, but Josie worried that might change when a high maintenance guy like Red was home all the time.

"Ma'am, can I sign you in?" a tiny voice said from behind her.

Josie turned to see a female uniformed officer, five feet and maybe ninety pounds, holding a clipboard. Josie was nearly six feet tall and never understood how any woman that small could feel confident doing this very physical job.

She signed her name and serial number. "Don't think I know you . . . Officer Hoffman . . . probationer?" Josie asked, looking at the woman's name tag.

"Yes ma'am."

"Be careful out there," Josie said, walking away and making a mental note to be certain the woman's training officer was big and nasty enough for both of them, at least until she learned to survive on her guile and wits.

Josie stood on the curb within a few feet of the body. In the early morning light, she thought under all that Halloween makeup the victim might've had an interesting face, actually better looking than Officer Hoffman, until she got close enough to see the gray stubble and dark lines under his eyes and layers of mascara. Even from a distance, despite the fact he was dressed in women's clothes, his thick wrists, slim hips and barbershop haircut were a giveaway.

"Got any ID yet?" she asked Behan, who was sitting on the steps of an apartment building now and searching inside the victim's small beaded handbag.

"Detective Martin has confirmed our victim was definitely not a woman," Behan said, grinning.

"Just looking at him should've done that," Josie said, and wasn't certain she wanted to hear the rest of this story. Ann Martin was a fairly new detective supervisor working on Behan's homicide table. She wasn't his first choice and although he never complained, Josie had heard from nearly everyone else in the station that they were not a perfectly matched pair . . . not even remotely close.

"She insisted on verifying, wouldn't call him a man until she knew he had a dick."

"And the coroner let her do that?" Josie asked.

"Yeah, he called it finding Wanda's Waldo. Took her a while to figure out where the deceased had tucked it . . . apparently Detective Martin hasn't spent much time in Hollywood's magical kingdom."

"Give her a break, Red. She's trying. Who's the dead guy?"

"Patrick Kessler, on special occasions Patricia," he said, showing Josie a driver's license. "High-end drag queen as far as I can tell . . . no life-altering surgeries, maybe started hormone therapy, but won't know if he's a wannabe transgender 'til the post. One of my guys will check with the director at the Gay and Lesbian Center to see if they know anything about him."

"Isn't Marge Bailey here?" Josie asked. Her vice lieutenant always worked late on Saturday.

"She was . . . took a look but didn't recognize him, went back to check her computer files."

"Witnesses?" Josie asked, checking out the few street people who were still hanging around behind the tape at dawn.

"A city block full, all deaf, blind and dumb . . . didn't see or hear anything. We're door-knocking all the apartments in this dump," he said, indicating the Regency Arms hotel behind them, and added, "and everything for at least half a block. He walked from that church to this spot right before he was killed."

"I wouldn't count on anybody volunteering much in this neighborhood."

"We've transported a dozen locals back to the station, but so far we've got nothing. That priest over there thinks he talked to the victim just before the stabbing," Behan said, pointing at a tall, emaciated, middle-aged man with thinning blond hair, blue eyes, and thick wire-rimmed glasses. He was wearing a black cassock that appeared to be much too heavy for hot weather and two sizes too small with a frayed clerical collar, and was standing inside the yellow tape, staring at his feet as if there were something wrong with them.

"He doesn't know whether or not he spoke to Kessler?" she asked.

Behan got up, stretched and moved closer to her. His eyes were bloodshot but she couldn't detect any odor of alcohol, yet.

"Took his confession . . . says it was too dark to see his face. Priest's name's O'Reilly . . . claims he followed our victim outside but didn't see anything . . . I think I scared him. Maybe he'll talk to you."

Josie shrugged and thought the priest seemed a little odd and at the moment very nervous. She didn't mind trying. Sometimes her rank made skittish people trust her and they'd say things they wouldn't say to a detective, especially one as cantankerous as Red. She walked over, tapped him on the shoulder to get his attention, startling him.

"Sorry Father, I'm Captain Corsino, commanding officer at Hollywood police station," she said and was surprised how frightened he seemed. His hand was trembling and clammy when he shook hers. Up close she could smell his nervous sweat and see old scarring on his face. She recognized the aftermath of childhood acne, a severe case that had left his skin raw and badly pitted. She'd gone to Catholic schools and remembered the nuns and priests as mostly opinionated and arrogant bullies. Father O'Reilly did not fit her stereotype.

"Is there anything you can tell us, Father, that might help unravel this terrible mess?"

"No . . . I told the other policeman . . . I don't know him. I don't know anything," he whined.

"What made you go after him?" she asked.

"I, I couldn't . . . the church doesn't . . . he was troubled. I thought I could help, but . . . I, I didn't see anything." He was stammering, wouldn't look directly at her and blushed like a teenage girl, which made his skin condition look even worse.

"Can you remember anything he might've said? Was he afraid of someone? Did he tell you anything that might help?"

"I can't talk to you about his confession. I can't do that."

If she kept questioning him, Josie worried he was going to cry or throw up or both. He might settle down in a day or two and Behan could try again. She thanked him, gave him her business card and went back to where the coroner was lifting the dead body onto the gurney. The victim was a big man but, unlike most transvestites or cross-dressers, had delicate features under all the makeup. But she guessed that at two A.M. in a dark bar, even after a lot of heavy drinking, he still wouldn't pass as a woman. She'd heard stories from an older policewoman who had worked in the Van Nuys women's jail during the early seventies about a gorgeous Mexican transvestite who'd been booked as a woman. The female officer who'd strip searched him never realized he was a man. The arrestee finally got nervous about the consequences of being unveiled and confessed, causing the officer who searched him considerable embarrassment for the remainder of her career. Josie knew there were men who could pass as women even without hormone treatments, but she'd never seen a Santa Monica

Boulevard transvestite that anyone would mistake for a genuine woman.

Although she was certain Behan would work this case as if Kessler were the most important person in Hollywood, history told her a satisfactory outcome was doubtful for victims who lived in this shadowy underworld. His demise would most likely go unnoticed in Los Angeles's expansive, disconnected city, and barely mourned, especially among his fellow street dwellers who accepted untimely death as the cost and probable outcome of their lifestyle. It was difficult enough telling a family their loved one had been murdered, but shame usually surpassed grief in this sort of circumstance.

Detective Martin was talking to the coroner's assistant and taking notes but stopped and hurried to catch up to Josie as she headed toward her car.

"Ma'am, have you got a minute? Can I talk to you?" Martin asked, matching her stride.

Josie stopped. She'd heard that request at least a dozen times a day, every day since she'd been promoted to captain. It was never just a minute, but not listening wasn't an option. Everything that took place in Hollywood division was her responsibility. She knew when officers stopped talking to her bad things could happen. Ignorance was always dangerous, but somehow she knew that if past experience were any indicator, whatever Detective Martin wanted would be important only to Detective Martin.

"Morning Ann," Josie said. "Need something?"

Martin was a head shorter than her, a lean, serious woman. She wore her long curly hair tied back in a ponytail and always dressed in bland nondescript pantsuits like a nun on weekend pass from the convent.

"I just wanted to thank you again for giving me this opportunity," Martin said, slipping her glasses on top of her head.

"You've worked hard; you earned it."

"I know Red wanted someone else, but I promise I won't let you down."

"Just do your job; that's all I ask."

"Yes Ma'am," she said. "I am trying."

As she watched Martin return to the coroner's van, Josie hoped she hadn't made a huge mistake. Martin was by all accounts a good detective, but she was becoming a distraction. Josie had pushed for her promotion because Red always resisted having a female supervisor on his table. He wanted the guys around him he knew and had worked with, but this time Martin was far more qualified than anyone else who'd applied for the position. But then Ann Martin's skills were never an issue. It was always her grating personality. She saw sexism everywhere and thought every rebuke or criticism had to be because she was a woman.

Josie knew Red Behan wasn't a sexist. Years ago, he'd been her supervisor in narcotics when she was a new detective. He was an equal opportunity grouch, set in his ways, who'd give you a hard time if he thought you weren't doing your share of the workload or did it badly, but hand you the keys to his house if you needed a place to stay. Josie worried that in trying to do the right thing she might've miscalculated this time and forced totally incompatible personalities to work together, which usually meant a lot of extra work and headaches for her.

BY THE time she got to Hollywood station it was nearly noon. She was starving and stopped to pick up donuts and coffee at Starbucks and finished a cream-filled éclair before getting out of the car. There were melted smears of chocolate on her Levi's and the car seat but it was Sunday and her admin staff wouldn't be working today, so she cleaned off the seat and didn't worry about the Levi's. A few uniformed officers were in the admin office using the computers for reports, but they didn't care how she looked on what should've been her day off, and any chance of citizens seeing her, or department staff officers coming in on Sunday, was minimal.

She deposited the rest of the sugary heart-attack pastry by the coffee machine in the watch commander's office knowing she was one of the few people in the station, among these young health-conscious cops, who would eat them. Her metabolism allowed her to eat anything, as much as she wanted and never gain weight on her tall, bony frame. It was a gene she'd inherited from her tall skinny Italian father. Her bad-tempered Irish mother had certainly given her the excessive-wine-drinking gene.

The secretary wouldn't be working on the weekend, but the door to Josie's office was open so she guessed the watch commander had needed someplace quiet and private to write rating reports or he had raided her file cabinet again looking for candy bars or jelly beans and forgot to close the door. She never locked it anyway. Cops were too resourceful and nosy. They'd find a way to get in if they were curious about a new special order or policy change from the chief, or wanted the snacks she'd stashed mostly for their benefit.

The desk was clean, but that wasn't a surprise either. For the last year the office had run smoothly because her secretary Maki was that rare civilian creature in the police department bureaucracy who possessed top-notch skills and relished hard work. She was a computer geek, had a BA in English from the state university in LA, and was happy being a secretary. Josie took full advantage of her talents using her as both an adjutant and secretary and assigning a clerk typist or two to help with the workload.

The officers liked Maki because she was young and perky and her brother was an LAPD cop in another division. Josie suspected that the male-dominated police department with a ready supply of young eager dating partners had contributed greatly to her secretary's job satisfaction.

Four hours sleep had definitely not been enough. Josie's eyelids felt heavy and she worried she couldn't make the drive home to Pasadena without resting a few minutes. She shut the door to her office and dropped onto the couch. She leaned her head back, closed her eyes and stretched out her long legs on the coffee table.

Her mind needed a few minutes to reset before going home and this couch had become a favorite place to sleep. It was a necessity when callouts and late night investigations made it impossible to get to a real bed, but since her husband had moved out of their house and pretty much out of her life, sleeping on the couch or in bed at home didn't seem to make any difference. Jake left complaining he wanted a real wife, not someone who'd drop in when it was convenient. They'd been married almost twenty-five years, as long as she'd been a cop, but sometimes she thought the argument about spending too many hours at the police station was longer and more intense than their marriage. She sat up and opened her eyes. Even when she tried to nap, he invaded her thoughts and made her feel guilty about doing the job she loved.

There was a light knock and the door opened a little. Marge Bailey peeked in and was grinning.

"We didn't sleep again last night, did we?" Marge asked, handing her a mug of coffee. "Still thinking about that asshole you married?" she added and dropped on the couch beside Josie.

"No, I was sleeping just fine until the phone rang and I had to drive here in the middle of the night," Josie said, knowing she was at home in the den drinking brandy when the call came in at four A.M.

"You're such a bad fuckin' liar," Marge whispered.

Josie shook her head. Lieutenant Bailey was a tall blonde with beauty queen looks whose salty language made hardened criminals blush. They'd been friends for years and Josie knew Marge was not only tough, but smart, and could smell bullshit like a bloodhound. Nevertheless, she didn't want advice on how to live her life, so she'd keep trying to convince herself, as well as Marge, that everything was fine.

"Did you find our victim on file?" Josie asked, determined not to talk about Jake.

"Nope, Kessler was never arrested by Hollywood vice . . . never been arrested period as far as I can tell, not even a traffic ticket."

"That's strange, don't you think for his lifestyle? Maybe it's a random killing . . . someone who hated men with no fashion sense who dressed like women."

"That narrows the suspect pool down to most of the fuckin' civilized world."

The door opened wider and Behan was standing just outside the office with Detective Martin. "Gotta minute, boss?" he asked, coming into the room with Martin trailing a step behind.

Marge got off the couch, making room for him, and moved to Josie's worktable on the other side of the room. Josie knew there were some unresolved issues between the homicide supervisor and vice lieutenant. They'd had a brief affair last year before Marge put an end to it hoping to help Behan salvage his latest marriage. It didn't take a genius to see they still had feelings for each other, but Josie stayed out of it because their personal problems hadn't seemed to affect their work.

Josie got up too and opened the wardrobe closet. She pulled out a clean uniform to get it ready for Monday morning while they talked. It was a time-consuming boring project reattaching all that shiny paraphernalia—buttons, silver captain bars, name tag, badge.

"We've got an interesting development . . ." Behan said, as he filled the spot she'd vacated on the couch.

"Our victim was chief of staff for Jeff Flowers, the LA city councilman," Martin said, interrupting him.

Josie avoided eye contact with Behan. It wasn't necessary. She knew the "why the hell did you do this to me" expression would be all over his face.

"Have you notified the councilman?" she asked, turning her attention to the uniform, but she knew immediately this low-profile murder had suddenly become a lot more interesting.

Behan leaned back and folded his arms. He was annoyed and had temporarily stopped participating.

"Yes, ma'am," Martin said sheepishly after an uncomfortable silence. She knew she'd spoken out of turn. Red was the lead detective. It was his job to brief the captain.

For a second, Josie almost felt sorry for her. It wasn't a big deal, but the department was all about seniority and respect. Let the other guy take the credit, don't brag, step back and show the boss he or she is truly in charge. There was a certain feel for this job that included knowing the natural pecking order, but Josie believed you couldn't teach it. Good cops did it instinctively.

"Isn't Hollywood part of Flowers's council district?" Martin asked, recovering quickly.

"No," Josie said, explaining she had three city council people who represented different parts of the Hollywood area, but Jeff Flowers wasn't one of them. If everything she'd heard about the man was true, she considered it good luck not to work with him. Other captains claimed Flowers was arrogant and demeaning toward command officers in the areas he represented.

"We're meeting him at his district office Monday morning after the post, and he made it clear he's not happy about that," Behan said.

"Need me to come along?" Josie asked, knowing Red could handle it, but she wanted to be there as backup if Flowers lived up to his reputation. There wasn't much on her schedule for Monday and it helped her sanity to get away from the paperwork occasionally and participate in hands-on police work. Her bureau commander tried to discourage her from going out in the field except to oversee or supervise subordinates, but Josie knew if police work ever became primarily a desk job, she'd retire. She was a cop and needed the occasional adrenaline rush as well as the feel of a .45 semiauto in her hand.

"I'll let you know," Behan said.

"Does Kessler have family?" she asked.

"Wife and two grown kids . . . I'm going over there now. I'll try to make sure everyone gets notified before we release his name to the media."

He got up off the couch slowly, grunting like an old man. He looked tired and nodded at Josie and Marge before leaving, but ignored his partner. Martin looked embarrassed and maybe a little miffed but after a few seconds she took a deep breath, composed herself and followed him.

"What the hell was that all about?" Marge asked when she and Josie were alone again.

"Red's not pleased," Josie said.

"No shit. Is Miss 'Nobody-respects-me-because-I'm-a-woman' being a pain in the ass again? It's so boring; she needs to get over herself," Marge said.

"I don't understand why she can't just work and stop worrying what everybody thinks or says or doesn't say. She's a talented detective, but you'd think she'd be smart enough not to mess with Red."

Marge got up but didn't say anything until she was almost outside the door. "Maybe you shouldn't wait too long to deal with that situation, boss," she warned and was gone before Josie could respond. There really wasn't any need to talk about it. They both knew how close their friend was to falling into another whiskey bottle, but Josie had a station to run too, and she wouldn't allow Red to chase away competent detectives.

When she put away her uniform and closed the wardrobe, Josie took a long look in the full-length mirror hanging inside the door and then wished she hadn't. Her stringy black hair needed washing and was pulled back, making it easier to see the dark shadows under both eyes, and although it could've been the florescent lighting that made her skin look pale and unhealthy, she knew it probably wasn't.

She'd fallen asleep on the lounger in the den again last night dressed in the clothes she was still wearing before she woke up, and then poured a brandy to help her get back to sleep. The outfit was wrinkled and had a certain Goodwill quality to it, and these same Levi's that were tight a few weeks ago, after a steady diet of wine and junk food, were baggy on her skinny frame and had new chocolate stains. Without Jake around to nag her about healthy meals, Josie had developed the bad habit of forgetting to eat or convincing herself that ice cream was a good substitute for dinner. The holster on her belt hung too low on diminishing hips . . . it was the sad image of a malnourished, badly dressed, urban gunfighter.

Jake was gone and seemed to have taken most of her pride with him. She grabbed her briefcase and purse and slammed the closet door shut. The watch commander must've heard the loud bang and came running.

"Are you all right, ma'am," he said, standing a few feet away, wide-eyed with his hand resting on his holstered gun.

"Sorry, I'm fine," she said. Or I soon will be, she thought.

THREE

In less than an hour shopping at Albertsons market, Josie had filled her city car with a week's worth of groceries and cleaning supplies. She parked in the attached garage at her home in Pasadena, a city just north of downtown LA, and removed all the heavy paper bags that were covering the shotgun locked securely on the floorboard. She was certain most of the perishables would die in the refrigerator before she got a chance to cook them, but it was important to try.

Although Jake had done most of the cooking for the last few years, she did know how to make a simple meal, no rich sauces or exotic side dishes like the ones he made, but it would be edible and healthier than the usual nightly ration of potato chips.

She filled trash bags with the spoiled contents of the refrigerator before washing the shelves and restocking with fresh food. The clothes hamper in the laundry room was overflowing, so she took off her jeans and put on a clean pair of shorts, a tank top and running shoes before dumping a load of clothes in the washer.

The bed sheets hadn't been washed for a couple of weeks and although Jake was the last one who'd slept on them, she stripped the bed and piled everything on the floor with all the dirty clothes she picked up off the closet floor and the back of the bedroom chair. Jake's half of the closet was empty except for a few hangers. It made her feel bad not seeing the row of expensive suits and perfectly tailored shirts hanging there.

His tennis bag wasn't thrown in its usual spot in the corner near the nightstand and the trophy he'd won shortly after he retired from the district attorney's office and went into private practice wasn't sitting on the dresser any longer. He'd earned the seven-inch plastic statue by outlasting a bunch of gimpy geezers at a local parks and recreation tournament but treated the thing as if it were the Wimbledon dish.

The one thing he did leave behind surprised her. It was a picture of him and their son, David, taken a year ago in San Francisco. They'd gone there without her and looked very happy together. That's probably why the SOB left it, she thought, to show her just how unimportant she was in their family.

She gathered the dirty linen and clothes and carried the bundle down to the laundry room. The three-story house needed a good cleaning, but Josie figured that could wait since nobody had really been living in most of the rooms for weeks. David was still in San Francisco with Kizzie and Josie knew her son's girlfriend would keep him away from Pasadena and his mother as long as she could. She'd be surprised if Kizzie hadn't already convinced him to marry her. David was a six-foot four-inch talented artist and pianist, but he was a twenty-four-year-old nonparticipant when it came to functioning in the real world. Kizzie was Josie's age, not young or beautiful, but she gave David what he really wanted—someone who would make all his decisions and support him.

It was best not to think about her son. She could feel her stress level rising and that usually meant opening a bottle of wine. Instead, Josie went into the kitchen and washed some vegetables and a couple pieces of chicken for an early dinner. While the chicken was roasting, she intended to go for a two- or three-mile run at the local high school track but finished half that distance and walked home exhausted. Getting back in shape, much like cleaning house, was going to be a slow painful process.

AFTER DINNER, she straightened up the kitchen, put the clean clothes away and made the bed. She hoped the results would make her feel better, but all it did was remind her how lonely she was in this big empty house. It was still too early to sleep, so she took a shower, tucked a holstered four-inch revolver in the waistband of her clean Levi's, covered the weapon with a light shirt and walked to Old Town Pasadena. Although this was the touristy part of town, her favorite bar, the Carriage Inn, was usually empty except for the one or two locals who didn't need or want ambience and didn't mind sticky table tops and a bartender who for the most part ignored them.

"Get what you want," Tyler yelled from the back room after Josie got tired standing in front of the chipped granite bar and shouted his name.

She found an open bottle of Cabernet on a shelf and poured a full goblet, filled a large bowl with cashews and carried everything to a booth in the corner. The place was deserted except for a couple arguing at one of the tables and two women sitting in another booth. Tyler finally came out from the back room, took a look around and went back. It wasn't much, but at least she wasn't drinking alone. She checked her cell phone for messages, nothing from work, her wandering husband or her son. David rarely called since he'd been in San Francisco. She tried to convince herself it was a relief not to have to deal with the young man's disappointing life but she missed him and that nagging solitary feeling wasn't helping.

The bar was about to close when her cell phone rang and Josie recognized the familiar number of the Hollywood station watch commander. She stared at the phone.

It was two A.M.; she was tired and a little drunk but knew she had to answer.

"Captain, we got another homicide on Santa Monica Boulevard. Detective Behan asked me to notify you," the young lieutenant said, after apologizing, with the mistaken belief he had disturbed her sleep for the second consecutive night.

"Where on Santa Monica?"

"Regency Arms."

"Why do I know that name?" Josie asked, trying to clear her head.

"It's the same dirtbag hotel where that queen got stabbed yesterday . . . only this guy was killed inside on the second floor."

The bartender was standing beside her booth when she finished the call. He had a ring of keys in his hand and was dangling them in front of her eyes, his subtle way of saying, "I'm closing. Get out." When he leaned over the table to pick up her empty glass and nut bowl, Josie could smell his cheap cologne and whiskey breath. Both his arms were heavily tattooed, and she suspected most of his body looked the same. She could see a ring of colorful inked pictures peeking out from the neck of his tee shirt. He was an odd character with his dyed blond hair in a ponytail and diamond studs in both ears, but there had been a lot of nights and early mornings he'd kept the inn open until she was ready to go home.

"You got coffee?" she asked.

"I got something in the kitchen that used to be coffee ten hours ago."

"Can you heat some in the microwave?"

"Yeah, but why'd anybody wanna drink that shit."

Josie waited until Tyler returned with a Styrofoam cup full of a bad smelling, steaming black liquid that looked and tasted nasty. She thanked him, put twenty dollars in his hand and left. She swallowed as much of the concentrated caffeine as she could tolerate on the drive back to Hollywood and was grateful her stomach had been coated with half a pound of cashews.

The Regency Arms was in Hollywood's area but bordered on Rampart division and was the portal for many of Rampart's drug and prostitution problems oozing into her division. Marge Bailey and her vice officers were moderately successful in keeping the prostitutes operating on the other side of that invisible line between divisions. If they dared cross Normandie Avenue to do business in Hollywood, the vice officers pounced on them. Lieutenant Bailey couldn't prevent them from living in the Regency, but she didn't make it easy for them to do business in their own backyard. Most of the crimes associated with that hotel happened in Rampart, but Josie wasn't surprised when a killing or any other serious felony occurred on the Hollywood side of the boulevard.

Yellow police tape blocked the walkway outside the Regency, but except for the half-dozen legally parked police cars and uniformed officers, the street and sidewalks were empty. Josie spotted a few camping tents in the alley beside the hotel and a couple of young men huddled in a doorway, but otherwise it was a very different scene from the sideshow less than twenty-four hours ago.

Before entering the lobby, she stood on the doorstep and noticed the lights of St. Margaret Mary's church were on a few blocks away. She could see a figure that seemed to be looking in the direction of the hotel standing in the light of the open doorway, but it was too dark and too far away to recognize anyone. After a few seconds, the figure disappeared inside the church; the lights went out and the massive wooden doors were closed. Josie guessed either Father O'Reilly or one of the other priests heard all the activity and was curious.

As soon as Josie entered the Regency, she inhaled the stench of dried vomit, urine and mold mixed with accumulated layers of dust that had piled up over the years and filled every crevice of the building. It caused her already dodgy stomach to feel much worse as she climbed slowly to the second floor. The door to the room at the end of the hallway was open with two uniformed officers standing outside. As she walked down the hall, Josie saw broken locks and splintered wood on several of the door jams, telltale signs that at some time those doors had been kicked open either by her officers serving search warrants or drug dealers collecting tardy payments.

She didn't think the smell could get any more disgusting until she stepped inside the victim's room. Concentrated filth was so much worse. Behan and Martin both wore surgical masks, and he handed one to Josie when she entered. The floor was covered with rotting food in broken containers and a nervous puppy that cowered in a pile of dirty clothes. The animal had peed and left generous diarrhea deposits on a carpet that was so stained it didn't seem to matter.

The body of Henry Trumbo was lying on a ripped mattress on the bedroom floor. There were no sheets, only a stained blanket that partially covered Trumbo's face. The victim was on his back wearing only a bra and women's panties. His throat had been slashed from ear to ear, so deeply the bone was visible, and blood had coagulated around his head and shoulders. Trumbo was a big man—Josie guessed over six feet tall and muscular, as if he knew his way around a weight stack. A bloody butcher knife had been left, jammed into the mattress a few inches from the victim's nearly detached head.

"What else do we know?" Josie asked Red, handing back the notes he'd given her. Her voice sounded strange and muffled under the mask. It was hot in the room and breathing with the thing over her mouth and nose was making her lightheaded so she took it off, hoping at some point her senses would overload and she wouldn't notice the unpleasant smells anymore. In any case, it wasn't as bad as suffocating.

"We have his buddy back at the station . . . Marvin Beaumont. He's the one called 911," Behan said, finding the name in his notes. "One of my guys and Marge are taking his statement. He says Trumbo was supposed to meet him in this shithole. Trumbo was dead by the time Marvin got here."

"For real . . . his name's Marvin Beaumont? Is Marvin a suspect?" she asked.

"Not yet."

"Any connection to the Kessler murder?"

"Not yet."

"How about Councilman Flowers?"

Behan shook his head.

"So you kept me from getting a good night's sleep just to ask you a lot of stupid questions."

"According to his buddy, Trumbo's a former cop."

She hesitated, not wanting to hear the answer, but asked anyway, "Ours?"

"Beaumont claims Trumbo retired from LAPD. Martin's going to pull his personnel package tomorrow . . . actually that's later today, after the post on Kessler."

Josie watched Detective Martin in rubber gloves and surgical mask searching through the disgusting debris that covered nearly every inch of the room. The woman was so focused and deliberate that Josie began to feel a little better about foisting her on Red.

The camera crews and web media had been out briefly the day before when Patrick Kessler's body was sprawled on the sidewalk, but not a single media-type person appeared while the yellow tape blocked the sidewalk in front of the Regency Arms. Josie was surprised, but pleased no one had noticed or cared enough to find out what was happening. Behan reminded her it was probably because he hadn't released Kessler's name or his connection to

Councilman Flowers yet and none of the media had been allowed to get close enough to see the body.

By late morning, the technicians and the coroner had finished their work and the hotel was open for business again, so no one would know about Henry Trumbo's death occurring in the same vicinity as Kessler's until Behan was ready to reveal it.

"I'm beat; I need to get some sleep," Behan complained to Josie as they walked to their cars and then asked, "Martin's gonna be busy doing the work-up on Trumbo this afternoon. You wanna come with me to Flowers's office when I get back from the Kessler post?"

"You've got time. Let's grab a quick bite to eat first," she said, knowing unless he ate something he would stop at his favorite bar for a pick-me-up on the way back to the station. She didn't want to spend all morning worrying if this was the day he'd decided the life of a drunk was better than being a detective.

"I'm not that hungry."

"It's not a request, Red. I'll meet you in back of the station, and we'll walk across to Nora's."

He gave her that I'm-not-a-baby glare, but they both knew her tolerance had worn thin and she wouldn't allow him to drink his way to a premature retirement. He didn't argue, got into his car and drove away, leaving ugly rubber streaks on the asphalt.

Josie noticed Detective Martin had been sitting in her car across the street watching the exchange with Behan. It made Josie uncomfortable having to babysit the homicide supervisor, and she certainly didn't want an audience while she did it, especially one that might be taking notes for a lawsuit someday. She didn't like thinking that way, but too many women in the department had sued for much less. Taken out of context, Behan's gruff demeanor and drinking were fodder for lawsuits, and in many ways he was a dinosaur in the new, kinder-gentler, less forgiving and politically correct LAPD. There was a time when unusual characters that were as talented and valuable as Behan were allowed to survive, but no longer. The liability-sensitive department culled them out in favor of dull and predictable.

Partly for selfish reasons, she needed to keep him on this investigation. Hollywood's detective lieutenant had retired and his replacement wouldn't arrive for another deployment period on the transfer, for at least four weeks. Behan was acting detective commanding officer as well as homicide supervisor and did a great job with personnel— Martin being a glaring exception—and he breezed through the paperwork. She didn't have anyone else who could fill the position. If she asked the bureau for help, her boss would likely send the lamebrain lieutenant that West LA station was always trying to dump and Josie would be forced to deal with him for a month.

More importantly, after nearly twenty-five years of police work, she could almost smell when a case might be more than it seemed. After the killing tonight, she figured these two homicides would take someone as good and experienced as Behan to solve them. She realized Martin was a wild card. If the troublesome detective decided to play her hand and claim she was being treated unfairly, it would become a distraction, maybe an obstacle to keeping Behan in the game. Josie had to acknowledge she might've made a mistake in promoting Martin and that her good deed, as it usually did, was going to come back to bite her.

She had no doubt about what to do if Martin's behavior interfered with Behan's investigation. Josie would move her off the homicide detective table and deal with the inevitable messy consequences later.

THE BEST thing about Nora's Restaurant was its proximity to Hollywood station. Except for breakfast and hamburgers, the food wasn't great, but the bar was a Hollywood cop hangout and Josie's favorite place to unwind if she couldn't make it back to Pasadena. This morning, she and Behan sat at a table as far as possible from the stock of liquor bottles.

It took several minutes for Behan to relent and speak to her. They both avoided the subject of his drinking and talked about the investigation.

"I'll go to Flowers's office with you," she said, as he nibbled on a slice of toast, and added before he could disinvite her, "How's Martin working out?"

"Fine," he said, taking a bite of scrambled egg and pushing the dish away.

She started to say something about him not eating enough, but didn't. I'm not his damn mother, she thought. One son who didn't listen to her was plenty.

"Good," she said. "All I want is to give her a chance."

"My guy would've been better."

"Problem is you've never interviewed a woman you liked better."

"So?" he asked.

"You're telling me with all the positions you've filled over the last three years you never found a woman that was the best candidate?"

"That's what I'm telling you."

"Too many women with good reputations have applied and you turned all of them down. You've got to see that forces my hand. What could you possibly be looking for that you haven't already seen?"

"You."

Josie hadn't blushed since she was twelve, but he surprised her and she felt her face starting to warm. She also knew it wasn't flattery because Red didn't do that. They had worked well together as detectives. He wanted what every cop wants—a partner he trusted.

"Thanks," she said. "But you've still got to give her a chance or the next time the bureau will fill the position and we'll both be sorry . . . only . . ." She hesitated but wanted to tell him to be careful, not do anything that could be construed as . . . what? Everything Red did could be misunderstood. He was direct, irritable, impatient and sometimes disagreeable, but other cops respected his talent and gave his personality a pass. How could she tell him not to be himself? Warning him wouldn't be fair to Martin either. What if she weren't writing a little black book on him and Josie's fears were groundless? Just making the suggestion would poison any chance they had of working together.

"Only what?" he asked, after waiting for her to finish her thought.

"Nothing, forget it."

"Flowers agreed to meet with me at sixteen hundred. Does that work for you?" he asked and she nodded. "I should know more about Trumbo and Kessler by then," he said, got up and left without making any attempt to pay for food he never wanted.

Although he had barely touched his meal, Josie was starving and finished an omelet, potatoes and toast before Marge Bailey tracked her down.

"Your secretary said you'd probably be here," Marge said, waving at the lone waitress who brought a menu but she ordered without looking at it. "Saw Red going into the cot room before I left . . . he looked shitfaced but I didn't smell booze."

"He's tired . . . too many dead people for one weekend."

"Trumbo's not in the vice file either, but did you get a close look at his body?" Marge asked taking a mug of coffee from the waitress and all the toast from Behan's plate before the woman could clear it off the table.

"Unfortunately I did; what about it?"

"He's wearing expensive Victoria's Secret lace panties but his legs look like a fuckin' tarantula and he's a body builder. Manly muscles are the last things most of these cross-dressers want. His nails were dirty and no manicure or polish . . . like he'd never had a manicure in his life. I don't know . . . guess it's not all that unusual but it just didn't feel right."

"You don't think he was a transvestite?"

"Don't know . . . just didn't look like he was planning on dressing up to go out last night, but there he was, a half-dressed drag queen in fancy undies."

"That wasn't his room either. Maybe Mr. Beaumont can enlighten us."

"I took his initial statement. No revelations there either," Marge said, as her breakfast arrived.

"Who actually did rent that room?" Josie asked.

"Who knows? It's the Regency, aka communal living in a toilet. First shithead off the street gets the best room . . . no register to sign, all money transactions under the table. Damn city won't shut them down. I've tried . . . low-income voucher housing for Rampart's cockroaches."

"What did Red do with the puppy?" Josie asked. The puppy being in the room had bothered her for a lot of reasons. First, she hated seeing a helpless animal live that way, but more importantly, the room wasn't set up to accommodate a dog—no water dish, bed, toys. She mentioned it to Behan but he believed it was probably a stray that had wandered inside the hotel off the street and stayed.

"He had Martin take it to station. Somebody will want the little flea bag."

Josie waited until Marge finished, and they walked back to the station together. She intended to nap for a least an hour but Maki was waiting in her office at the worktable with a pile of projects and letters to sign.

"You look tired. We can do this later," Maki said, as soon as Josie sat across the table from her. The young Asian woman had her short black hair pinned back with pink barrettes this morning which made her look about sixteen years old. She wasn't very pretty but her family was wealthy and her lifelong hobby was shopping. Her clothes were expensive and stylish and an outgoing attitude made up for what she lacked in beauty.

"Sign the letters for me and leave the other stuff. I'll do it in a few minutes," Josie said, struggling to keep her eyes open.

Maki picked up the stack of papers, shut off the lights and closed the door on her way out. Without windows, the office immediately became pitch black and quiet. Josie rested her head on the table and fell into a deep sleep. Her cell phone beeping woke her up two hours later. The air conditioning was barely functioning and her clothes were damp with perspiration, strands of wet hair stuck to the side of her face. There was a missed call from her son, but no message. She thought about calling him back, but didn't. She wanted to talk to him, but would do it later, away from the station, where there were fewer distractions.

She was rested but hoped the kink in her neck and sharp pain in her spine would eventually go away. She'd slept so soundly she hadn't moved and felt as if every muscle in her sweaty body were permanently twisted into an awkward sitting position. There was still a little time before Red left for Councilman Flowers's office so she went to the locker room, took a long cold shower and changed into her uniform. Behan hadn't returned from the Kessler autopsy when she finished her paperwork, so she went upstairs to find Lieutenant Bailey.

The vice office was empty, which wasn't unusual. Marge didn't allow her officers to hang around. The miniblinds covering the windows to the lieutenant's inner office were closed, but the door was open so Josie went in and wished she hadn't.

The elegant, white-haired Victoria Behan was there in the cramped room with Marge—Red's current wife and his ex-lover were sitting side by side having what looked like a confidential chat. Josie tried to back out, but Marge saw her.

"Boss, look who's here, Vicky Behan," Marge said, standing. The stress was clearly visible on her friend's face.

Josie gave the older woman a quick hug and said, "What a surprise. How are you Vicky?"

"I should go. I know you two have work to do, and I have a board meeting to attend," Vicky said, slipping her purse under her arm and moving around Josie. "Thank you, Marge, and good-bye Captain," she said, staring at the floor as she hurried out of the office. She was a beautiful woman, but there were dark lines under her eyes, and she looked as if she'd been crying.

"What's going on?" Josie asked, after waiting a few seconds for Marge to volunteer information.

"It's complicated," Marge whispered.

"Is she leaving Red?"

"How should I know?"

"What'd she say?"

"She's unhappy and lonely."

"What are you supposed to do about it?"

"She wants me to talk to Red, find out what's wrong."

"We all know what's wrong. What'd you say?"

"I said I'd rather suck on a .357 magnum until it went off and blew my fuckin' brains out."

Josie sat in the wooden office chair behind Marge's desk. She knew this conversation was going nowhere so she asked, "Do you still have a copy of Marvin Beaumont's statement?"

"What was I supposed to say? I'm not gonna grill the sonnofabitch about his love life with his wife," Marge said and kicked at her file cabinet knocking over a signed picture of her hero, the outspoken former police chief, Daryl Gates.

"Red's not your problem anymore. You were right not to let her drag you back into their lives."

Marge opened the top drawer of the cabinet, took a folder out and gave it to Josie. "Easy for you to say, Corsino."

The file included a copy of Marvin Beaumont's statement and pictures of both the Trumbo and Kessler homicides.

"You talked to Beaumont, right?" Josie asked.

"Yeah, just for a few minutes, he admitted going to the hotel to meet Trumbo. He didn't know, but thought Trumbo was going to buy drugs. He was going to a party that night and Trumbo was supposed to go with him. He gets to the room, finds Trumbo's body, calls 911, and doesn't know shit about any drug dealer or what kind of drugs Trumbo was buying. Swears the guy was dead when he got there."

"Did Trumbo have cash on him?"

"Couple hundred and credit cards in his wallet . . . wasn't a robbery. Somebody just wanted his ass dead."

"Does Beaumont have a record?" Josie asked.

"Nope."

"Your people ever arrest Trumbo?"

"Nope, he's a downtown dweller, has a condo somewhere near Little Tokyo . . ." Marge stopped talking and was staring outside the office.

After a few seconds, Behan leaned in the doorway and asked Josie if she was ready to go. Before she could answer, he was gone again. She got up, handed Marge the folder and left. There wasn't much she could or would say as long as their past relationship didn't affect their work, but Miss Vicky's visit was another matter. Red's family problems, like his drinking, didn't belong in her station and Josie knew she'd have to deal with both issues.

COUNCILMAN FLOWERS'S district office was in Van Nuys, the hot humid valley area north of downtown near one of the larger and older LAPD stations. Behan drove and on the way told Josie what the autopsy on Patrick Kessler had revealed. Kessler had been stabbed three times in the chest before he collapsed on the sidewalk. The last wound cut deep, hit a major artery and he bled to death before the ambulance arrived within minutes after the assault. His body didn't show signs of hormone treatments, but the coroner wouldn't know for certain until the lab tests were completed. There were no defensive wounds on his hands or arms, so it appeared he hadn't seen his assailant or knew the person and didn't expect the attack.

"So we've probably got one killer," Josie said, as Behan exited the freeway.

"Probably . . . there was a crowd around him. After he went down, they scattered and the murder weapon was gone."

"Can it be the same knife that killed Trumbo?"

"Coroner doesn't think so. Victims had different kinds of wounds, and Kessler's looked like the blade wasn't as wide as the knife we found in the mattress near Trumbo. The coroner's certain the one we recovered from the bed was used to kill Trumbo."

"How about video on the street?"

"It's the wrong end of Santa Monica. If it were the west end, we'd have security cameras everywhere, but we only found two and the quality sucks."

"Odd both victims would get killed in such close proximity. Don't you think?" Josie asked.

"Not really, it's where a lot of these guys hang out."

"Have you talked to Marge?"

"Yeah, I agree with her. Trumbo's body looked staged to me too. His clothes were thrown on the floor like he wasn't planning on wearing them again, and if Beaumont's telling the truth, we know he was going to a party. The women's stuff wasn't big enough for him either. Marge is going to pull in a few of her snitches, see if anybody knew him or Kessler."

"Good," Josie said, relieved that at least she didn't have to give the lecture about working together. After giving it some thought, she decided not to mention Miss Vicky's visit. She knew how Red would react and it wouldn't help. It would be better to arrange a meeting with his wife and talk to her.

THE COUNCILMAN'S district office was on Roscoe Boulevard in a strip mall with a dry cleaner on one side and US Bank on the other. It was a plain brick building with tinted windows and the city seal on the front wall over his name and district. The receptionist seemed surprised to see them and said they'd have to wait a few minutes because the councilman was meeting with constituents.

Fifteen minutes later the door to Flowers's office opened and three men in business suits walked out followed by the councilman. Josie recognized one of the men, but couldn't remember where she'd seen or met him. He seemed to know her too, but didn't stop or say anything. The secretary whispered briefly to Flowers and he immediately came over to Josie and held out his hand.

"Captain Corsino, I didn't know you were coming. I apologize for making you wait," he said.

"You know Detective Behan?" she asked, moving aside.

Flowers took them back to his office. It was a large room with bookshelves filled with rows of law books, a well-stocked liquor cabinet with cut-glass doors in the corner near a wet bar and a big-screen television mounted on the wall. His polished mahogany desk was clean with not a piece of paper or pen in sight. Leather chairs and a couch were set around the room, conversation style. Josie's immediate thought was, this isn't a place where busy people work. It was an expensively furnished man cave.

"Can I get you something to drink, Captain, Detective?" Flowers asked, going directly to the bar.

She and Behan declined and sat beside each other on the couch.

"What can you tell us about Patrick Kessler?" Behan asked.

"He was my chief of staff," Flowers said, his face twisting into a weird pain-filled expression, maybe a failed attempt to look distressed, Josie thought.

He was shorter than her, heavy set, balding, with a round permanently pink face, and reminded her of a fat hummingbird as he flitted from one end of the room to the other before finally perching on the arm of a chair facing them. "Pat was my friend. He worked hard. I don't know what else I can tell you."

"Did you know he was a cross-dresser hanging around Hollywood alleys?" Behan asked.

"No," Flowers answered quickly and slid off the arm onto the chair cushion. His eyes narrowed and he leaned forward staring at Behan. "I don't want Pat's wife, Susan, or his family bothered with any of this," he warned.

"I'll keep that in mind," Behan said, sarcastically.

"I'm depending on you, Captain Corsino, to make certain she is not dragged into this mess," Flowers repeated, turning to Josie.

"Why do you suppose that would happen?" Josie asked.

"Patrick comes from a very wealthy family. His father is Seymour Kessler . . . the downtown developer," Flowers said, looking from Josie to Behan's blank expression. "In any case, this indiscretion shouldn't taint his father or wife. It will only draw media attention if you allow it."

"Indiscretion," Josie said. "His son was murdered."

"I've talked to your bureau commander. He assures me the family will not be bothered and this investigation will be kept low key," Flowers said, as if he hadn't heard her.

"I need to look in Kessler's office," Behan said, getting up. His tone was clear. He didn't want any part of whatever the bureau commander had promised.

"I need some reassurance first from you, Captain, that your subordinates will protect the Kessler family," Flowers said.

"Detective Behan will do whatever it takes to find the killer. That's all I can promise," Josie said, and got an angry glare from Flowers. He was unhappy and didn't bother to hide it. Apparently, her answer wasn't the one he wanted.

"Frankly, that's not good enough," Flowers said, pushing a button on his phone to summon his secretary. "Miss Mabry, show these officers Mr. Kessler's office," he said, turning his back on Josie as soon as the woman entered.

"What a prick," Behan whispered as they stepped into the hallway.

Josie caught a quick smirk on the secretary's face so she figured the woman had heard Behan and didn't disagree. Miss Mabry was a middle-aged heavy-set woman who had a nervous habit of pulling at her skirt as she walked. She led them to an office on the other side of the building and unlocked the door.

"I thought this guy was Flowers's chief of staff," Josie said, after the secretary had opened the door and stepped aside. "This looks like a storeroom."

"Patrick liked this arrangement. He wanted this office," Mabry said and hurried away.

The space was small and cramped with a couple of file cabinets and bookshelves filled with notebooks and some office supplies. It was a hovel compared to his boss's office.

Behan was quiet as he opened the desk drawers and searched the file cabinets. Josie looked in a couple of the notebooks while she waited and found old projects and research data pertaining to the councilman's district. There was nothing personal in the room, not a picture or certificate on the walls. Nothing that said they were in Patrick Kessler's space.

"This is bullshit," Behan finally said. "Either Kessler was never here or he didn't do anything when he was. Besides, have you ever seen a chief of staff's office this far away from the boss?"

"No point confronting Flowers. He obviously had all this arranged in case you wanted to see it. The question is why? What's he hiding?"

Behan shook his head. "I'm guessing it has more to do with him being a sleazebag politician than hiding evidence about Kessler's killing."

"Did you recognize the fat gray-haired guy that came out of Flowers's office when we first got here?" Josie asked.

"You mean Doug Miller. He's a director with the Protective League."

"What's a police union guy doing hanging around here?"

"It's what they do, boss, hobnobbing with the powers that be . . . setting up that cushy job for retirement."

"Well, we aren't going to find anything here. Do you have an address for Kessler's wife?" Josie asked. She didn't want Behan to start his tirade about the police officers' union again. She knew too many of the directors were disgruntled officers, who were looking for a place to hide from police work, but she thought one or two actually did a decent job; however, nothing she'd heard about Miller made her think he was one of the better ones.

"Maybe I should handle that interview alone, Corsino," Behan said. "You heard what the man said, and my career's already pretty much in the toilet."

Josie didn't argue; she didn't have to because they both knew she was stubborn and that Flowers's bullying and ordering her and Behan not to interview the victim's family meant that's exactly what she was going to do.

FOUR

Behan had no trouble finding the Kessler home. He'd been there the day before to notify the widow about her husband's death. It was a rambling two-story house in Brentwood, northwest of downtown Los Angeles in a neighborhood where Josie knew the LA district attorney and mayor both lived.

He parked on a narrow street that lacked the convenience of sidewalks or curbs, an illusion of country life in wealthy suburbia. The homes were set back on large properties, some hidden behind walls and heavy shrubbery. People who lived here walked their dogs in the middle of the street alongside nannies pushing their kids' buggies, all of them confident only residents and servants would dare use these private secluded roads.

A housekeeper answered the intercom at the front gate and told them to wait while she informed Mrs. Kessler. A few seconds later, the gate buzzed open. They walked up the driveway and found Susan Kessler waiting for them on the porch. She was an attractive, blonde, slightly overweight woman who had that dull, puffy, morning-after look of a heavy drinker. Behan introduced Josie. The widow gave her a quick nod but was more interested in speaking with the red-headed detective.

"Please make yourselves comfortable," Mrs. Kessler said, pointing at the expensive-looking wicker furniture on the porch and giving Behan a faint, but seductive smile.

"We're sorry to bother you," Josie said, feeling less guilty about disturbing the woman who was openly flirting with her detective.

"I understand. Actually, I've been expecting you to come back," she said, sliding onto the chair closest to Behan. Her skin was lightly tanned and Josie thought her low-cut, sleeveless white dress was a long way from grieving attire.

"Do you know if anyone threatened your husband or did he mention someone he was afraid of or was avoiding for any reason?" Behan asked.

Mrs. Kessler shook her head, "No, but apparently there was quite a bit I didn't know about Pat."

"You weren't aware of his cross-dressing."

"I knew there was something wrong in our relationship . . . lack of a relationship. He hadn't had much to do with me since the kids went off to college."

Josie sat back and watched as Behan questioned Kessler's wife. She was cooperative and matter-of-fact about her husband's lifestyle. Josie was waiting for some show of warmth or words of loss from the widow, but Susan Kessler was icy cold. Her children didn't live at home. The daughter was married, the son away at college. She wouldn't allow them to come home for the funeral or "sideshow" as Mrs. Kessler described it.

"He talked to a priest before he was attacked and seemed distraught. Do you know why?" Behan asked.

"Haven't got a clue."

"Do you think his father might have some idea of what was going on with him?"

Mrs. Kessler laughed, a little too long and then said, "Hardly."

"Didn't they get along?" Josie asked.

"As Detective Behan knows from his last visit, we stay here with Pat's father. This," she said, with a sweeping motion indicating everything around them, "this is all

Seymour's and he never allowed Patrick or me to forget it. How do you think they got along?"

"Is your father-in-law here?" Behan asked.

She didn't answer, got up, entered the open french doors and disappeared inside the house. While she was gone, the housekeeper came out with two tall glasses of iced tea. Josie was grateful and finished hers in a few gulps. Summer temperatures were setting records and her dark blue uniform felt like a wool blanket. She saw beads of sweat trickling down the sides of Behan's face, but he didn't touch his glass. Josie guessed he'd rather have had a cold beer.

Twenty minutes later, about the time Josie figured they'd been abandoned, an older man came out of the house. He was big and good looking like his son and walked with a slight limp directly toward Behan and shook hands.

"She said you wanted to talk to me, detective. Do you know who killed my son?" he asked in a tone that said he expected results.

"This is my boss, Captain Corsino," Behan said.

The older man inspected Josie from head to foot then said, "A woman," and turned back to Behan as if he'd just discovered a big blue turd standing on his porch.

"We're hoping you might be able to help us," Josie said. She had almost blurted out a sarcastic remark but stopped herself, remembering the rude man had just lost his son. "Do you know anyone who might've wanted to harm your son?"

"Of course not, what kind of question is that," he said.

"It's a good one," Behan said. "Your son's dead. Did he have enemies?"

"No," he said and took a sip from the glass of iced tea Behan had abandoned. "Obviously, the boy was having mental problems . . . dressed up like that." His voice trailed off and Josie thought Mr. Kessler suddenly looked smaller and less intimidating.

"Would he have any reason to be in that area of Hollywood?" she asked.

"I think he had friends there."

"Do you know their names, addresses, anything?" Behan asked.

The old man shook his head and seemed to crumble onto the closest chair. For a moment, Josie thought he was sick, but soon realized he was exhausted.

"What difference does it make," he said, with an angry sneer, snapping back to his irritable self. "My son is dead."

"I want to know who did it and why. Don't you?" Behan asked, sitting on the railing directly in front of him.

Kessler got up. He stood still for several seconds staring at the floor as if he were confused or deciding where he wanted to go. "There was a man . . . came here one time a few weeks ago with Pat. I didn't like him," he said, looking at Behan. "My son was afraid of him . . . I could tell. I ordered him out of my house. He never came back and Pat never mentioned him again, but I don't believe that was the end of it."

"Do you know his name?"

"Pat called him Hank, that's all I know . . . except he was one of yours."

"A cop?" Josie asked, immediately thinking of the late Henry Trumbo.

"Big man . . . looking around all the time like you all do, talked tough like one, so I asked him if he was a cop . . . he just grinned at me but didn't deny it." Kessler hesitated before adding, "He had a gun too, under his shirt, but no matter, he left quick enough when I told him to get out of my house."

Seymour Kessler's tone softened a little as they talked, but he refused to believe his son willingly participated in the "unnatural practice of wearing women's clothes." He insisted either Patrick was drugged or forced to dress that way, and it was done solely to humiliate his father.

He had no evidence to support his theory, but insisted his son was weak and could be easily manipulated. The senior Kessler admitted having enemies. He'd made a lot of money developing parts of downtown LA by outbidding contractors who didn't like to lose. He suspected they had retaliated through his son.

Josie watched Red's body language and knew him well enough to understand that, like her, he probably wasn't buying into any of this. Murder wasn't usually that complicated.

Despite Seymour Kessler's bitterness, she could sense loss and genuine grief coming from him, emotions clearly lacking in the widow. He was sad, and at the same time, angry with the police and the world for allowing his son to die. She had also decided he was a bully accustomed to getting results his way, who wouldn't be satisfied until every question had been answered and every loose end tied up in a manner he understood and accepted.

"Are you going to show him Henry Trumbo's picture?" she asked Behan as the driveway gate closed behind them. Susan Kessler had never reappeared, but it didn't matter because Seymour had proven to be much more helpful.

"Uh huh."

"It might be him."

"Maybe."

Behan took off his jacket when they got into the car. Josie saw perspiration stains on his shirt and his face was a shade redder than usual.

"Are you okay?" she asked, turning the air conditioning vents in his direction.

"I'm fine, just thinking I need to find out what Martin's dug up on our second victim. Trumbo getting killed in the Regency is looking less like a coincidence if he did know Pat Kessler."

"Have you checked out Trumbo's residence yet?" Josie asked.

"Martin was getting the search warrant. We'll probably serve it as soon as we get back. Wanna come?"

"Love to, but I've got captain stuff to do, bureau meeting."

J OSIE WAS surprised to find her boss, Commander Perry, waiting in her office when she returned. His meeting had been scheduled in the Wilshire area with the four captains, including herself, who worked for him. West Bureau was without a deputy chief and Perry was a temporary replacement until a new one could be promoted, but Josie didn't care if another deputy chief was ever selected. Perry was that rare staff officer who actually understood cops and had been on the streets and done real police work. He let captains run their stations with little interference, then held them accountable for the results. He'd been acting deputy chief for two months and life had never been better for Josie because, unlike some of her peers, she wasn't afraid to make decisions and was willing to live with the consequences. Hollywood station was thriving, but she knew, based on past practice, her independence wouldn't last.

Perry was sitting at her worktable watching a cable news station where the ubiquitous young blonde woman was reporting on the death of Seymour Kessler's son. The story was mostly about the elder Kessler's prominence in the Los Angeles business community, probably because Behan had been careful not to reveal many of the details related to the homicide. His media release carefully avoided any mention of how Pat Kessler was dressed or a detailed description of the area where he was killed. Josie waited until the story was over before turning off the television and shaking hands with her boss.

"Did I get the wrong info on our bureau meeting?" she asked, sitting across from him.

Perry was a retired marine who still looked like a military man in his freshly pressed class-A police uniform. He was compact, tan and fit with short gray hair and clean-shaven. He rarely smiled but never had a harsh word for anyone unless all else had failed. A solid company man, he supported the chief of police but knew how to navigate political waters and survive in that quagmire called civil service. He looked directly at her and seemed reluctant to speak, something she had never experienced with this man.

"Meeting's canceled. I came to tell you Robbery-Homicide is taking over the Kessler investigation. Chief thinks it's too high profile and time consuming for Hollywood."

"I don't remember complaining," she said, still locked in his dead man's stare.

"You didn't. It's fucked up, but that's what the old man wants so that's what we'll do."

She was quiet, her thoughts ricocheting like an errant bullet in her brain. There were too many x-rated versions of what she wanted to say, what she knew she should say and finally did say, "I want to keep it."

"That's not up to you . . . or me."

"We have a second homicide that might be connected. What about that one?"

"It's yours until you hear differently," he said, getting up. "How's Behan doing?"

"Fine, why?" she asked. "Is he the reason they're taking it?"

"No. Calm down, Corsino. A lot of important people have taken an interest in this case. I think the old man wants to have it downtown, closer to him."

"Where no one will ruffle any political feathers," she said in a tone that sounded nastier than she'd intended.

"I'll let that go because I know you're not the sort to bad-mouth the chief."

"Behan does better work than a roomful of RHD detectives," Josie said, wanting to change the subject because she knew as soon as Commander Perry was out the door, she'd be bad-mouthing the chief to Behan and Marge.

"Detective Richards will be here later today to meet with your detectives about transferring the case," Perry said, as he was leaving. He stopped near the door as if he wanted to say something, but didn't, and was gone.

Josie figured he'd thought about commiserating, but that wasn't his style. It didn't help. She went back to the detective squad room but Behan and Martin had already left to serve the search warrant on Trumbo's apartment. She wasn't going to call them back just to tell them bad news. RHD would have to wait until they finished because Trumbo's investigation still belonged to Hollywood, and it had suddenly become her priority.

She started to go up to vice, but changed her mind and instead went back to her office. Marge didn't need to know or worry about any of this yet. The vice lieutenant would remain an important player in solving both of these homicides. This was definitely in her territory. When the time came, Josie would insist her headstrong friend employ her resources to assist RHD as well as Behan if that's what it took.

Maki stopped Josie outside her office to tell her that the detective from RHD was waiting inside. He hadn't wasted any time getting there which put her in even a worse mood. She had wanted to talk with Behan first and give him an opportunity to adjust to the idea of losing the Kessler investigation before he had to hand it over to someone they both knew wouldn't be as good as he was. It was stupid to separate Kessler from Trumbo's murder, but she figured if Behan kept Trumbo, chances were good he'd solve both murders, probably long before RHD even got a whiff of finding the killer.

The name should've registered when Commander Perry told her who would be handling the investigation, but Josie never associated the Richards she knew with RHD. She was surprised and speechless finding Sergeant Kyle Richards in her office. He had been a supervisor working in Hollywood until nine months ago. He was her friend, a good friend, and the only man she'd ever even considered cheating with in all those years of marriage. His departure from Hollywood patrol came when she made it clear she loved her husband and there wasn't any possibility of a future for them. He immediately transferred to another division, saying it was too difficult to stay in Hollywood and be around her every day.

It was different now. Her husband was most likely out of her life forever. Any feelings she might've had for Jake didn't make much sense anymore, even to her.

Richards stood when she entered. He was taller than her with salt-and-pepper hair and those penetrating gray eyes. A two-inch scar beneath his left eye was barely visible under day-old stubble. She couldn't hide how happy she was to see him, but was surprised how quickly all those emotions she'd suppressed for so many months had surfaced.

"Sorry about this," Richards said. He still had that laser gaze that made most people look away.

"You're working with Robbery-Homicide?" she asked, trying to ignore the nervous rumblings in her stomach.

"On loan from surveillance to this homicide task force," Richards said and reminded her that he had dual status as a sergeant and detective supervisor. He also admitted that, so far, this hastily formed task force consisted of him.

"I guess I should've known or guessed when Commander Perry said the name Richards, but I was so upset about losing the investigation I guess I wasn't really paying attention. When did RHD put this task force together?" Before he could answer, she sat on the corner of her desk and said, "Let me guess; it was as soon as Behan made it clear he wasn't going to kowtow to Kessler's father and would work this case the same as any other murder."

"Captain at RHD told me he didn't want to see Seymour Kessler's name on the eleven o'clock news."

"So they expect you to bury it?" she said.

"Nobody said that, but I am wondering why they gave it to me. I'm a good cop and a fair detective but I'm not Red Behan."

"But surveillance is a good fit for you . . . plenty of action," she said, having heard from Behan that, like Commander Perry, Richards had a background with the Marines' Force Recon. His mysterious past in several different countries before joining the department always made Josie suspicious that at some point in his life Richards had also worked with the CIA or some other federal intelligence agency. "How's Beth?" she asked, remembering his smart, pretty daughter.

"Sixteen and discovering boys . . . dad's no longer the center of her life. My mother's taken her to visit relatives in London for the summer. They can drive each other crazy for a few weeks." He sat on the couch and finally looked away.

"I'm glad to see you," Josie admitted, after a few seconds of uncomfortable silence. "But I'm still pissed you're taking my investigation."

"Where's Red?"

"Finishing up a warrant . . . he'll be here."

"If it's okay with you, I'd like to work with him on this."

"Won't you get pushback from your boss?" she asked.

"They told me I can pretty much bring in anyone I need. Nobody said it couldn't be Red."

"You can try, but it's going to be hard flying under the radar on this one."

"You look good, too skinny though," he said, and got up. "Everything okay . . . the family?" he asked, standing a few feet away. They both knew he was asking if she was still with Jake. It was no secret her marriage was wobbly when he left.

"David's still in San Francisco with his girlfriend." Josie stopped herself from saying she didn't know Jake's whereabouts and really didn't care anymore. She was pretty certain beginning that conversation would create a whole new dynamic between them, and it was really difficult for her to think about a fresh start when she hadn't quite figured out how to clean up the mess she'd made of her marriage.

"All right," he said when it became obvious she wasn't going to offer any additional information.

"You can hardly see that anymore," she said, pointing at the scar on his face but mostly wanting to say anything that would change the subject.

"I heal pretty fast," he said with a wry smile, and she wondered if he was still talking about his old injury.

Behan and Martin came into the office a few seconds later with a box full of items they had removed from Henry Trumbo's apartment. The homicide detective shook hands with Richards and seemed pleased to see him again until Josie explained what was about to happen to his murder investigation.

"What genius made that decision?" Behan asked, but he wasn't nearly as disappointed as Josie had anticipated. He seemed almost too comfortable with the change.

"The chief," she said.

"I doubt that. He's been on the streets. I worked with him. Somebody's pulling strings, pressuring him," Behan said.

"Chief has to be a politician to get another term. He knows the mayor won't keep someone who doesn't play well in the city sandbox," Josie said.

"Does Seymour Kessler have that much influence?" Richards asked.

"Apparently, or it might be Councilman Flowers," Josie said, glancing at Martin who was sitting at the worktable, not saying anything but listening intently.

"So, how does this work? I hand over everything I have and you fuck it up?" Behan said, staring at Richards.

"That might be the department's master plan, but I'd rather work with you if you don't mind."

Josie and Richards sat at the table with Martin while Behan went back to the detective squad room to retrieve the murder book and his notes. Josie told the watch commander to track down Lieutenant Bailey, ask her to join them and bring any information she had on the two homicides.

"Sonnofabitch," Marge said with a wide grin as soon as she arrived and spotted Richards. "Are you back?" she asked, giving him a quick hug. She had briefly dated him when he worked in Hollywood, but unlike her affair with Behan, it was never serious for either of them.

Richards nodded but didn't answer and seemed uncomfortable. It was an awkward exchange, which told Josie these two probably weren't seeing or talking to each other for the first time since his departure.

It took hours to review all the material Behan had accumulated since the two murders. None of the witnesses had admitted to seeing Kessler get stabbed which wasn't a real surprise to anyone, and Father O'Reilly was still reluctant to reveal any conversation in the confessional.

"As far as I'm concerned you're still lead detective on Kessler," Richards said when they finished going through the paperwork. "My captain doesn't want this can of worms anyway, so he won't be watching that closely."

"But the chief will. Keep the old man informed. I don't want any heat coming down on Red. If it does, you've got this investigation back in your lap," Josie said.

Martin had been quiet during Behan's review of the Kessler case, but when he started talking about Henry Trumbo she had plenty to say. Trumbo's LAPD personnel file painted a picture of a troubled man who had somehow evaded elimination in his background investigation and was briefly allotted a spot in a police academy class. He survived the process another two months before his probation was terminated. Beaumont was wrong. Trumbo hadn't retired; he hadn't even made it out of the police academy.

She told them that Trumbo was a freelance carpenter by trade, but actually had been making his living as a male escort. Occasional jobs from local contractors had been embellished on his department application to account for his income. He'd admitted to marijuana use but had been a frequent abuser of prescription drugs and neglected to mention that detail. He did manage to keep fit and somehow passed the physical and psychological examinations. The notes from his entry interview said he was "articulate, enthusiastic, had a pleasant demeanor, exuded confidence and command presence—a candidate for an LAPD recruitment poster."

His application photo didn't remotely resemble the man Josie had seen sprawled on that mattress at the Regency Arms. When he died, his clean-cut handsome face had day-old stubble and the hair on his almost shaved head in the police academy had grown out and was styled, but thick and nearly shoulder-length. If he hadn't been wearing women's lingerie, the buffed-up Trumbo would've looked more like a casting poster for a mob hit man.

"Which interviewer wrote that note?" Josie asked.

"John Castro. He's a homosexual sergeant who sits on a lot of the entry boards. He brags about actively recruiting other gays," Martin said.

"Talk to him. See if he knew Trumbo before the interview. Find out who did his background investigation.

Whoever it was missed some obvious disqualifiers. One of them should be able to shed some light on this guy," Josie said.

"We're interviewing Marvin Beaumont again in a few minutes," Behan said. "He's the guy who was supposed to meet Trumbo at the Regency."

"Have you shown Seymour Kessler a photo of Trumbo?" she asked. "Is he the one Seymour threw out of his house?"

"He thinks so, but he's not positive," Behan said. "I think old Seymour's got a bit of selective memory syndrome. I get the feeling he's paying for some investigating of his own."

"A private investigator?" Richards asked.

"I don't know, but he's just the guy to do something stupid like that."

"Throw his wrinkled up old ass in jail if he interferes," Marge said.

"That'll make the chief happy," Behan said.

"What did you get from Trumbo's room?" Josie asked, not wanting to consider what the repercussions would be if Seymour Kessler had to spend any time in Men's Central Jail, but knowing she'd be the first one in line to sign the booking slip.

"Pictures of him and people we don't recognize, bills, letters . . . got a safe-deposit box at Bank of America, membership card to Nicola's, some club in Hollywood, other assorted junk. Martin will go through and sort it out," Behan said.

Martin stood and picked up the box. She left abruptly without saying anything, but Josie noticed Behan and Marge exchange a quick look as soon as she was gone. Josie had managed cops long enough to know that, despite her immediate warning and her friends' adamant denials, she had just witnessed the beginning of an unlikely alliance to deal with an unpopular coworker that would come to no good and inevitably would result in monumental problems.

FIVE

Josie's secretary had the instincts of a good adjutant and never went home until she was certain her captain didn't need anything. It was late when the meeting finished, but Maki was at her desk waiting patiently.

"Your son called twice," Maki said, handing Josie a stack of messages. "He asked if you could call him." She was struggling not to smile as she added with a decent imitation of David's sarcastic tone, "When you can pull yourself away from more pressing police matters."

"That's my kid."

"Claims he's been calling your cell phone all day, but you won't answer."

"So he has," Josie said, looking at the half-dozen missed calls on her phone. "I turned it off, guess I forgot to put it back on. You go home. I'll call him."

"Yes, ma'am," she said, locking her desk and picking up her purse practically in one motion. "Oh, I almost forgot. On his way out, Detective Behan said to remind you he was interviewing Mr. Beaumont."

Josie wondered if there was something wrong with a mother who'd rather be listening to Marvin Beaumont's interview than talking with her only son. Of course Marvin wasn't going to ask for money or want to live in her house with his annoying girlfriend. She wasn't certain that's what David wanted, but the odds of having a conversation with her son that didn't include him asking for money, food or a place to sleep were never good.

She closed the office door and called him. He was still in San Francisco with Kizzie. Jake had been staying with them for a few days, but he was on his way back to LA to prepare for a trial. David paused after revealing that bit of information, maybe hoping she'd ask about her husband, but she didn't.

"Are you coming back, too?" Josie asked with mixed feelings. She really wanted to see him, make certain he was healthy and reasonably happy. She wasn't eager to spend time with Kizzie, but putting up with his girlfriend was a small price to pay to have him closer to her.

"I have a job in LA. I'm starting next week. That's why I called. I wanted to stay at home for a few days until we find an apartment . . . if that's okay."

"No problem, of course," she said, fixated on the improbable words, "I have a job."

"Great, we'll leave early tomorrow morning," he said, and added, "Love you," before hanging up.

She had questions. What kind of job? Did it involve music? Had he finally dumped his tiny ancient girlfriend and found someone his age and size? She actually knew the answer to the last one, but kept hoping.

Thanks to her latest resolution to get back into shape, the refrigerator was full of healthy food and the house was reasonably clean, so her son couldn't report back to his father that she was falling apart without him. Josie had to admit she didn't miss Jake's nagging about working too many hours, not eating right and not getting enough sleep. It was convenient having someone who'd pick up after her and have dinner waiting, but other than their occasional intimacy including great sex, she was discovering there wasn't much Jake could offer she couldn't live without or find somewhere else with less aggravation.

Marvin Beaumont was not what Josie had expected after reading both Marge Bailey's and Detective Martin's initial interviews. She saw him for the first time on a video feed from the adjoining interrogation room where Behan and Richards were questioning him. He was a tall, handsome black man wearing what looked like an expensive tailored suit. While Henry Trumbo had a rough appearance, his friend seemed . . . stylish.

As Josie listened to the interview, it only took a few minutes to discover why Beaumont presented himself so well. He was an attorney, a very successful trial lawyer if his own immodest assessment was accurate.

"I had no idea Henry was going to the Regency Arms for drugs," he answered in response to Behan's question. "He asked me to meet him there . . . Frankly, I was late because I took one look at the place and fled."

"But you went back," Behan said.

"I tried to call but he wasn't answering his cell phone . . . guess I felt guilty and went back to extricate him."

"That night you told my partner you knew he was going there for drugs," Behan said.

"No, I guessed as much when I saw the hotel. What other reason would he have to go to a place like that?"

"Weren't the two of you headed to a party that night?"

"I was. Henry was my security man."

"Why would an attorney need security?" Richards asked.

"I've handled a few high-profile nasty divorce cases where the husband wasn't happy with the outcome . . . it was just a precaution."

"So your security guy tells you to meet him at a dirt-bag hotel," Behan said.

Josie could hear the sarcasm in Behan's voice and understood why. She wasn't buying that story either, but Beaumont seemed unfazed by his tone.

"Henry said he had to get something on the way and wanted me to pick him up there, so I wouldn't arrive at the party before him. Until I saw the place, I never thought about drugs. He was just out of rehab. He promised me all that was over."

"What was your relationship with Trumbo?"

"He was my friend; he worked primarily as an investigator but provided security when it was necessary."

"Nothing else," Richards persisted.

"No, if you're asking what I think you're asking. I did not have a physical relationship with Henry. I'm not certain what was going on in that hotel room but I don't believe any of it. He wasn't that sort of man."

"Did you know Patrick Kessler?" Richards asked.

"I know his father. I handled Seymour's divorce several years ago, but I never really knew Pat. Why? Do you believe they were killed by the same person?"

"Can you think of any business Trumbo might've had with Patrick Kessler?" Behan asked, ignoring his question.

Beaumont had a puzzled expression. He shook his head, but Josie thought he didn't really seem surprised that Trumbo might've known the younger Kessler. He answered the rest of their questions and never appeared defensive or reluctant to tell them what he knew, but Josie sensed he was keeping some of the more interesting details to himself. She couldn't explain why, but thought it odd that his answers were so deliberate and carefully constructed as if he were afraid to misspeak or knew just how much he could say without stepping over some self-imposed line.

When the interview was over and Beaumont had left the station, Josie went into the interrogation room where Behan and Richards were comparing notes.

"What do you think?" she asked, looking from one to the other.

"I'm not buying the hotel story. I'm betting he knew what Trumbo was doing there," Behan said. "And it wasn't drugs. No self-respecting drug dealer would've left that much money in his wallet."

"Is he as good an attorney as he thinks he is?" Josie asked.

"Your basic ambulance chaser," Richards said. "Finds rich unhappy wives and gets as much as he can from the husband."

"That's not unusual," Josie said.

"I spoke to a few lawyers who worked with Beaumont at his last—and actually his only—law firm. That's where he was when he handled Seymour Kessler's divorce. Seymour's wife got very little of his fortune. The firm's partners told me Beaumont had been politely asked to find another place of employment because his MO was to uncover compromising pictures or a mysterious witness pretrial and then get the husband, or wife in Seymour's case, to settle out of court."

"Again, isn't that standard practice?" Josie asked.

"According to one of the partners there were too many suspect cases where the other party claimed he or she was set up or the witness lied," Richards said. "Nobody ever proved anything, but they dumped him, so I'm guessing they suspected at least some of the sleaziness and gutter tactics were happening."

"Beaumont has his own practice now and, as far as we can tell, his only employee besides a secretary was the late Mr. Trumbo," Behan said. "He claims Trumbo told him he was a retired LAPD cop, but he never bothered to verify because Trumbo showed him a badge and ID and he did such a good job there was no reason to doubt him."

"What did he say when you told him Trumbo never made it out of the police academy?" Josie asked.

"But detective, he possessed an authentic badge and gun," Behan said, mimicking Beaumont's formal speech pattern.

Behan confirmed that Trumbo's cell phone, badge, gun and police ID hadn't been found in the hotel room where he was killed or in his apartment. They figured either the killer had taken them or less likely, Trumbo had everything stashed somewhere.

They all agreed it was an interesting question how Trumbo got an LAPD badge and ID, since he was fired before the badge was issued and the ID should've been taken back at the academy. Josie knew there were plenty of lost or stolen badges he might've bought on the street. His money, driver's license and credit cards were still in his wallet after he died, but the police ID and badge weren't. If he was protecting Beaumont that night, she figured they should've been there or somewhere nearby.

"We need to talk to Patrick Kessler's wife again," Behan said to Richards as they were leaving the interview room. "If she was planning on divorcing Kessler, and Beaumont was involved, they'd have plenty to embarrass the old man . . . get him to pay her big bucks not to make his son's lifestyle public."

"Beaumont's never going to admit it, but that might explain why Trumbo was hanging around Patrick Kessler, maybe intimidating him, threatening to embarrass the family if he or his father didn't give Susan Kessler a huge settlement," Josie said, and added quickly, "but let Richards set up this interview with Susan Kessler. At least try to make it look as if RHD's running the investigation now."

"Yes ma'am," Behan said. He was annoyed, but Josie knew the Kesslers had enough influence that if they thought Hollywood still had the case, Susan or Seymour would make a call to the chief's office and that would be the end of any involvement by her detectives.

When Behan had gone, Richards asked if she had a few minutes to have a drink with him before she went home. She agreed to meet him at Nora's for a glass of wine after she changed her clothes.

For a lot of reasons, she knew it was a stupid thing to do, but Josie told herself she wanted the wine and didn't want to drink alone again. No, the truth was she'd missed him. The bar was still serving food and she was hungry, too. Besides, they were working together and there were legitimate things to discuss. Her resolution this morning to go for a jog tonight didn't have much chance of happening anyway.

She changed back into her Levi's and was walking through the watch commander's office when Marge caught up to her.

"Wanna get something to eat?" Marge asked, holding the lobby door open.

"I'm meeting Kyle across the street. Come with me," Josie said, knowing it wasn't what she wanted but it would quash rumors if anyone from the station saw them. She never liked being the object of gossip.

"No, you go. I'll grab something on the way home."

"I want you there," Josie insisted.

"What the fuck's wrong with you Corsino? Kyle's a great guy and he's crazy about you."

"I'm not buying a new model while the old one's still running and cluttering up my driveway."

"Trust me on this one, boss. That clunker you married stopped running years ago. Just drive the sonnofabitch off a cliff and be done with him."

Richards was sitting at the bar when they got to Nora's. Marge drank one glass of wine and excused herself to go to the restroom. She never came back. Josie wasn't really surprised. She ordered her favorite meal, a half-pound hamburger, french fries and a bottle of wine. They moved to a table near the back of the room and in a few minutes the waitress brought her meal and a steak with french fries for Richards.

They finished half a bottle of wine before Josie felt as if she could relax and enjoy his company. She stopped thinking about Jake and David and the last couple of years watching what she thought was a loving relationship fall apart. It was enjoyable getting to know someone with an expectation there might be a future and not constantly worrying about how to preserve a past that just wasn't relevant any longer.

"Is Beth dating yet?" she asked, as the waitress cleared the table.

Richards closed his eyes and shook his head.

"I don't think so, but who knows. She's very pretty . . . like her mother."

He took a picture out of his wallet and showed it to Josie. A taller Beth than she remembered was dressed in an evening gown. Her auburn hair was pinned up and she looked beautiful, movie-star elegant.

"That's her prom dress," Richards said. "The boy was a tall, handsome redhead. He reminded me of Behan, only sober and without a highly developed brain."

Josie laughed, almost choking on her wine. "Beth's a smart girl. She'll figure it out."

"Marge and I have kept in touch. She told me Jake moved out," he said, abruptly.

"Lieutenant Bailey has a big mouth," she said, putting her glass down.

"I wanted you to know that I knew, but I promise I won't pressure you to do something if you're not ready. I'm pretty sure pressuring you doesn't work anyway. But, you need to know I haven't changed how I feel, and I'll gladly wait until you've decided what you want to do."

"I'm not into casual relationships, Kyle, and I'm not going to make promises I can't keep," she said.

"I know. Don't worry about it. I want us to be friends no matter what. I've missed you. I haven't felt this way about another woman since my wife died . . . that's all . . . thought you should know," he said, shrugging.

Josie had to admit she'd missed him too. They were friends. She cared about him and could already see their relationship developing into something real and lasting.

"Be patient," she said. "I'll get this sorted out in a way I can live with and still look in the mirror without feeling as if I've fucked up the last twenty-four years. I've got to make some sense of it."

"I get it," he said, standing and putting money on the table. "Gotta go, need some sleep. I'm visiting the widow Kessler tomorrow morning." He leaned over, gave her a quick hug and left.

She sat there for a few minutes having felt more affection in that hug than she'd had from Jake in months. It made her realize maybe she was looking at her situation completely wrong. She didn't have to make a decision about walking away from her commitments. Jake had already done that for both of them, but he was too cowardly to make their separation permanent. He was leaving his options open, but in a rare moment of clarity about her personal life, she'd just decided it was time to close those options forever.

SIX

This wasn't the first time Josie had thought about leaving Jake, but it was the only time she'd actually decided to do it. She slept soundly that night and realized her decision, even if it was the wrong one, was better than constantly second-guessing herself. She never had a problem making choices at work. In fact, she was eager to make every call, and Commander Perry had noted that, although she wasn't always right, no one doubted her ability and willingness to move forward on the best course of action. Maybe her personal life would finally benefit from those endless hours she'd spent doing her job.

She got up early enough to run a couple of miles before eating a healthy breakfast of cereal and orange juice and even made coffee at home to avoid encountering the evil Starbucks bear claw. Her mind felt clear for the first time in weeks, but before she started the process of making the separation with Jake official, she knew she'd have to talk to David tonight. Her son's range of emotions was stacked as high as his gangly frame, and she was hoping to ease him into accepting an outcome that should've been understandable even to him.

As soon as she arrived at the station that morning, the watch commander told her she had a visitor who had gone up to the coffee room and would be back in a few minutes. He gave her a business card for Doug Miller, a director from the LA Police Protective League, the rank and file union.

Josie told the desk officer to let her know as soon as he returned and wondered why a league director wanted to talk to her. She'd never been that friendly with the league and it was well known she didn't think they did enough as an organization to help those officers who really needed them. She remembered Miller had been with Council-man Flowers the morning she and Behan were there, but doubted he had any information on the Kessler murder. It had been so long since the man had done any real police work she doubted he'd know a clue if it showed up on his e-mail, but like everyone else in the city, she'd be polite and listen to him. The police union wielded a lot of power and right or wrong they could make life miserable for anyone who crossed them. She didn't mind a good fight, but never considered a battle with the Protective League worth the time or trouble.

She and Maki were reviewing the day's scheduling when Miller finally made his appearance. He knocked and walked into her office without waiting to be asked. Apparently he didn't care whether or not she had time to see him. Maki ignored him and continued her briefing. Josie looked up and nodded but kept her attention on the adjutant until she finished.

Miller looked around at the pictures on the wall for a few seconds, then sat on the couch and pouted. There were one or two items left to discuss, but neither Josie nor Maki wanted to talk about them in front of him, so the adjutant got up and gathered her paperwork.

"All yours," Maki said as she walked out, clearly not pleased.

"Hope this isn't a bad time," Miller said, struggling to get his substantial mass off the couch and move closer to Josie, whose first thought was that he'd definitely been living the good life on the officers' union dues. The back of his expensive-looking jacket stayed stuck above his hips when he stood and his fleshy handshake felt limp and damp. He was clearly uncomfortable in an office with barely a hint of circulating fresh air and dabbed at the perspiration on his face as he talked.

"Good as any," she said. "What can I do for you?"

He attempted to be charming telling her how well thought of she was among the league directors, the officers who worked for her and generally throughout the department and practically the entire civilized world. She didn't respond or react. Flattery never impressed her and Josie knew her reputation would be built or destroyed by her alone. It didn't matter what he or his buddies thought. All she could control was what she did.

"There is one matter I would like to bring to your attention," he said, his beauty contestant smile quickly mutating into a somber frown.

"Really," Josie said, with phony surprise but caring less what he had to say every minute he remained in her office.

"Detective Ann Martin met with one of our directors and expressed some discomfort in her situation on your homicide table." Josie must've looked as if she was about to pounce because he added quickly, "She isn't making a complaint against anyone. I thought I'd just give you a heads up."

"If she isn't making a complaint, what's the problem?"

"She's uncomfortable and wanted counseling."

"Because?" Josie asked, determined to coax something relevant from the man.

"The way I understand it is she feels like nobody really wants her here."

"Does she base that feeling on anything concrete?"

"Not that I'm aware of."

"Did she mention why she hasn't brought her concerns to me?" Josie asked and kept herself from saying, "since I'm so wonderful and everybody's so damn crazy about me."

"She was hesitant to cause problems for you, but I thought you'd probably want to know. Our paralegal did advise her to discuss the matter with you and even offered to sit in on any meeting."

"She didn't think going to the league might cause me problems? What paralegal?" Josie asked, knowing there wasn't a good answer to her first question, but grateful for not having to deal with the league's general counsel who'd been a mediocre cop before law school, and in her opinion was a terrible lawyer.

"Gabriella Johnston, she's in our attorney's office and is incredibly good in these situations. She can usually get the officer back on board without bad feelings or lawsuits."

"Great," Josie said, getting up. "I have no idea who she is but tell her to call me and set up a meeting with Detective Martin."

She got up and moved around her desk hoping it would be a not-so-subtle clue she was done talking, but it took escorting him out the door to deliver the message. He continued chattering until they got into the lobby where she shook hands, thanked him for his assistance and retreated back to her office.

"Commander's on line one," Maki said as soon as Josie stepped inside the admin office. "I told him you were away from your desk. He wanted to wait."

"Just keeps getting better," Josie said.

She picked up the phone, and for the next few minutes, she listened to a lecture on following orders and the danger of allowing emotions to interfere with intelligent decision making. Josie didn't attempt to interrupt Perry because that would've prolonged the speech. She waited patiently until he ran out of words, mostly adjectives.

"Are you still there?" he asked, after a lengthy period of silence on her part.

"Yes sir," she said.

"Are you going to tell me what kind of game you think you're playing here?" he asked.

"Detective Richards asked for Behan's assistance and I didn't see any reason to deny the request."

"Mr. Kessler called the chief this morning and said Behan was still in charge as far as he could tell. Apparently your detective interviewed his daughter-in-law again today. Is that correct?"

"Detective Richards set up the interview. Behan went along only to assist."

"Don't play games with me Corsino. When I give an order, I expect you to do as you're told."

"It's Detective Richards's investigation," she said calmly. "If you think a surveillance detective with very little homicide experience can handle a major murder investigation on his own, just tell me and I'll pull Behan off. He has plenty to do without this."

There was silence on the other end of the line and Josie could almost picture the commander pounding his head against his desk. She knew he wanted her to behave like a good little soldier and do whatever she was told, but she was a cop, not a soldier, and would do whatever it took to catch a killer.

"I have four captains under my command, Captain Corsino. Why is it you're the only one that makes me feel like I have no idea what you're doing and no matter what I say you're going to do things your way."

"I have a lot of respect for you, sir. I'm sorry you feel that way," she said as sincerely as she could, knowing he was probably right.

Before ending their conversation, Commander Perry put Josie on notice again that if he found out Behan, instead of Richards, was running Kessler's murder investigation, she would answer to him, and, "It won't be pretty."

Josie didn't want the commander as an enemy, but everything about this investigation was beginning to smell like day-old garbage. What was the department afraid Behan might uncover? She couldn't believe anyone thought protecting Kessler's reputation was worth letting a killer escape, maybe the same killer who was responsible for Trumbo's death.

She recognized the dull pain developing above her eyes as a lack of caffeine, or food, or it might've been Perry's tirade. Change of watch was unusually noisy this afternoon with uniformed officers filling the hallways and watch commander's office, yelling at one another, banging doors and putting the decibel level somewhere near a rave party. Normally she enjoyed their activity. There was edginess in the turmoil that signaled to her the young officers were primed and ready to do battle with whatever they might encounter on the streets, but today it was just adding to the throbbing in her head.

It was getting late and her stomach was making those sounds that led to making microwave popcorn while avoiding any of the health-conscious unappetizing snacks that filled most of the space in vending machines these days. She remembered the pale skinny reflection in her wardrobe mirror, called Marge in the vice office and told her to meet at Nora's in five minutes. Her friend never turned down an opportunity to eat and was already munching on garlic fries when Josie arrived.

The bar area was empty except for a couple of burglary detectives who were paying their bill as soon as Josie got to Marge's table. They stopped to chat about a particular problem they were having in the Hollywood Hills and asked if they could have an extra car patrol the area. Josie explained daily deployment was up to the lieutenant watch commander, but promised to discuss the problem with him. She was careful not to make promises, but knew the lieutenant would find a way to help. Her patrol lieutenants were new and eager to demonstrate their worth.

"Don't these fuckers ever give you a break?" Marge asked when the detectives had gone.

"What are you talking about?"

"You're eating. Can't they wait and bitch about their problems later?"

"I don't care. At least I know they're trying to deal with problems."

"It's like being on patrol again. You just sit down to eat and some woman comes up and wants to discuss her neighbor's barking dog, or her nephew's drug habit, or wants you to make her asshole kid behave."

"Comes with the job."

"You're too nice. Tell 'em to fuck off."

"Yeah, like I'd ever do that. What do you have on Nicola's?" Josie asked. She was never certain how much of Marge's outrageous behavior was for effect. There were never any complaints from citizens or suspects so Josie guessed a lot of her friend's off-the-wall comments were done strictly for her reaction.

"On who?" Marge asked, taking a bite of hamburger.

"That club Nicola's where Trumbo had a membership card," Josie said, watching the waitress put a hamburger, chocolate malt and garlic fries in front of her.

"I'm going there tonight. It's a mystery . . . wasn't on my radar at all so I drove by . . . it's on Cahuenga near the freeway."

"Is that where the Greek restaurant used to be?"

"No, this looks like a business office on the outside. Wanna come?"

Josie groaned. "Yes, but my kid's coming home tonight. I want some time with him."

"We'll be done early. Red asked me to see what kind of place it is. He wants to find out what they know about

Trumbo or Kessler without telling them it's the police asking."

"How do you know it's not a private club, and they won't let you in?"

"It's not. I pulled their permits and licenses. They serve liquor and charge a club membership fee . . . a hundred dollars."

"A year?"

"A night, Corsino . . . our Secret Service fund can handle us . . . of course I'm out of business for the rest of the month."

"I'll get the bureau to advance you cash. What do I wear?"

"I watched the place last night . . . very informal, looks like a bunch of after-work business geeks. Some of them were in casual clothes, some dressier. You're good like that, better if you can show more skin," Marge said, pointing at her blouse. She hadn't had any inclination to put on a uniform and was still wearing her Levi's and boots. She felt sorry for patrol officers who had to wear that dark blue uniform, but she intended to keep her casual look until the heat wave passed.

They finished eating and walked back to the station. There were still several hours before they had to leave for the club, and she wanted to call David to tell him she'd be late, but didn't. The food had cured her headache. The thought of disappointing her son over having to work late wasn't appealing, and it was a sure formula for regenerating the pain in her head. He'd figure it out when she wasn't there. He would be staying with her, so they should have plenty of time to talk.

Maki was waiting when Josie returned. Her desk was clean and she was chatting with one of the police officers who had been loaned to detectives. Josie thought they both looked, and were acting, like teenagers. He'd been taken out of patrol because of an injury. His torn hamstring was mending but he couldn't go back in the field for several weeks, so she had assigned him to detectives to help with their paperwork. It was a way to get him out of the house where he was going crazy and teach him something new, but his contribution other than flirting with her adjutant had been minimal. His ingratitude was irritating.

"Go away. Leave my adjutant alone," Josie said, in a half-kidding voice as she walked past them into her office.

He blushed and disappeared into the hallway.

A few seconds later, Maki carried a stack of papers into her office and said, "Boss, you scared him."

"Good," she said. "He shouldn't be bothering you."

"I don't mind."

"I do. He needs to earn his keep or go home. This is a chance for him to learn something and he's wasting it."

Maki left the papers in a neat pile on the desk and turned to leave.

"Sorry," she said, staring at her hands and nervously pulling at her watch band.

"Maki," Josie said, and the young woman stopped fidgeting and looked up. "You are the best adjutant I've ever had. I'm very happy with you and your work, but he's not a good cop yet. I need to make him better, so he lives long enough to get that pension money the city takes out of his paycheck every two weeks."

"Okay, boss," she said, smiling.

"Go home if you're caught up."

"Yes, ma'am, but I can stay if you need me."

"No," Josie said.

She recognized too much of herself in Maki. Her adjutant never wanted to miss anything and would work all night without being asked just to be at the station when the officers came back with arrestees in tow and stories to tell. Police work and everything connected to it was addictive. She knew Maki thrived vicariously on the excitement, but watching wasn't a substitute for living. Josie couldn't save herself from a lifetime of adrenaline overloads, but she liked Maki and wanted her to go home at night, have a family and a normal life . . . whatever the hell that was.

Josie had started to sort through the stack of papers when the watch commander interrupted and said there was a priest, Father O'Reilly, at the desk who wanted to see her.

"I told him it was late and you might be getting ready to leave. He said he doesn't mind coming back tomorrow," the young lieutenant said, giving her a look that suggested, "I'd put this off if I were you."

"Let him in. I know Father O'Reilly," she said, pushing the paperwork away.

In a few seconds the lieutenant returned with the priest trailing. The man looked tired and thinner than Josie had remembered. He wasn't wearing the collar tonight and could've passed for a nerdy college professor in jeans and light knit polo shirt. When they shook hands he looked away and seemed just as nervous as he'd been the morning of Kessler's murder.

He sat at her worktable and didn't speak right away. Josie offered him coffee, which he declined. She asked how he'd been, saying she hoped everything was okay at the church. She was trying to help him relax but failing miserably.

"I've been thinking about that poor man. I, I thought maybe . . . there were things I should've told you," he said, attempting to control his stutter.

"What sort of things?" she asked, thinking Behan ought to be here, but she didn't want to scare the priest back into silence by suggesting she call him.

"I haven't been well . . . taking medication . . . my . . . my nerves."

Josie listened quietly as he haltingly described his condition, his exhaustion and the church's refusal to move him away from a place that he believed was destroying him. It was a painful recital for both of them, and his stuttering got worse as his anxiety grew.

Finally she got him to stop talking by standing and leaving the office. Maki had a water cooler near her desk. Josie filled a glass and brought it back.

"Drink this and sit back for a minute," she said, giving him the glass. "You don't have to talk, just sit there and try to settle down."

He thanked her and took two pink capsules from a small pill container in his pants pocket. He swallowed them with a sip of water, leaned back and closed his eyes. Her cell phone rang and she reached over to her desk and turned it off without looking at the caller's number.

"Thank you," O'Reilly said, opening his eyes after several minutes. "I have . . . never mind. This is not about me. I'm ashamed to admit I lost a soul that night," he said. His stutter was more controlled now and his hands had stopped trembling. Josie wondered what was in those little pink pills.

"I don't understand," she said.

"Mr. Kessler came to confess . . . but I didn't permit him to make his peace with God."

"You refused to hear his confession?"

"Worse . . . I allowed him to think I was listening until he realized . . . he asked me to help him fight the Devil. My disgust kept me from hearing and understanding until after he was dead." Father O'Reilly folded his hands tightly and pressed his knuckles against his lips. The tips of his fingers were red from the pressure.

"I'm sorry, I still don't understand what you're telling me. Did he feel his lifestyle was sinful?"

"No, no that wasn't it at all. He knew something about another man . . . someone I thought at first he feared, but then it seemed as if he respected him too. He was clearly suffering, but to my shame all I could see was his perversion."

"Did Kessler tell you anything else about the man or why he might've feared him?"

"I don't remember exactly, but I have a feeling it was an influential or powerful person . . . someone who could control him, make him do things he didn't want to do. It was all very confusing. I was trying to shut out the words, but I believe he had made a decision that he couldn't keep his secret any longer. He was about to do something and it frightened him."

"And he wasn't talking about his cross-dressing?"

"No, I'm certain that wasn't it. He expressed no remorse in believing God had erred in creating him as a man."

Josie could almost see the priest relaxing as he talked to her. It was warm in the office. The temperature was still in the nineties outside, and the air conditioning inside the station wasn't functioning at all now. Perspiration soaked through his shirt under the armpits, and his thinning hair looked damp and flat, but either the pink pills had done their job, or finally revealing what he knew had relieved his apprehension.

"Why did you decide you could talk to me?" she asked.

"I failed a sinner in life; I hoped to do something for him in death," he said and stood, using the chair to help support himself. "I don't think I'm betraying his trust. You see it wasn't a proper confession . . . I do feel this is the right thing. Don't you?" he asked, but she didn't answer because he didn't seem to want a response. He turned to leave, then stopped, came back, and sat again. "His confusion and pain frightened me; wanting something that's impossible, I can't understand," he said, shaking his head. "God makes these decisions, not man."

"It's all right, Father. What happened wasn't your fault," Josie said. He was becoming agitated again and she tried to say something to calm him.

"His fear was terrifying. I've never felt such fear in a grown man . . . as if he knew something very bad was about to happen. I abandoned him to face eternity without benefit of absolution . . . condemned by my arrogance. He wanted forgiveness. I failed him, failed my vows," he said and got up again, steady now. "Sorry Captain, I didn't mean to . . . I hope I've helped."

Josie touched his arm to get his attention again and asked if he'd be willing to come back the next day and give her homicide detectives a statement. She hoped they could make more sense out of his words. He nodded, and she escorted him back to the lobby, then watched as he walked slowly but steadily toward Sunset Boulevard. He seemed frail and vulnerable, bent over slightly with his arms folded tight in front of him moving alone on the empty sidewalk . . . an easy target for one of the many boulevard muggers, she thought, and turned away. She went back into the station convinced the priest had bigger worries than local street thugs.

Josie waited another hour before changing into a black silk tank top she had in her wardrobe. It was actually a chemise slip but looked great with her jeans and was perfect for a hot night. She slipped her badge and ID into her pocket and rummaged through the top shelf and found a leg holster for her five-shot revolver. It wasn't the safest way to carry a gun but she strapped it onto her left leg. Her outfit didn't really leave a lot of choices. Purses were too difficult to keep track of in club settings, and she wasn't going anywhere without a weapon. She had borrowed fake teardrop diamond earrings from Marge and put up her hair in a fashionable twist.

She checked herself in the wardrobe mirror and was surprised how good her outfit looked in a trashy sort of way. The leg holster was uncomfortable and difficult to reach in an emergency, but she knew it was her best option. Marge met her in the nearly empty detective squad room where Josie was surprised to see Behan still working on his case notes.

Marge wore a similar outfit only more risqué with a strapless top and tight black spandex pants.

"Where are you two going dressed like that?" Behan asked, looking up from his computer.

"Nicola's," Marge said. "You asked me to check it out."

"Thanks, for a minute I thought you might be supplementing your incomes."

"Another wisecrack and I'll make you come with us," Josie said.

"No you won't . . . men guests aren't allowed," he said, grinning.

"Really?"

"Women only," Marge said. "But Red actually could go since half these fuckers don't look any better in a dress than he would."

"We're going to a drag club," Josie said.

"Yep."

"Don't you think that's a relevant fact, something you should've told me before I agreed to do this?"

"You might've said no and then I'd have to go alone because all my female undercovers look like high school cheerleaders. I need mysterious and funky-hot, not cute."

"By the way, Red, Father O'Reilly came to see me and he's willing to give a formal statement. I didn't look for you; I was afraid he'd bolt. Actually I didn't think you'd still be here," Josie said and gave him a brief rundown of what the priest told her.

"So somebody might've had a reason to muzzle Kessler, or at least he thought so," Behan said when she finished.

"Influential powerful person covers a lot of fucking territory . . . his father, his boss, maybe even the widow. She's not exactly falling on his grave, crying her eyes out," Marge said, tugging on her top to pull it up a little and added, "We gotta go, boss. My snitch is waiting to get us into the club."

"Try not to be yourself Bailey and piss off everybody in the place before you get any good info," Behan said, still looking at his computer and missing the middle-finger response by Marge. Josie saw him almost smile. It didn't take a genius to figure out what Marge's reaction would be.

Marge drove one of her vice squad's undercover rentals, a new black Mercedes, because she intended to park it across the street from Nicola's where it could be seen. Her snitch was a drag queen who was not as flamboyant as many of those who roamed Hollywood's streets, but nevertheless unmistakably a queen. His name was Steven Petroski but he preferred to be called Ramona. He was waiting for them on the corner of Hollywood and Highland, wearing his best party dress.

The tourists coming out of the restaurants and theaters gathered around the man thinking he was obviously there for their entertainment. Ramona smiled and posed for cell phone pictures with retired old men from towns like Phoenix and Miami while their wives cringed but took the photos. It was no different from standing in front of the world's biggest ball of string to prove to the neighbors they'd gone somewhere and found something they'd never allow to exist in their own backyard.

Marge pulled the Mercedes to the red curb and parked. She got out and stood between the open driver's door and the car.

"Petroski!" she shouted over the sunroof. "Get your fat ass over here."

The sea of gray hair parted and Ramona in his bright red dress and platform shoes blew kisses to his fans as he sashayed across the open plaza toward the car. He wasn't a big man but a little overweight. It wasn't easy in the tight dress to get into the back seat, but he managed to contort his body in a sideways slide. The overpowering odor of cheap perfume immediately filled the car and Josie lowered her window a little.

"What the fuck did you do, shower in that shit?" Marge asked, getting back into the car and turning the air conditioner higher.

"A girl's gotta make an impression," Ramona said in a husky voice.

Josie turned in the seat to see him. He had a round toad face heavily made-up with red lipstick and dark mascara. His wig was black and long with hundreds of tiny ringlet curls covered in layers of sticky hair spray giving it a lacquered enamel appearance.

"How difficult will it be to get us into the club?" Josie asked.

"Sweetie, with that face, don't sweat it. But take mama's advice. Don't let those pissants near your drink . . . you neither sergeant . . . drop a roofie in your gin and tonic, find your pussy shanghaied to the highest bidder." His last sentence was a bad rap rendition.

Petroski didn't make much effort to disguise his voice but his mannerisms were Kabuki feminine with an abundance of hand movements and an occasional touch of one finger on Josie's shoulder to make a point.

"Did you know Henry Trumbo or Patrick Kessler?" Josie asked, turning just enough so he couldn't reach her.

"As I informed the beautiful sergeant, can't say I've had that pleasure."

"I'm a lieutenant . . . asshole. Get us inside, then stay away from me until I come looking for you . . . go about your business and let us work," Marge said, as she parked the car on Cahuenga across the street from the club. There was a large asphalt lot adjacent to the building, but Josie knew Marge would want to be where it would be easy to leave in a hurry if that became necessary. "Got it?" Marge said, glaring at Petroski in the rearview mirror.

"Yes ma'am, we are virtual strangers once I step over the enchanted threshold," he said, patting his porcupine hair with both hands.

They crossed the street but before reaching the front door of Nicola's, Marge stopped Petroski and said, "I forgot. Find a ride home. You're not coming back with me."

"Why, darling, would I ever leave with you?" Petroski asked dramatically, before giving the muscular doorman a peck on the cheek while ushering Marge and Josie into the club in front of him like a mother hen. The big doorman gave Petroski a playful pat on the butt and didn't seem to notice or care about the two women. "Behold paradise," Petroski said, raising his flabby arms as he stood under a huge chandelier in the lobby of the spacious club. Josie thought the place resembled pictures she'd seen of Roaring Twenties speakeasies, over-the-top cheap glitz with crystal disco balls, a shiny white marble bar with painted gold trim and white tablecloths with vases of long-stem roses everywhere. The male waiters wore makeup and costume tuxedos with tailored shorts and tails. It was gaudy and elegant at the same time.

"Sonnofabitch," Marge said, doing a 360-degree turn and trying to take in the strange setting.

"Tootles," Petroski said, walking away from them with an exaggerated hip sway and waving over his shoulder after Marge paid the cover charge for the three of them. He moved toward a white-haired, tanned old man with a long ponytail and lipstick, dressed in a business suit with an unbuttoned Hawaiian shirt. He had been loitering near the bar and gave Petroski a broad grin.

"His night's a success. Let's see what we can do," Josie said, following a man who acted like a maitre d' and did manage to find them an empty table in a spot where they had a good view of most of the club.

A jazz trio was playing toward the back of the room, but noisy conversations from too many drunken patrons and loud laughing at the bar nearly drowned out what sounded to Josie like some decent music. She was amazed by the number of people clothed in expensive business attire who seemed to have stepped out from an office at Seventh and Flower but were interacting with obvious drag queens and cross-dressers as if they were business clients and social equals, which they might've been.

Marge went to the bar to get them a couple of bottled beers. Josie had made her swear she'd watch the bartender open them in front of her. She knew a glass of wine was not an option in a place where roofies and other date-rape drugs routinely got slipped into drinks.

The vice lieutenant took several minutes making her way back to their table. Josie observed her working the room and was always impressed how Marge could get just about anyone to talk and confide in her.

Josie sat back and knew it might be awhile before she tasted that cold beer but didn't care because she hated beer anyway. Her role was strictly backup and protection for her friend. There was a time she enjoyed the role of undercover cop and would've been disappointed not to be out there making contacts and digging for information, but these days running Hollywood station was a big enough challenge. All her energy and creativity was directed at keeping her division functioning and her people safe.

A distinct odor of marijuana was in the air and Josie saw several people smoking joints. The traffic in and out of the restrooms told her there was probably more drug use and sex going on out of sight. Marge had settled in at a table with a few geeky-looking patrons so Josie wandered into the lounge area of the women's restroom to test her theory, and immediately interrupted two men, one of them bent over a velvet couch in a dark corner with his skirt pushed up to his waist exposing his huge naked ass to the world, as the other one who had his skirt down at his feet stood behind him with an erection and a silly grin.

"Ladies," Josie said nonchalantly, and walked past them into the stall area. They barely paid any attention to her, and she could hear them from the other room moaning and grunting.

She waited until it was quiet again, flushed the toilet and washed her hands, and when she came back through the lounge they were sitting on the couch now fully dressed sharing a mirror full of choppy little lines of white powder.

When Josie got back to her table, both Marge and Ramona were there.

"Where've you been?" Marge asked, looking worried.

"Had to use the restroom," Josie said.

"How much fun was that?" Ramona asked, winking.

"Seriously, you need to shut this place down," Josie said.

"You missed her. Mrs. Kessler was here," Marge said.

"The widow Kessler?"

"The same. She was with some other woman . . . fuck, I think it was a woman. Who knows down this rabbit hole," Marge said, taking her cell phone out of her pocket. She showed Josie a photo she'd taken of Susan Kessler and a woman Josie recognized immediately.

"That's Councilman Flowers's secretary," she said and concentrated for a moment until the name popped into her head. "Miss Mabry . . . Behan and I met her at his district office. Just let Red and Richards know tomorrow. You find anything else?" she asked.

This wasn't the sort of place she expected to find Susan Kessler especially so soon after her husband's death, but it wasn't unusual that a wife would know a woman who worked with her husband. It was significant that Susan Kessler acted as if she didn't know about her husband's "other life," and yet here she was romping in what was most likely his adult playground.

"I stayed away from them because the wife might know me but Petroski got up close and personal."

Petroski wiped his forehead with the back of a cocktail napkin leaving a dark beige smear of makeup. Nicola's wasn't well-ventilated or sufficiently air-conditioned. The temperature outside was mildly uncomfortable but with all the body heat it had to be ten degrees hotter inside the club. Beads of sweat ran down his face from under the heavy wig. The red dress had been soiled by perspiration and Josie could smell the stale odor of dry cleaning fluid every time he moved.

"I merely expressed my condolences to the widow," Petroski said.

"What did she say? Did she talk to you?" Josie asked.

"Bitch told me to fuck off," he said, and grinned before adding, "The other one seemed nice though."

"Did they talk to anyone," Josie asked.

"They went to the coat room . . . the bitch yelled at Frankie . . . came out, told me to fuck off and left."

"Who's Frankie?" Marge asked.

"The coat girl . . . we call her Frankenstein because she's had so many surgeries, hacking away to create that soft womanly look . . . but you know big hands, big feet, King Kong post-electrolysis . . . not much hope there," Petroski said, shaking his head.

"Why did Susan Kessler yell at him?" Josie asked, trying to keep the man's erratic thoughts on track.

"She claimed her husband left a briefcase in the coat-room, but Frankie swore he took it when he left that night."

"Which night?" Marge said, impatiently.

"The night he got stabbed, darling. Pay attention," Petroski said, as if he were talking to a child. He turned to Josie, looked at the ceiling, and shrugged.

Petroski explained that he heard Frankie tell Mrs. Kessler her husband had been in the club just hours before he died, and he showed his briefcase to a big man that everyone else in the club had pegged as a cop but then Patrick and the cop left together.

"The girls were on their best behavior until Officer Piggy was out of the house," Petroski said.

"We need to bring Frankie to the station and show him a picture of Trumbo," Josie said, when Petroski left the table. She was tired and ready to leave. They had been in the club three hours and had already established that both Patrick Kessler and maybe Trumbo had been there the night Kessler was murdered. Susan Kessler had lied to them. She knew about her husband's other life and apparently so did his boss's secretary.

They located Frankie in the coatroom, and discovered that Petroski's description of the man had been more than kind. Frankie lived up to his namesake, and Josie knew it would take a lot more than operations to make this man look like an ugly woman. He was taller than her, with a wrestler's muscular body and a boxer's battered face. His hair was shoulder length, curly and dyed red, and he wore a tank top and shorts exposing his hairy arms and legs. She wondered what he looked like before all the surgeries.

He agreed to go the station the next morning and look at a photo line-up, but his description of the man who left the club with Kessler the night he was murdered was dead-on for ex-cop Henry Trumbo.

SEVEN

Behan was gone by the time Josie and Marge got back to Hollywood station. It was nearly midnight when Josie turned on her cell phone and saw the missed calls from her son. She took off the sexy chemise top and put on the shirt she'd worn that morning, traded the leg holster for the one on her belt and a .45-caliber semiauto and felt dressed and comfortable again.

As much as she wanted to see David, Josie hoped he and Kizzie were tired and had gone to bed. She wasn't in the mood and didn't have the energy to deal with them tonight. She just wanted to shower and wash the smell of cheap perfume and body odor out of her hair.

Her son's beat-up Jeep Wrangler was parked in the driveway but, for a change, he'd left enough space for her to pull the city car into the garage. As soon as she turned off the engine she heard that wonderful mellow sound of the baby grand. She'd missed his music and the house seemed to come alive again as his perfectly played chords filled the empty rooms. She realized, however, all David's problems and his girlfriend came with his incredible talent.

Kizzie was waiting in the kitchen . . . five feet tall, ninety pounds, and forty-four years of snarky attitude. She smiled but didn't get up or pretend she was happy to see Josie. They understood each other. There was no real animosity between them, just the knowledge that Kizzie wasn't about to give up Josie's son, and Josie's belief that she was too old and in every way completely wrong for the young man.

Josie loved and worried about her son and had made it clear she believed he needed a woman who would encourage him to be successful and independent, and to develop his talent for music and painting into a good livelihood—for him, and hopefully at some point, his children and her only chance of having grandchildren. Instead he had Kizzie, who was a surrogate mother figure probably past childbearing age who supported his tendency to withdraw from life and responsibility and to depend entirely on her.

"Thank you for letting us stay," Kizzie said without a hint of gratitude.

"No problem," Josie said, dumping her purse and briefcase on the dining room chair. "What sort of job did David get?" she asked, knowing no further niceties were necessary between them.

Kizzie was wearing shorts and a skimpy halter top, sitting cross-legged and barefoot on the kitchen chair looking remarkably younger than her age. The tattoos now covered not only both arms and her back, but one leg had several pictures and some symbols Josie didn't recognize. It was obvious she didn't want to answer the question and finally mumbled, "Davy should tell you himself."

They conversed for a minute or two about the trip from San Francisco, but Josie was only half listening and couldn't help staring at the woman wondering how someone who was older than her managed to look that young. She knew there had to be health advantages to stress-free living, but who knew hanging out in coffee shops and selling homemade strings of beads at swap meets and flea markets kept your skin so smooth and wrinkle free. Josie did know two things for certain—first, there was no way she'd ever deface her body with permanent ink scribbling; and second, she'd never be capable of contorting her skinny six-foot frame to sit on the kitchen chair that way.

The music stopped, but David didn't show himself for several minutes. He probably heard them talking and was still hoping that if they spent more time together the two women in his life might eventually do more than tolerate each other.

"Hi mom," he said peeking around the kitchen doorway.

He looked healthier than the last time Josie had seen him. His skin was tanned and he'd gained a few pounds. She hugged him and kissed his cheek but was surprised when he hugged her longer and harder, as if he hadn't seen her for years instead of the few months he'd been in San Francisco.

"You look great, honey," she said, touching his short thinning hair. When he went to San Francisco, his hair was long and tied back in a ponytail. He looked handsome and happy.

"Kizzie's been taking good care of me," he said, smiling at his girlfriend.

"Actually, he's become a top-rate chef and we're eating like hogs," Kizzie said, uncrossing her legs and reaching over to rub his lower back.

"Top-rate chef?" Josie asked, remembering the young man who'd eat a loaf of bread rather than heat up leftovers in the microwave.

"First in his class at Sonoma's Chaillot Gourmet Cooking School," Kizzie said.

"So your new job involves cooking," Josie said, tentatively, hoping she'd drawn the wrong conclusion, but he nodded. "Anybody care for a glass of wine?" she asked, snatching an unopened bottle of Pinot Noir off the credenza in the dining room. Her vow not to drink too much was being tested. She opened it in record time and poured a little into three glasses.

"Let's toast the beginning of Davy's new career," Kizzie said, standing and holding her glass up.

Josie drank hers without acknowledging the toast and poured a little more before asking, "What about your music and painting?" She stopped herself from saying her son's name was David not Davy because she was convinced the woman took some weird pleasure in diminishing everything in her life.

"I love my piano. I'll never stop playing."

"You've been given a gift. It's selfish not to use it."

"You mean take advantage of it . . . make money off it," he said, not getting agitated like he usually did when they had this conversation. He was calm, so sure of himself.

"Yes," Josie said. "Better than sweating over a stove all day for minimum wage."

"That's not me. I don't want or need to be recognized as a great musical talent . . . I'm not," he said and held up his hand when Josie started to disagree. "I'm a good pianist. If I was willing to give up everything else in life and devote myself to music, then maybe I could be great, but I don't want to live that way."

"What about your painting?"

"What about it? I paint almost every day. You'll get one of my masterpieces for your birthday," he said, grinning at her.

"Great," Josie said, not sounding nearly as sarcastic as she wanted to, but it was disappointment, not anger, she felt. Her son was always so ambiguous about his talent and future, but now he seemed certain of himself. She was used to bullying him into admitting the error of his ways and getting him back on track, but it wasn't working this time.

Kizzie sat quietly sipping her wine. She'd obviously had time to make her case while they were living in San Francisco, and there wasn't any need for her to interject her opinion now. Josie feared David had found his tiny muse but she wasn't going to inspire him to play concerts at Disney Hall or hang his beautiful paintings in the Getty

Museum. Instead she'd move him to find exciting new ways to fricassee a chicken.

Josie kissed David on the cheek and gathered her belongings and the half bottle of wine that remained and slowly climbed the stairs to her bedroom on the third floor. She dumped everything except the wine on the chair near her bed and went back down to the den on the second floor and closed the door.

The bottle was empty, and she had just stretched out on the lounger and started to drift off when she heard the den door open and close. David sat on the matching lounger near hers. In happier days, she and Jake would sit side-by-side like that, drinking brandy and talking about their day until he'd get amorous and drag her to the couch where they'd make love and fall asleep in each other's arms. If she were going to change her life, she'd probably have to get new furniture or move some place where there weren't so many damn reminders of how happy she thought she'd been.

"I know you're disappointed, but this is what I need and want," David said, not looking at her. "Don't blame Kizzie or Dad. It's my decision."

"Is it?"

"Yes, I'm not nearly as impressionable as you seem to think I am."

Josie pushed the lounger into a sitting position, leaned on the arm and stared at him.

"We'll see," she said. "I want you to be happy, but I'm afraid twenty years from now you're going to regret this."

"I love you, just trust me," he said, getting up. "I know it's not your thing but let me handle my life my way. Everybody has regrets, but this isn't going to be one of mine."

She watched him leave and didn't say anything, but knew it wasn't in her nature to sit by quietly and let him ruin his life. However, she had to admit tonight was the first time she'd seen her son this passionate and committed to anything. It was a nice change.

She was tired and had to get out of this room before more good memories clouded the last year and influenced her decision to leave Jake. She went upstairs to the bedroom, changed her clothes and slept like a baby.

The next morning, Josie got up early and felt good. She went for a run at the high school and had breakfast, but there was no sign of her son or Kizzie. The door to David's bedroom was closed so she guessed they were still sleeping. She took a shower, dressed and was at Hollywood station before nine A.M.

Her adjutant looked surprised to see her so early without a dead body somewhere in the division.

"You've got to go back to detectives and see what Detective Behan has in the interrogation room," Maki said, following Josie into her office.

"What?"

"No, no, you've got to see for yourself."

Josie took the paperwork out of Maki's hands and threw it on her desk. "I'll look when I get my coffee. What else is going on?"

Her adjutant turned on the computer and pulled up the calendar for the day. There was a community meeting with the homeowners association at Father O'Reilly's church on Santa Monica Boulevard near the Regency Arms. Josie texted the senior lead officer for that area and he responded that he already had planned to be there. It would be a necessary waste of time. The people who lived in that neighborhood needed reassurance that their families were safe. Whoever had killed Kessler and Trumbo probably had little interest in the poor immigrant population, but Josie knew she had to deal with their fears and concerns. Occasionally, one of the residents actually knew something valuable about the crimes occurring in their area, another little piece of the puzzle that, by itself, meant nothing but might help create the bigger picture. Most of the time at that sort of event, Josie drank a lot of coffee, ate too many cookies and met a lot of decent people who just wanted to live quiet lives without their children stepping over dead bodies on the way to school.

She finished most of her paperwork, answered a few phone calls and was ready to get another mug of coffee. Several detectives were leaving the interrogation room where the video feed from Behan's interview could be seen. It was obvious that most detectives in the squad room had been in there to see it. Josie got her coffee and saw them pretending not to watch her go into the room and close the door.

Even on tape, there was no mistaking Frankie, the coatroom guy from Nicola's, sitting across from Behan and Richards and dressed in his finest couture—a professional wrestler's body stuffed into a pink silk pantsuit with ruffled white blouse and a tiny hat with white feathers perched on a mop of red hair with a face resembling a heavily made-up cabbage-patch doll.

They were just finishing the interview, and when Frankie stood to leave, he was bigger than either Behan or Richards. Josie waited outside the room until Frankie had left. She wanted the roomful of cops to see her standing there and prevent the snickering that might've been well-deserved but wasn't professional. Frankie didn't seem to recognize her and reached the hallway unscathed by the whispered remarks that would inevitably burst from those detectives' intelligent, creative minds as soon as he was out of the building and unable to hear them.

Josie went into Behan's interrogation room and closed the door. Unfortunately, Frankie's appearance would initiate a cornucopia of one-liners. Most cops could contain their cynicism only so long before it exploded like opening a pressure-release valve. She knew it was the way they coped with the strains on their sanity, so she allowed them some leeway, but not at the expense of another man's self-esteem. In Frankie's case, however, even she had to wonder if the man possessed any sense of worth.

"Were you listening?" Behan asked, as soon as she sat across from him. He was gathering his paperwork and a six-pack of pictures that included Henry Trumbo. Frankie's initials were under the one of Trumbo so Josie knew he'd identified the dead man as the one who left with Patrick Kessler that night.

"No, I got here just as you were finishing," Josie said, glancing at Richards.

"He ID'd Trumbo, so we know they were together about an hour before Kessler got killed," Richards said.

"Less than twenty-four hours later, Trumbo's dead too," Behan said, and added, "And the briefcase is nowhere to be found."

"Did Frankie have any idea what was inside the briefcase?" Josie asked.

"That dude is so messed up," Behan said, looking at Richards who nodded. "But he's not stupid. He remembered it was a hard case and had a combination lock. He said it felt heavy when he picked it up . . . like it was full of bricks. He watched Trumbo open it and look inside before they left Nicola's together."

"So who has it now . . . the killer?" Josie asked.

Richards stood and stretched. "That's my guess. What do you think, Red?"

"Haven't got a clue, but at least we can say the homicides are most likely connected, so we look for that common thread, something that ties these guys together."

"Kessler's father, his wife, Marvin Beaumont, suspects are endless . . . I wonder if Councilman Flowers knew Trumbo," Josie said, thinking out loud. She didn't get an opportunity to discuss it further because Maki interrupted to tell her she had a visitor waiting in her office.

She hadn't made an appointment, but Gabriella Johnston from the Protective League was in the neighborhood and wondered if Captain Corsino might spare her a few minutes to talk about Detective Ann Martin. Josie didn't want to deal with her insecure detective this morning but knew she had no choice. She understood what could happen if an officer felt as if his or her concerns weren't being taken seriously. It affected not only their work, but the entire station because people would inevitably take sides and the issue consumed time and energy. Josie knew it was better to deal with problems early and come to some conclusion. It was the uncertainty and feelings of neglect that caused anxiety and turmoil.

Gabriella Johnston got up as soon as Josie entered the office. She was as tall as Josie and as blonde and beautiful as Marge Bailey. She smiled, stuck out her hand and introduced herself as Gaby. Josie liked her immediately because unlike her boss, the league's general counsel, Gaby was confident and friendly.

"I apologize for barging in," Gaby said, running her hand through her short stylish hair and slipping an unruly strand behind one ear before sitting uninvited at Josie's worktable. "But I want to get this done. I've talked to Detective Martin and frankly . . ." She stopped and looked at the open door before whispering, "Frankly, she's very smart but a little high strung . . . don't you think?"

Josie had to smile. The woman was very disarming. Her voice was strong but not overbearing. "Maybe, but then Behan isn't a good fit for everybody," she said, closing the office door.

"That's what makes the world so damn fascinating; don't you think?" Gaby asked, taking an electronic tablet out of her briefcase and clicking through a few pages. "Let's cut through the bullshit, shall we? My recommendation is we meet without including Detective Behan . . .

just you, Martin and me. From everything I've heard, it's Martin who has to make the adjustment."

"I agree completely." Josie was impressed. Even without meeting him, Gaby had figured out Behan wasn't the problem or at least the problem couldn't be fixed by expecting to change him.

"Okay, so I'll set up our meeting for tomorrow morning if that works for you," Gaby said, switching off the tablet, and Josie nodded. "I'm certain that will be the end of it. I've checked; Martin has a history of heightened sensitivity issues, but she's also an excellent detective, I've been told, and worth all this trouble, yes?"

"I'd agree with that. It's definitely not her work ethic that's the problem," Josie said.

"Okay, we're done. I'll be out of your hair unless you allow me to buy you lunch," she said with that big smile.

"No, but we can walk across the street and have lunch together if you like. I'd enjoy that."

As soon as they left the station, Gaby started telling stories about her boss. She was a paralegal who had just taken the bar exam but had to hold his hand through most of their legal dilemmas. Josie believed her because she had worked with the general counsel on a couple of occasions and had been disappointed with the outcome.

Gaby was funny and told stories like a veteran cop. She had no qualms about making fun of her boss whom she called an idiot savant. "Sadly, his remarkable aptitude is avoiding responsibility." There was no effort to spare herself either as she told Josie about several cases she'd handled where everything went wrong.

"The first time I had to testify at an officer's trial board, I was so nervous my big feet tripped walking up to the front of the room," she stopped to lift up one foot and show Josie that she did indeed have big feet. "I knocked over a video camera on a tripod. It fell on the captain at the end of the table causing him to fling his full cup of hot coffee in the face of the female civilian sitting next to him. She panicked, jumped up and her fist whacked the captain on the other side of her breaking his nose. He screamed in pain, pushed his chair back, fell off the platform and sprained something in his back. Needless to say, nobody really cared what I had to say."

They were sitting at a table in Nora's when she finished the story and not only Josie, but the officers sitting at the table next to theirs, were laughing. Without knowing who they were, Gaby bantered with the men until they paid their bill and left.

"You don't take any of this too seriously, do you?" Josie asked.

"Not really," Gaby replied with that smile. "Life's too short. You've got to enjoy it."

Josie couldn't remember the last time she met anyone she liked so quickly. They swapped stories about police department personalities they both knew and Gaby wasn't shy about revealing every embarrassing detail she'd discovered about several staff officers who had to deal with the Protective League.

Before their lunch arrived, Marge walked into the bar area alone. Josie waved her over to their table and with some coaxing she joined them. It only took a few minutes before Gaby and Marge were comparing the men they'd recently dated. Josie thought they could be sisters, not only in appearance, but in demeanor. The salty language Marge used didn't seem to bother Gaby and toward the end of lunch, she might've taught the vice lieutenant a few choice words.

While they waited for the bill, Josie asked Gaby what she thought of one of her bosses, Doug Miller, the league director.

"He's in the city's pocket," Gaby said.

"In what way?" Josie asked.

"I heard Jeff Flowers has offered him a spot on his council staff when Miller retires from the department this year; and when Flowers runs for mayor, he's promised to keep Miller with him."

"Big fucking surprise," Marge said.

"Did you ever deal with an academy recruit Henry Trumbo?" Josie asked and then added, "He got fired from the academy several months ago." The question should've occurred to her before since part of Gaby's job was to counsel troubled cops.

Gaby had a perplexed expression as if she were trying to remember and finally said, "Big guy, kind of dull looking . . ." She hesitated and then smiled and said, "Yes, the handsome escort who was a carpenter by trade."

"That's the one. What do you know about him?"

"Not much, he came to the league for support when he got fired . . . claimed sexual discrimination because he was bisexual, but that wasn't why he got fired. He lied on his application and it didn't help he was dumber than road kill."

"Did you interview him?"

"I think the boss did first and then gave him to me. I told Trumbo there was nothing we could do. You lie you're gone. Cops can't lie . . . at least they can't get caught lying," Gaby said, pushing her chair back and standing. "Hate to eat and run girls but I've got another crisis to attend downtown." She put enough money on the table to pay for her lunch and slipped the strap of her purse over her shoulder. Before leaving, she shook hands with Josie and Marge, a firm confident handshake.

"Where the fuck did you find her? She's great," Marge said, putting her cash on the table.

"She's working with the union handling officer disputes. She's going to mediate between Martin and me."

"Mediate what?"

"Martin thinks nobody likes her."

"Damn straight. What's to like?"

"You're obviously not invited to participate in this mediation process."

"I'd rather be eaten alive by starving piranhas than sit and listen to Martin whine how shitty it is to be a woman in a man's world. Glass ceilings only bother assholes too stupid or weak to break them."

"So you're not buying into this whole sisterhood thing?" Josie asked, but only because she knew the answer would be entertaining.

"Fuck 'em, I don't remember any sisters offering to help me when I got my ass kicked by that seven-foot Australian pimp last week."

They walked back to the station together and Josie didn't mention Martin again. She would never say it out loud, but she agreed with Marge. Nowadays, nobody paid much attention to your gender if you were good at what you did. Most cops were willing to give anyone a chance at the job, but in the policing world, she also knew women like Gaby or Marge would certainly have an easier time than the uptight ones like Ann Martin.

The door to her office was closed when she got back and Maki told her Martin had asked to borrow it to interview the recruitment sergeant John Castro.

"She told me it would only take an hour, but they've been in there since you left . . . almost an hour and a half. Sorry boss," Maki said.

"Don't worry about it. Is Behan still around?"

Maki didn't know, so Josie went to the detective squad room and found him at his desk making notes on his yellow legal pad.

"Won't you allow your partner to use the interrogation rooms?" Josie asked, sitting on the desk near his.

"What?" Behan asked, looking up.

"She's interviewing Sergeant Castro in my office."

"Don't blame me. You hired her."

"It's not a problem. I just wondered why."

Behan shook his head but didn't respond. He put his pencil down and said, "Kyle Richards and I interviewed Councilman Flowers's secretary Miss Mabry this morning. She said she's known Susan Kessler since high school. Kessler asked her to go to Nicola's last night to pick up her husband's briefcase. She said Kessler claimed there were important papers in there she needed to close his estate. That's all she knew. She'd never been there before and didn't know how Susan Kessler knew the briefcase would be there. Her story pretty much checks out. They did go to the same high school and according to witnesses they were only in the club a few minutes," he said.

He leaned over as if he had seen something in the hall-way and shouted Ann Martin's name.

Without hesitating, Martin did a pirouette to change directions, came into the room and stood in front of Behan's desk.

"Morning Boss," Martin said to Josie and pretty much ignored Behan. "Sorry about taking your office. I didn't want to bring Sergeant Castro into an interrogation room. He's gay and ultrasensitive about being treated unfairly, so I thought it might be better to find neutral ground."

Josie avoided looking at Behan. She knew they would be thinking the same thing, wondering how Martin could say that without recognizing any similarity to her behavior.

"Good thinking," Josie said. "Did you get anything interesting?"

"Castro claims he didn't know Trumbo before the entry interview, didn't know he was gay or bisexual and hadn't talked to him since that day. He said he wrote the comments about Trumbo being a poster boy candidate because that's what he believed at the time."

"You believe him?" Behan asked.

Martin shook her head and waited a few seconds before answering.

"I don't know. He had this smirk all the while like he knew something important but he wasn't going to tell me. I don't know how to explain it. It was an odd interview. The man can't sit still and he talks ninety miles an hour . . . very unusual."

"Pull Castro's personnel package. See if there's someplace he and Trumbo might've crossed paths . . . maybe outside organizations . . . anywhere they could've been together," Behan said.

"What are you thinking?" Josie asked.

"Trumbo had somebody in the department that got him a badge and ID. Castro's in Personnel Division. He has access to that stuff."

"True, but tread carefully. I don't need a grievance because he feels like we're discriminating against him."

"Richards is good at sniffing around without causing dust storms," Behan said, going back to his notes.

"Oh, I almost forgot," Martin said. "I've been interviewing Trumbo's academy classmates and we have one of them here in Hollywood . . . an Officer Hoffman."

"I met her the morning of Kessler's murder," Josie said, remembering the woman who seemed too small for the physical challenge of policing the streets. "Have you talked to her yet?"

"No, she works a late watch. Thought I'd do it tonight."

"Use my office again. I want to see how she's doing."

THE COMMUNITY meeting was scheduled to begin in a little over an hour and Josie had changed into her uniform and was preparing some comments in her office when Marge called and asked if she had a few minutes to spare.

Josie put the notes in her uniform shirt pocket and calculated she had about thirty minutes before she had to make an appearance before the homeowners. There weren't too many details she could reveal about the murders but wanted to tell them enough so they felt as if they weren't being ignored. Their concerns were legitimate, but Josie was fairly certain these two killings wouldn't impact a neighborhood whose streets already produced as many crime stats as a small city.

Marge was in her office with Steven Petroski, aka Ramona. Petroski was in a tank top and baggy shorts. Without a wig and fresh makeup the illusion was gone. His pudgy face was unshaven, and the eyebrows had been plucked clean, replaced by black liner resembling a pair of McDonald's arches. Traces of red lipstick and smeared mascara told Josie the guy probably hadn't bothered to wash his face since last night. His thin brown hair was short, dirty and hadn't been combed recently.

"Oh my," Petroski whispered when he recognized Josie in uniform. "Where's my queen of the night?"

"Doing her day job . . . What's up?" Josie asked.

"Tell my boss what you told me," Marge said.

Petroski scratched his head vigorously with both hands. "Sorry, I'm so nervous," he whined. "Your costume . . . you know, it makes me crazy."

"Trust me it's not the uniform that makes you crazy," Marge said. "He's saying Kessler and Trumbo weren't the only two drag queens who've been attacked in that area. There were more of them, but they didn't die so nobody reported it."

"When?" Josie asked.

Marge looked at Petroski but he stared at his folded hands, so she said, "Within the last month . . . two were stabbed on Santa Monica but they were able to get away."

"Do we have names?"

"Street names," Marge said. "But he can point them out."

Petroski crossed his legs like a woman and folded his arms. "All right," he said and sighed dramatically. "I'll do it, but they can't know it was me."

"And how the fuck would they know it was you unless you told them?" Marge asked.

"They're victims, not suspects. What difference does it make?" Josie asked.

"Loose lips will kill my sexy hips, honey . . ." Petroski said, and looked sheepishly at Josie. "Sorry your honor, sir."

Marge told Josie she would advise Behan, then take Petroski out to locate the other victims. If they had been attacked by the same suspect and lived, they might have a description of their assailant or have seen something that might help identify him.

"I'll see if Martin can come with us. Nobody's going to pay much attention to two women and him in a car," Marge said, pointing at Petroski.

"I can get dressed up and we can be three beautiful women," Petroski said.

"Yeah, let me think about that one," Marge said and quickly added, "Fuck no."

JOSIE GOT to St. Margaret Mary's meeting room just as Father O'Reilly was concluding his welcoming remarks to a group of about forty people. He spoke tentatively, barely above a whisper and Josie could see people leaning forward trying to hear him. She was surprised by how many had attended. This sort of gathering usually drew a dozen or so of those active older neighbors who paid attention to what was going on because they didn't have much of anything else to do.

Everyone turned around as soon as she walked into the crowded room adjacent to the church's side door. The windows were open and fan blades were whirling in every corner, but it was still stuffy and warm and smelled like a gym. The walls were covered with children's crayon drawings and a bookcase had what looked like picture prayer books stacked on the shelves. Being Catholic, Josie recognized a space that would probably be used as the infant's crying room and a catechism class during mass.

Father O'Reilly, in a louder voice, introduced her midsentence, and Josie walked to the front of the room. She took the notes out of her pocket and glanced at the faces in front of her. They were mostly Latinos and possibly a handful of Armenians. The difficulty was in addressing their concerns, but not letting the discussion degenerate into a bitching session about somebody's last speeding ticket.

She began with a brief summary of the two homicides and emphasized that the police had no reason to believe the neighborhood was in danger from this killer. She hesitated a moment, thinking about the stabbings she'd just heard about that hadn't been reported, but she still believed Kessler and Trumbo were targeted and not random.

There were one or two geriatrics in the crowd but most in the audience were young couples, some with small children and a number of adolescent boys. She figured the boys were the altar boy contingent. Given how transient the population was in this area, she was surprised at the direction the questions took.

"We're afraid our kids will get hurt walking to school. Men who come to that hotel are bad. They don't care who they kill. Why don't you shut it down?" one young father asked.

Josie explained how they had tried and described everything Marge had done to close the Regency Arms. The houses around Santa Monica Boulevard were mostly bungalows or apartments filled with illegal immigrant families. They lived with gangs, drugs and prostitution and in the past didn't expect much from the police, but this group was vocal and not happy with the service they were getting.

"These guys come off the boulevard now and into the neighborhood. My nine-year-old daughter, she sees condoms on the lawn when I take her to school. That's not right."

Josie didn't have an answer. She promised more patrols by uniformed officers and vice but knew she was lying. Too many resources already went to this area and conditions rarely got better. It would improve if the people who lived here started painting out graffiti, stopped dumping garbage on the street and kept their sons inside doing homework instead of hanging around street corners selling and buying drugs, but they were poor people with too many mouths to feed. They worked day and night and the gangs and pimps raised and abused their kids. Prostitutes walked their streets because nobody complained. The good neighbors were afraid to call the police because they were here illegally and feared deportation. She explained all that, and they stopped asking questions.

"If you were on the street the night Mr. Kessler was killed and you saw anything, I'm asking you to talk to me. You don't have to worry about your legal status. I just want to catch a killer," she said, before concluding her remarks.

They clapped politely but Josie knew there was little chance anyone knew anything that might help or had any incentive to share it with her. They had come wanting something she couldn't promise them—a safe clean neighborhood. All the demographics were stacked against them and until that got adjusted there would be little change. She wasn't going to bullshit them just to get information.

The participants gathered into smaller groups talking in their own languages. One or two came up to Josie and shook her hand, thanked her. Father O'Reilly moved hesitantly around the room, speaking only to direct the altar boys to pass around the coffee. Josie watched and could see he was uncomfortable in a social setting but after a few minutes he was approached by a tattooed, tough-looking young man who wore his pants so low she wondered how they stayed up. She thought it very unlikely he was one of the altar boys. The boy got into an animated discussion with the priest and Josie was about to intervene when Father O'Reilly came over to where she was drinking coffee and stuffing her face with stale chocolate cookies.

"I'm sorry Captain . . . could I speak to you over here?" Father O'Reilly said, talking slowly and trying not to stutter. His face was sweaty and she noticed a brown stain on the edge of his collar—makeup? It wasn't unusual to try and hide the terrible acne scarring, but the vanity of it surprised her. He pointed at the young man who was pacing like a hungry lion.

The priest introduced the boy as Rago. He was Latino, maybe sixteen years old. His body was covered with tattoos, a few Rampart markings she recognized as one of the more active, violent gangs. He wouldn't look at her, but spoke in Spanish directly to O'Reilly.

"He says he saw the stabbing that night," Father O'Reilly said.

"Why's he telling me?" Josie asked. "Suddenly overcome with civic duty?" She knew the little thug spoke English, but this was his way of trying to keep an advantage. What is this kid up to, she wondered.

"He hates those men . . . you know, that kind," Father O'Reilly said, shaking his head as if he didn't want to explain. "He admits he's been arrested before for attacking them."

"So?"

Rago was getting agitated and gesturing with his hands as he told his story to the priest. It was obvious he didn't like her but was surprisingly deferential to the priest.

"He says he was there that night the man was killed. He's afraid the police will find out and think he did it, but he didn't."

"Tell him we'll definitely find out if he did it. Ask him what happened."

Father O'Reilly asked and Rago started speaking so fast the priest had to stop him and said it was too difficult to translate unless he slowed down. He continued, telling the story a few sentences at a time. Josie grew up hearing her father speak Italian with relatives and that language was similar to Spanish, but she couldn't understand a word the boy said. It was a kind of street slang he spoke.

Rago told the priest he was sitting on the steps of the Regency when Patrick Kessler walked by dressed as a woman, but everybody knew he was a man.

"Nobody ain't that stupid," the boy said in English.

It was a hot night and there were lots of people on the sidewalk. There were several groups of young men who said things to Kessler, but he ignored them and kept walking. When somebody yelled the name "Patricia," Kessler turned around and came back toward the hotel. Rago said he thought about jumping him just for fun, but before he could do anything, Kessler stopped and bent over. When people moved out of the way, Rago saw Kessler standing there, staring at the blood soaking through the front of his blouse. A few seconds later, he collapsed on the sidewalk.

The boy said he ran away before the police arrived and didn't see the killer, but he did see a woman pick up the knife and run past the Regency.

"Would he recognize the woman if he saw her again?"

"He doesn't know. It happened so fast he can't be certain."

Josie called the station and Kyle Richards was still there. He came to the church and took Rago into the priest's small vestibule behind the altar to get his statement.

Richards spoke excellent Spanish and didn't need Father O'Reilly's assistance. The expression on Rago's face was clearly apprehensive as Richards grabbed his skinny arm, pulled him into the room, and closed the door. She went along not because she didn't trust Richards but Josie knew if he spoke to Rago alone there was always the possibility the boy could make a complaint later. She wanted to be a witness.

"Sit there," Richards ordered and pointed at the only chair in the room. Rago sat immediately. There was no pretense of not speaking or understanding English. Boys like Rago knew when the game wouldn't work. "What lies are you telling my boss?" Richards asked before Rago could get comfortable.

"I ain't fucking lying," Rago whined and repeated the story he'd told Josie through Father O'Reilly.

"You're full of shit," Richards said when the boy finished. "You killed that guy and you're making up this stupid story."

Rago was twisting on the chair whining and protesting his innocence. The stench of nervous sweat filled the closet-sized room and beads of water drizzled down Rago's face and arms. His hair was wet and dripped onto the sides of his neck. After almost an hour of Richards's relentless prodding and accusations, the boy was silent and covered his face with both hands. He was exhausted and scared. Richards winked at Josie.

"Find the woman," Richards said.

The boy looked up. "Huh?"

"By Friday . . . I want the name of that woman who picked up the knife or you tell me where I can find her."

"Damn, I ain't got no fuckin' way . . ."

"That's the deal. You want me off your back . . . find the woman and don't try running. You don't want me chasing you."

WHEN JOSIE and Richards finally finished the interview, everyone had gone and the church was deserted except for the two of them sitting together in the last pew. She hadn't spent much time in a place of worship since her early teens when she was forced to go to Mass every Sunday. There was something peaceful, soothing about an empty church, the low lights, vivid stained-glass windows, statues with kind, forgiving faces. It was a place to take stock of your life and make adjustments. She thought about Patrick Kessler who had come here wanting absolution . . . for what, Josie wondered.

"Do you think he's bullshitting?" she asked, watching Richards finish his notes.

"I don't know. Lying comes so naturally to kids like him it's hard to tell. I talked to Rampart's gang sergeant before I came out. Rago's been in and out of trouble since he was nine, mostly petty stuff, but his father's in the Mexican Mafia, serving time for murder. His mother's been arrested for prostitution and his big brother got killed last year in a drive-by. His juvenile rap sheet has arrests for battery and hate crimes."

"But why lie about this? He wasn't in trouble. We weren't even looking for him. Why come forward?"

"I'm guessing he's worried someone saw him hanging around the Regency that night. He's street savvy and knew we'd find his record for beating up drag queens . . . or he killed Kessler and he's sending us on a wild goose chase to cover his ass."

"Maybe," Josie said, but she didn't think so. Rago might be a gangbanger with bad genes, but something, maybe her motherly instinct, told her this was one of those rare moments in Rago's screwed-up life when he might be telling the truth.

"Before I let him out the door, I whispered in his ear he'd better come up with that woman or he's my number-one suspect," Richards said.

"Nice touch," Josie said, lifting her feet up onto the padded kneeling rest and leaning back with a groan. It had been a long day and she was tired. "Aren't you afraid he'll run, disappear?"

"No. If he tries to hide in Hollywood, he knows someone will give him up, besides he can't survive outside the hood. Want to change and get something to eat?" Richards asked.

"Are you done for the night?"

"Behan wants me to work on Sergeant Castro, but I can start tomorrow."

"Martin is supposed to interview one of my probationary officers who was in Trumbo's academy class. I told her I'd sit in," Josie said, looking at her watch. It was only seven but seemed like the middle of the night. "Let me see how long that takes and I'll get back to you, if that's okay." She did want to go with him but her weary body was telling her it wasn't going to happen tonight. "But don't count on me. I'm really tired."

Richards didn't say anything, but she could see he was disappointed. Her new life was beginning the way the old one had ended—with frustration.

Officer Hoffman and Martin were waiting in her office when Josie returned.

"Did Marge talk to you?" Josie asked Martin, who was sitting at the worktable with a very uncomfortable-looking Officer Hoffman.

"We're leaving as soon as I'm done. Petroski's complaining about low blood sugar so Marge is getting him a hamburger and fries while we finish up here," Martin said.

"How are you doing?" Josie asked the young officer, patting her gently on the shoulder before sitting across the table.

"Fine, ma'am," she said, but Josie knew she was having problems. Josie had been following her progress by reading entries in her probationary book. Her attitude was great, but police work required more than desire. She had trouble qualifying with her weapons, wasn't aggressive in situations where command presence was critical and couldn't quite handle radio communications. Her training officer was one of Josie's best, but he was losing patience.

"Do you remember Henry Trumbo from your academy class?" Martin asked.

"Yes ma'am, he only lasted a few months but I do remember him."

"What exactly do you remember?"

"He was big and not too smart . . . stayed mostly to himself . . . good looking but kind of slimy."

"Slimy?" Josie asked.

"Always taking shortcuts . . . ways not to work too hard."

"Did he have any buddies . . . friends he hung out with?"

"Not in class, but Sergeant Castro from recruitment was always at the academy checking up on him . . . watching . . . talking to instructors."

"How do you know Castro was there for Trumbo?" Josie asked.

"Recruits all talked about it . . . the way Sergeant Castro met with him after physical training and how he'd stand behind Trumbo on the shooting line checking his scores . . . not all the time but a lot. The day before he got fired they had lunch together at the counter in the academy café. We all figured with sergeant's help Trumbo was a cinch to make probation, but then he didn't."

"Did you see him with anybody else?"

"No, ma'am."

The interview took half an hour. As soon as Officer Hoffman had gone, Martin looked at Josie and said, "Castro sat where you are now and told me more than once he never saw Trumbo after the entry interview."

"Apparently, he lied," Josie said.

"But it's such a stupid lie. Anybody at the police academy could've seen them talking."

"Has anybody confirmed what Hoffman saw?"

"I've only talked to a couple of his classmates, but no, not yet. They claim they don't remember Trumbo or didn't pay much attention to him. You know how recruits are. They're afraid to open their mouths."

"Finish interviewing the other classmates, see if anybody can back up what Hoffman says. I'm afraid she's not going to be around much longer. If her next rating is as bad as the others, she's not going to make probation either."

"Too bad," Martin said. "I like her. She tries hard."

"Richards should still be here. Let him know what Hoffman said before he starts the workup on Castro tomorrow."

Josie was out of her uniform and back into Levi's minutes after Martin left her office. Neither of them had mentioned the meeting with Gaby Johnston the next morning and Josie was grateful. She believed the mediation was a waste of her precious time and she just wanted to get it done without having to pretend she thought it was a good idea. The only thing that made it worthwhile was spending time with Gaby again. She knew Marge already considered Gaby a friend and wanted the three of them to have lunch after the meeting.

She located Richards in the detective squad room with Behan. She just wanted to say good night, but listened as they were attempting to come up with a strategy for interviewing Mrs. Kessler again the next day.

"She won't like it if you're not there," Richards said, nodding at Josie as she sat on a stack of boxes near Behan's desk.

"Who won't like what?" Josie asked.

"Red doesn't want to be there tomorrow when I interview her."

"If Seymour Kessler finds out I'm involved he'll bitch to the old man again. Commander Perry will yell at you and I'll lose my investigation," Behan said.

"Take Martin," Josie said. "Or better yet, if this is about Nicola's, go with Marge."

"Bailey is sure to piss off Mrs. Kessler, and then she'll refuse to say anything," Richards said. "Besides, we've all seen how she flirts with Red; he's the one she really wants to see."

"In the last interview did you ask her if she was divorcing her husband?" Josie asked.

"She denied it," Behan said. "I asked Beaumont, and he claims it was Seymour Kessler who asked him if he'd be willing to handle Patrick's divorce, but Patrick never contacted him."

"Some family," Josie said.

"It's looking like Beaumont might be our link between Trumbo and Kessler, but I'm short on motive why anybody would want either one of those guys dead."

"Susan Kessler had motive," Josie said.

"I don't see it. Even if Patrick threatened to divorce her, he's the one wearing lace undies from Fredrick's of Hollywood. She'd take him to the cleaners," Behan said, and added quickly, "But we do need to know what was in that briefcase. She knows and I'm guessing it has nothing to do with her husband's estate and something to do with why he and Trumbo are dead. Why don't you go with him?" he asked, looking at Josie.

"Go where . . . with who?"

"Interview Mrs. Kessler with Richards . . . Martin and Bailey are okay but you're better. She won't intimidate you."

"I'm mediating tomorrow morning."

"The interview is in the afternoon at her attorney's office," Richards said, shrugging. "It's a good idea."

"If Gaby Johnston can make Martin happy with this mediation and Red promises to try harder to make her feel welcome on his homicide table, I'll do it," Josie said, and saw Behan's face immediately turn the color of his hair.

She didn't wait for an answer. Talking to Behan was a lot like talking to her son, neither of them was willing to alter his perception of the world even if it made life better. Denying and rationalizing were so much easier than changing.

Thinking about the expression on Kyle Richards's face when she turned down his dinner invitation, Josie had a pretty good idea where her son might've picked up those traits.

EIGHT

David had prepared a gourmet meal that night and Josie arrived just as he was taking the osso buco out of the oven. He was surprised to see her home so early and in time for dinner, but she noticed there were three settings on the dining room table.

"If you've got company, I can go upstairs and get something to eat later. I'm beat," Josie said, thinking the food smelled great but a nap and late dinner would give her an excuse to avoid Kizzie.

"I've made enough for at least six. I'll just add another setting. Dad's in the den with Kizzie," he said cautiously and waited to see her reaction.

"Jake is here?"

"I asked him. Is it all right . . . it's only dinner. If you're uncomfortable, I'll tell him he has to go," David said.

Her son had supported her when her husband walked out. It had been one of the more pleasant surprises in her life. Father and son were always close, but David was candid in telling his father how disappointed he was when Jake left.

Much to her surprise, Josie didn't really care if her husband stayed or not and figured it would be a test to see if she could keep her food down while he acted as if breaking up their family was no big deal and best for everyone, especially her.

"Don't do that. I'll add a setting for me and go get him," she said.

David was staring at her as if he wasn't certain she was as calm as she seemed and while she put another plate and wine glass on the table he peeked into the dining room and asked, "You're sure? I'll toss him out with a doggie bag if you want. Just don't shoot him," he said with a painful smile.

"Tempting but probably not appropriate . . . I promise not to shoot him or push him off the third-floor landing," she said, giving her son a loving pat on the cheek.

THEY WERE in the den, Jake and Kizzie, sitting in Josie's loungers drinking a couple of whiskeys and chatting like professors in the university lounge.

Kizzie saw her first and got up quickly as if she were doing something wrong. "Hi, you're home early," she said, coughing on the whiskey she hadn't quite swallowed. "Does Davy know?"

"We're all having dinner together," Josie said with a tight grin. "Won't that be nice." She went to the wet bar and poured herself a glass of whiskey from an expensive bottle of Jim Beam.

Now Jake was standing too, but didn't seem the least bit uneasy.

"How are you Honey? I'm glad you're home," he said.

"I'll see if Davy needs help," Kizzie mumbled and left so quickly Josie couldn't tell her dinner was ready.

"What's up?" Josie asked when they were alone.

"The kids asked if I'd come over . . . they thought you'd be working . . . you know . . ."

"The kids?" Josie asked, sarcastically. "The woman's older than me, Jake."

"I forget. She seems . . . you know she acts young. You look great . . . a little skinny. Are you eating right?"

"David said you're working on a case, anything interesting?" she asked coldly, ignoring his question. It irked her that he always looked so good. He was ten years older than her and his hair was gray, but he didn't have an ounce of fat on his six-foot athletic frame. He was handsome and smart and just the sound of his laugh used to make her smile, but at this moment he was annoying the hell out of her.

"No, pretty routine stuff . . ." He crossed his arms and stared at her the way a father might with a young child. "Maybe we should have a serious talk, just you and me, after dinner. I think it's time we made some decisions," he said.

"Not necessary," she said, putting her empty glass on the bar. "I'm filing for divorce."

He looked surprised which she thought was peculiar. They hadn't lived together, barely spoken for months. He was a lawyer; he of all people should realize actions have consequences.

David called to them from downstairs that dinner was ready. But her husband seemed reluctant or unable to move.

"Not hungry?" Josie asked, walking away.

DINNER HAD the aura of mealtime at a cloistered monastery where monks had taken a vow of silence. Jake was usually the chatterbox at the dinner table, but he gave the veal his undivided attention, barely looking up except to take healthy gulps of Chianti. Josie noticed the "kids" exchange worried glances, but neither of them said a word.

When Kizzie picked up the empty plates and carried them into the kitchen, Josie finally said, "That was the best osso buco I've ever had. You are definitely a good cook. The wine's great. What's for dessert?"

"Humble pie," Jake mumbled into his napkin.

He didn't wait for dessert and told Josie he'd call her in the morning to arrange a meeting with their lawyers. She agreed, even though she didn't have an attorney. The divorce announcement was almost as big a surprise to her as it was to Jake. The words came out of her mouth more as a reaction to his indifference and condescension than something she'd planned to say that night, but nonetheless Josie knew it was right. One of them had to step up and put this dying marriage out of its misery.

She told her son later that night and was relieved he not only accepted her decision but agreed with her. The good news for the evening was his surprise announcement that he and Kizzie had found an apartment in downtown Pasadena and would move there the next day. Her house was about to be empty again—no husband, no son, no obnoxious little person, but to her surprise, she wasn't as pleased as she thought she'd be about David finally establishing his independence. Her function and relevancy in his life was changing. It made Josie happy for him and a little sad for herself.

David's apartment was unfurnished, so at breakfast the next morning Josie gave her son enough money to rent a U-Haul truck and told him to take his bedroom furniture and anything else he needed in the house except her bed and the loungers in the den.

Allowing him to move the piano was a difficult, heart-breaking decision. She relented but insisted on hiring a professional mover to bring it to his apartment. The prospect of hauling the finely tuned instrument in the back of a rented truck wasn't acceptable. She and Jake had purchased it on the installment plan when their son was eight years old, and they had suffered through years of tedious lessons until eventually the pleasure of listening to his music made it all worthwhile. Josie wanted her son to have it but had a premonition that, when the piano was gone, he was really gone. She would never admit it, but thought she might miss his music as much as him.

The restaurant had given David a salary advance and Kizzie had saved enough from her funky jewelry-making business to afford a decent two-bedroom apartment. It was in a nice area and would be his first real home away from the family home, albeit only a mile away. Josie drove by to see the place on her way to work, and they showed her the second bedroom where he intended to put the piano.

Everything she'd learned in over forty years of living warned Josie her son's newest endeavor, like all the others he'd attempted in his young life, had a high probability of failure, but she made herself a promise not to say anything and do everything she could to help him and Kizzie succeed. He was happy and working, so she'd be there to support him even if her fears came to fruition.

Besides, at the moment, she had her own life-altering debacles to handle. It had been easy to give away furniture because unless Jake was willing to give up his half interest in the house, she'd have to sell it after the divorce was final. Every room was filled with items carefully chosen to fill her family's needs and desires over the last couple of decades. Now it was just more stuff connected with too many memories that she might have to move into a place where they didn't belong.

It was almost time for her meeting with Gaby Johnston and Detective Martin by the time Josie got to Hollywood. The station was always busy, but the lobby was full of media cameras and reporters.

"What's going on?" she asked a veteran desk officer who was taking a report and ignoring the disturbance.

He motioned for her to move to the end of the counter away from the activity and noise and out of earshot of the nosy reporters.

"They told the lieutenant they want a statement on Hollywood's serial killer," he said, shrugging. The officer was almost sixty years old and had spent most of his career on the front desk. Nothing surprised or interested him any longer.

"We have a serial killer?" she asked, sarcastically.

"Yes ma'am, according to the *LA Times* and NBC, we do."

"Get them and all their equipment out of my lobby. Tell them somebody will make a statement as soon as they're set up outside," she said, not actually knowing what anybody might say.

Her adjutant was in the watch commander's office with several uniformed sergeants huddled around the lieutenant's desk. They all turned to look at Josie when she came in and stopped talking.

"We have a situation, ma'am," the watch commander said with a nervous laugh. He was a new lieutenant, a career paper pusher who'd been promoted and couldn't find his job of choice in the administration building. Without the benefit of field experience, he discovered the world of policing had suddenly become a little too real and complicated.

"First thing you need to do is get them out of the building. Your desk sergeant is doing that," she said, as the lieutenant started to get up. "Does Behan know what this is about?"

"No ma'am."

Josie told Maki to put Gaby Johnston and Detective Martin in her office when they arrived and keep them entertained until she got back. She found Behan upstairs in the vice office with Marge Bailey.

"Fuck," Marge said as soon as she saw Josie.

"That bad?" Josie asked.

"Shithead Petroski needed money . . . snitched to that asshole cop-hater Greenburg at the *Times* we had a serial killer targeting queens, but we weren't telling anybody because we couldn't make an arrest and it made us look bad."

"Tell them it's not true," Josie said.

"I did. They want to hear it from you," Behan said.

"Fine, I'll tell them it's not true."

"Are you sure about that?" he asked.

"About what?"

"Are we sure we don't have a serial killer?"

"Is that what you think?" Josie asked.

Marge got up and started pacing. "Look," she said, "last night Martin and me went out with shit-for-brains Petroski. We found three drag queens that had been attacked . . . knifed on Santa Monica Boulevard. It was random, none of the usual business dispute crap."

"Seriously hurt?"

"Superficial cuts . . . suspect hit and ran off."

"So do you think we've got a serial killer?" Josie asked.

Behan got up. "Not really," he said. "But I think somebody wants us to believe we do. None of the victims had real injuries . . . minor cuts on their arms and hands. They all said someone jumped out of the shadows, took a couple of swipes, and ran away."

"Did they see anything that might help us?" Josie asked.

"One of them thinks he punctured the suspect's right thigh with his spiked heel," Marge said, and seeing Josie's confused expression, added, "He does karate and instinctively kicked at the guy's balls, but asshole turned and the spike heel stuck in his leg . . . at least that's what the victim claims."

"What do you want to do, Red?" Josie asked.

"Go along with the serial killer charade. Maybe somebody is targeting drag queens, but I don't believe that's why Kessler and Trumbo were murdered. If the killer wants us to believe that, let's pretend we do. Maybe he'll make a mistake if he thinks we're buying into this fantasy."

Josie left them in the vice office and went outside to the front of the building. She had learned after years of running a police station how to talk to the media without really saying much. She left open the possibility of a serial killer by advising caution on the streets. The senior lead officer for the east end of Santa Monica Boulevard already was working with the Gay and Lesbian Center to get the word out. The media had their sound bite for the early news programs and Josie was certain by the weekend she'd see at least a half-dozen television feature news stories on the dangerous world of drag queens.

A few officers stood near the front door of the station while Josie gave her interview and she noticed Gaby and Marge were sitting on the top step watching. They got up as soon as she finished and met her at the bottom of the stairs.

"You're good at this," Gaby said, shaking her hand.

"Department teaches bullshitting 101 at command development school," Marge said, grinning at Josie.

"Good to see you again," Josie said to Gaby, ignoring her friend. "Are you ready for this?" she asked, knowing it was the last thing she wanted to do.

"You bet. I'll get Martin and meet you in your office," Gaby said and went back inside the station.

"Shut up," Josie ordered, looking at Marge's smirk.

"Yes ma'am. I'll wait upstairs and we can mosey over and have us some lunch when you're done with all this touchy-feely crap."

They were waiting in her office when Josie got there. Maki had set a pot of coffee and mugs on the worktable and Josie wondered if that was her adjutant's idea or Gaby's. Coffee meant someone was expecting this to last awhile, a possibility that had never crossed Josie's mind.

Detective Martin began by apologizing for "causing all this trouble," and then proceeded to itemize every instance in her estimation Behan had snubbed or offended her. It was an impressive list even for someone as cantankerous as Red to inspire.

"How do you get any work done?" Gaby asked as soon as Martin finished. "You must be writing notes constantly."

"Have you told him these things bother you?" Josie asked, amazed at the volume of petty offenses.

"No . . . he doesn't seem interested. He treats me like I'm stupid or not there."

"Have you noticed how he treats everyone?" Gaby asked.

"Not really. Why should that matter?"

Josie rubbed above her eyebrows. She felt a headache building slowly as Martin talked. It had become clear to her that Gaby's intervention was pointless. There were certain women in police work who simply did not belong. They were smart and physically fit enough to do the work, but somewhere hidden in their subconscious minds, they expected and wanted to be treated differently because they were women. They would do whatever was necessary to get the job, but at some point when they felt secure, the truth would surface. Their gender was a factor and everyone had better deal with it—mistakes would be balanced by hormonal excuses until there were different standards and quality was sacrificed to achieve equality at any cost.

Not in my station, Josie thought.

"So Captain Corsino is that agreeable with you?"

"What?" Josie asked looking up at Gaby. She hadn't been listening.

"Detective Martin will immediately bring her concerns to you instead of writing them down and you'll work through them with her."

"No," Josie said, turning to Martin. "You're going to talk to Behan. Tell him what's bothering you and work it out. If you can't do that, I'll put you on another table or sign your transfer to another division."

The mediation went downhill from there.

Ten minutes later, an unhappy Martin went back to detectives and Gaby sat alone at the table staring at Josie who was scrolling through the messages on her Blackberry. The coffee sat untouched.

"That went well," Gaby said sarcastically, breaking several minutes of silence.

"Sorry, guess mediating isn't my strong suit."

"It's not you I'm concerned about; it's Detective Behan. You've left Martin no alternative but to make a complaint."

"That's not true. She can do what I told her and work it out with Red."

"Admittedly, I don't know her as well as you do, but with the list she's compiled, I don't see that happening."

"Fine, but I'm not going to negotiate away the ability to run my station."

Gaby didn't respond. She closed her notebook and tapped her long polished nails on its hard cover repeatedly like a neurotic woodpecker. The process wasn't working, and her body language said she felt frustrated with no viable options. Settling disputes required both parties to give a little, but the league's ace mediator just got a taste of the headstrong Hollywood captain who had a propensity to do what she thought was right regardless of the outcome.

"I'm hungry," Gaby said and slipped the notebook into her briefcase on the table. "If you won't work with me, at least feed me."

They walked to Nora's together and met Marge in the bar. Their lunch was a lot more subdued than it had been the first time, no raunchy stories or jokes this afternoon. There was some light teasing between Marge and Gaby, but Josie didn't participate and didn't have much to say. The subject of the serial killer came up again and Marge mentioned Petroski and the other two stabbing victims she'd interviewed. Josie interrupted before she could finish her story.

"This probably isn't something we should be talking about here," Josie said, glaring at Marge. Gaby Johnston sounded and acted a lot like a seasoned cop and Josie understood how easy it might be to get comfortable around her, forget that she was a civilian and not privy to information. There was no legitimate reason to tell her anything about their murder investigation.

Josie was surprised. It wasn't like her vice supervisor to blab details about a case even to a friend. Marge immediately changed the subject and asked how the mediation went, but the paralegal's curiosity had been piqued, and she persisted with another question that Marge joked about but this time avoided answering.

Shortly after finishing her meal, Josie excused herself saying she had a meeting. She knew they would gossip about the failed mediation as soon as she was gone, how she had undermined Gaby's efforts to placate Martin and save Behan from a nasty personnel complaint, but Josie didn't really care and was confident Marge would defend her decision to scuttle the whole process. Hopefully, Marge could convince Gaby to talk her client into not pursuing any further action.

Actually, Josie wanted to get back to the station before Richards left to interview Mrs. Kessler. After thinking about it, she'd decided Behan might've been right last night. The widow was unpleasant, difficult to question and seemed to have an inflated view of her own importance. Having a high-ranking officer present might make the interrogation go smoother and be more productive.

The business with Martin had made her antsy. She needed to get out and do something that resembled real police work. Participating in the interview would allow her to do the work she loved for a few hours, then come back and run her station without feeling as if her head were about to spin off her shoulders.

She didn't have to look far for Richards; he was waiting in her office. He explained that Behan's suggestion was the most logical approach to dealing with Mrs. Kessler and he guessed she'd probably come to the same conclusion, so he waited for her to come back from lunch.

"Besides, I figured you'd need to get out of here after this morning," he said.

"You heard about the disaster."

"No, but Martin was acting like a zombie and didn't hang around afterward so I made an educated guess."

"I just hope my stubbornness doesn't hurt Red," she said and knew that wasn't an admission she'd make to just anyone. She trusted Richards completely, something she couldn't say about any other man in her life.

"Red's a big boy. Let him handle this one."

That was an interesting proposition, one she hadn't even considered. Red Behan had manipulated and outmaneuvered some of the city's most clever killers and their high-priced attorneys. Surely, he could handle Ann Martin. Maybe this time, she should step back and let Behan do his magic. It wasn't really her way, but her approach wasn't having much success so why not.

They were scheduled to meet Mrs. Kessler at her attorney's office on Grand Avenue in downtown LA. The office turned out to be a two-story white house with a red lacquered front door on north Grand in Chinatown. It was located two blocks north of Cesar Chavez Avenue and across the street from a senior-citizens' home where elderly Chinese walked arm-and-arm up and down the sidewalks.

There were exactly fifteen stairs leading to the front door. Josie counted them as she climbed. The attorney's name was etched on the bronze plaque mounted on the exterior wall under an antique light fixture. It should've been a surprise, but Josie had had a premonition Marvin Beaumont was destined to be a prominent player in this investigation. Once inside, she had to admit he had an impressive office. The home's living room had been transformed into a lobby with stained concrete floors and a high ceiling with natural wood beams. The reception desk was set in a corner facing a seating area highlighted by a modern sculpture that Josie thought resembled a crazed one-legged peacock crashing into a tree. A ten-foot wall separated the lobby from the rest of the house downstairs, but it was obvious Marvin had spared no expense in creating an upscale space for his work environment. His taste in art and furnishings leaned toward the modern, not her taste but it felt welcoming. Two huge oil paintings had been hung behind the desk and although Josie guessed someone had splattered paint on them with a squirt gun, she did like the colorful effect.

An older serious woman in a business suit immediately came from around the wall to greet them. She introduced herself as Mr. Beaumont's personal assistant and offered to bring them coffee or anything else they might like. They declined, so she asked them to follow her back around the wall down a wide hallway and into a conference room. Like the lobby, the walls in that room were covered with original modern paintings and the chairs looked expensive but uncomfortable. Ten minutes later, Beaumont joined them with Mrs. Kessler by his side.

Susan Kessler immediately shook hands with Richards, holding on a little too long while she chatted about nonsense and rubbed his arm with her other hand. She barely acknowledged Josie, but whispered to Richards as if he were an intimate friend. She was wearing a skimpy summer dress, cut low enough to expose a lot of her ample breasts, and she made a point of turning her body so the taller Richards could get a good view.

"Thank you for meeting with us again," Richards said, pulling away. "You never mentioned Beaumont was your attorney."

"That's because I wasn't until this morning," Beaumont said, with a half smile.

Josie sat at the conference table and wondered if this woman flirted with every man she met or just found Hollywood detectives irresistible.

Beaumont pulled out a chair for Mrs. Kessler and sat beside her. Richards continued pacing behind them. He seemed preoccupied as if something were bothering him.

"Why don't you sit somewhere, and we'll get started," Beaumont said, nervously looking over his shoulder.

"I'm curious why you think you need an attorney, Mrs. Kessler . . . I mean since no one has accused you of anything," Richards said, sitting beside Josie.

"I'm representing Mrs. Kessler to make certain no one infringes on her rights during this process." Beaumont attempted to pat his client's hand but she moved it.

"You knew your husband was a cross-dresser. Why did you lie to us?" Richards asked.

Mrs. Kessler stared at the table a few seconds before answering.

"Not something I was eager to admit," she said, looking at her expensive manicure.

"Who told you your husband's briefcase was at Nicola's?"

"I saw him leave home with it, and it wasn't at work."

"What made you go to Nicola's?"

"I knew he stopped there every night."

"What was in it?"

"I'm not certain."

"That's not what you told Miss Mabry," Richards said. He wasn't giving her any time to think and Josie could see she was becoming rattled.

"Linda Mabry's an idiot. I doubt if she remembers anything I told her."

"She seemed pretty competent to me," Josie said, forgetting her intention to stay out of the interview.

Mrs. Kessler glared at Josie and said, "Linda's lips are permanently glued to Jeff Flowers's butt. The woman hasn't had an independent thought since she started working in that council office."

"What was in the briefcase?" Richards repeated.

"I told you I don't know." Now there was nastiness and anger in her tone.

"Then why go to a place like Nicola's in the middle of the night to retrieve it?" Josie asked, wondering what might happen if she pushed a little harder.

Mrs. Kessler sat quietly for a few seconds and Beaumont must've thought it was his cue to step in so he started to protest the question, but she stopped him.

"I went there because I thought some of Patrick's personal papers and effects might be in the briefcase. I was worried he might've had pictures . . . compromising pictures. I didn't want anyone to find items that could've been embarrassing for the family . . . for me."

"Why was Trumbo meeting your husband?"

"They were friends," she said.

"They were?" Beaumont asked, looking at Josie and then to Mrs. Kessler. "Henry never told me he knew your husband," he added, defensively.

Mrs. Kessler laughed quietly. "There was plenty Henry didn't tell you or anyone. He was quite a mysterious young man."

"How well did you know him?" Josie asked.

"Well enough," she said with a smirk. "Real charmer that one."

"What did your husband give Trumbo the night he was killed? He had something in that briefcase. What was it?"

There it was, that nervous look away. Suspects always did it during interrogations when they were about to lie. Josie knew Mrs. Kessler wasn't going to answer that question. Richards must've seen it too. He tried asking again, but there was no response, and Mrs. Kessler refused to explain what she meant by calling Trumbo a "mysterious young man." She had secrets and intended to keep them. Richards tried for another thirty minutes but couldn't pry or cajole the truth out of her. Finally, she sighed and glared at her attorney. Beaumont reacted to what was an obvious, if unspoken, demand from her and called a halt to the interview.

The receptionist appeared immediately to escort them back to the lobby. Josie asked to use the restroom, and the woman accompanied her there too, but en route, Josie managed to see more of the house. There were stairs in the back of the house that the receptionist said led to Beaumont's living quarters. An office door was open, and she could see he had obviously taken down walls to create an enormous space. It put Councilman Flowers's office to shame. It was bigger and far more extravagant with a modern work module that could've accommodated three or four people. She caught a glimpse of a glass table and chairs near a full bar with leaded-glass cabinet doors, exotic lighting fixtures that hung from the ceiling and a sitting area that was bigger than Josie's living room.

A closed door with Henry Trumbo's name on an engraved plate was directly across from the restroom.

"He kept an office here?" Josie asked, stopping in front of the door. It never occurred to her that Trumbo would've worked from Beaumont's office, but getting a search warrant for an attorney's office was not an easy task—bad luck.

"Yes," the receptionist said pointing across the hall. "There's your restroom."

Much to her surprise, when Josie came out of the restroom, which she really didn't need to use anyway, the elderly receptionist was nowhere in sight. She looked both ways in the hallway but the woman wasn't there or in the empty conference room.

Josie tried the door to Trumbo's office. It was open and with a quick glance toward the lobby she went in and closed the door again. She wasn't entirely certain what she hoped to find and if she'd even have time to look, but the opportunity was there so why not try.

The space wasn't as impressive as Beaumont's, but still nicer than her office. The furniture was more traditional with a big oak desk, leather chair and two more leather chairs in front of the desk. There was one file cabinet and the top of the desk was clean except for a small lamp and a laptop computer.

She quickly went through the four drawers of the cabinet and found the top drawer contained fewer than a dozen folders, and she didn't recognize any of the names on those files. The two middle drawers had magazines and an assortment of brochures on cars and clothes. The bottom drawer had a .45-caliber Glock 21 in a holster, a wallet with police ID in the name of Sergeant Henry Trumbo, and a sergeant's badge. She memorized the number on badge 1144, left it there and closed the drawer.

The computer was tempting, but she knew there wasn't enough time to access it and wondered why no one had come looking for her. Almost immediately upon having that thought, she heard knocking on the bathroom door across the hall. She pressed her ear against the door to listen and tried not to make any noise.

"Captain Corsino, are you all right?" the receptionist asked and knocked again.

There was silence and then the sound of high heels clicking on the cement floor. Josie quickly slipped out of the room and was a couple of yards from Trumbo's office when the receptionist and Beaumont came around the lobby wall toward her.

"We were worried about you, Captain," Beaumont said, looking over her shoulder down the hallway.

"Stomach problems . . . raw fish," Josie said and could see skepticism on the receptionist's face; she wasn't buying it.

They all went back to the lobby where Richards was waiting. He got up and opened the door for Josie but she hesitated and turned back to Beaumont.

"I noticed when I went to the restroom that Trumbo had an office here. Would you mind if Richards and I took a quick look around for anything that might help us find his killer?"

"I don't know . . ." Beaumont said, sucking in his bottom lip. "There's my clients' privacy to consider."

"Of course we wouldn't read any paperwork that might pertain to your cases. Actually, it would be best if you looked at every item first, let us know what we could or couldn't examine," Josie said. "A lot of times victims know their killers . . . more often than not they do."

"I suppose it would be all right . . . if it helps," Beaumont said. He looked as if he was trying to remember exactly what might be in there.

Josie followed him back to Trumbo's office and couldn't believe the lawyer was actually going to let her search. She looked back at Richards, and from his expression, she could tell he didn't believe it either.

Beaumont tried the door and seemed surprised it wasn't locked. He stopped for just a few seconds, glanced at the restroom and his eyes narrowed. Josie figured the light had finally gone on in his brain, but he opened the door and allowed them to enter anyway.

As soon as he was in the room, Beaumont stepped out of the way, made a sweeping gesture with his right arm and said, "Take your best shot. I doubt you'll get another chance."

"What about the computer?" Richards asked, standing over the desk.

"Take it. It has nothing to do with me or my business."

"Do you want to look in the file cabinet before I do?" Josie asked.

"Probably," Beaumont said, opening the top drawer. He examined each of the folders and stepped back. "Take them. They're not my clients."

Josie removed the files and put them on one of the chairs. As soon as she closed that drawer, Beaumont opened the second drawer and chuckled.

"Wanna buy a car?" he asked, holding up an advertisement for Chevy trucks. He closed that drawer, then opened and quickly shut the third one when he discovered more brochures. "I think I might've allowed the boy too much free time," he said and was still grinning when he opened the bottom drawer. The smile slowly faded as he stayed bent over, staring at the contents.

"We wondered where the heck those went," Josie said.

"Why . . . Why is that here?" Beaumont said, looking from Josie to Richards. "I swear I didn't know. I had no idea."

She could tell from the way he began fidgeting and nervously backing away, shifting his weight from one leg to the other, the lawyer probably didn't know the gun and badge were there.

"You haven't been in his office since he died?" Richards asked, taking his pen to flip open the wallet with the badge and ID.

"No, why would I," Beaumont whined. "There's nothing in here that concerns me."

"He worked for you," Josie said.

"Not that way . . . he was protection. He couldn't afford his own place so I let him use this. I'd never trust him with confidential client information . . . I'd never do that. The man was a simpleton."

"Right," Richards said, "a simpleton with a gun and badge that you hired. Do you have any idea why he'd leave this here if he was supposed to protect you that night?"

"No, of course not."

"You don't mind if I take the computer and flash drive," Richards asked, as he carefully slid the gun and wallet into a large manila envelope.

"Take it," Beaumont said too loud. "Take everything in this room. I don't care."

When they left, Josie had the stack of files. Richards carried the envelope containing the gun and wallet, and tucked the computer under his arm. The receptionist gave Josie a dirty look as she held the door open for them.

"Don't think she likes you much," Richards said, as they loaded everything in the trunk of his car.

"Go figure," Josie said.

"What if Beaumont had said no?" Richards asked.

"Guess we'd still be looking for Trumbo's gun."

"Some of us would."

NINE

They took the items from Beaumont's office back to Hollywood. Behan asked Josie if he could store everything in her wardrobe closet overnight and then book it into property in the morning. He wanted an opportunity to go through the files and computer first. She agreed. Her closet was big and could be locked. Marge had the only other key.

"I need to get Sergeant Castro back here tomorrow," Richards said. He was sitting at Josie's worktable studying Trumbo's police ID and badge. "This ID looks legitimate. Getting a badge would be easy. Grab one off the shelf in the retirement office and claim it's lost, but someone had to issue this sergeant ID."

Behan was sitting across from him and stopped shuffling through the files. "I'll have one of my guys pick him up in the morning and bring him here. Can I have Martin run the names on these folders or has she resigned from my homicide table?"

"Ask her," Josie said and saw Richards nodding.

The lieutenant watch commander knocked lightly on the open door and stepped inside Josie's office.

"Ma'am there's a television crew out front that wants an update on the drag queen serial killer, and I left some messages on your desk from a couple more that wanted to speak with you. Want me to handle it?"

Josie and Behan exchanged looks. This night watch lieutenant had been promoted from Metropolitan Division. Metro cops were different. They were hard-charging and extremely competent. Unlike the day watch lieutenant, nothing overwhelmed this guy.

"What will you say?" Josie asked.

"How much do you want them to know? That's what I'll say."

"Behan will give you a short statement in a few minutes and then the media are all yours," she said and added quickly, "Thanks."

He gave her a hasty salute and was gone. One thing she'd learned about the Metro cop mentality was you couldn't possibly give them too much to do; they volunteered for everything, and the more difficult or dangerous an assignment, the better they liked it. She knew he'd be back in Metro as soon as his probation period was over, but while he was assigned to Hollywood, Josie intended to take full advantage of his talent and energy.

"That's one headache you won't have," Richards said, grinning. A former Metro cop himself, Richards understood the breed.

"Did you recognize any of these names?" Behan asked. He was still rummaging through the folders and not paying any attention to anything else.

"No," Josie said. "Do you?"

"We're going to have to do some checking on their backgrounds. It's just a lot of online information and some newspaper or magazine clippings. If she shows up, I'll have Martin do it in the morning."

Josie's guilt meter was registering off the scale. She felt bad about blowing the mediation this morning. She had an opportunity to calm the situation, but couldn't make herself play that game . . . even for Red. There was nothing she could do about it now, but because of stubborn pride, she felt as if she'd failed her friend.

"I'm beat," Behan said, gathering the folders and stacking them on top of the computer. "I'll write a few talking points for the lieutenant then I'm out of here."

He put everything on the shelf in Josie's wardrobe closet and was gone. The wallet with the badge and ID were still on the table with the gun. She picked up the ID and looked at the picture of a clean-shaven, closely shorn Henry Trumbo. He had that wide-eyed look of a new recruit, so it was probably the photo that had been taken in the academy. If there was something going on between him and Patrick Kessler, it was beginning to look as if that something was lethal enough to kill both of them.

"What are you thinking about?" Richards asked, taking the ID out of her hand and putting it back in the envelope with the gun and badge. He placed the envelope on the shelf near the computer and files and closed the wardrobe.

"I'm thinking whatever Kessler knew was probably about either his father or Flowers," she said. "Big men have big secrets."

"Could've been his wife," Richards said.

"Susan Kessler was implying she'd slept with Trumbo. Why would a good looking guy like that have anything to do with her unless he wanted something?" Josie asked. She was trying to focus on a murky thought that had been forming in the back of her mind all day. The picture they were getting of Trumbo was a man who took shortcuts and used people to get what he wanted. Maybe this time he'd met his match in Susan Kessler and she used him to get rid of her husband because she found out her father-in-law was pushing his weak son to divorce her. Josie wondered if Susan Kessler got Trumbo to kill her husband and then she lured Trumbo to that hotel room and killed him.

Josie sat back, closed her eyes and sighed. It was a good theory, but the lack of any real evidence made it just that—a good theory.

"Are you okay?" Richards asked, and was staring at her when she opened her eyes.

"Other than maybe putting Red's career in jeopardy, ending my twenty-four-year marriage last night and losing my son to a card-carrying member of the lollipop guild, I'm fine," she said, and had to smile at the bewildered look on his face. She didn't think it was possible to do that to Kyle Richards.

"Sorry," he said.

"Don't be, but you wanna know the worst thing that happened in the last twenty-four hours?" she asked, and before he could respond said, "Giving away my piano. My son wanted it and he should have it, but I love that piano."

"Get another one."

"Why, I don't play the piano."

Now he laughed and Josie did too when she realized how lame that sounded.

"Think maybe it's time for me to go home," she said, getting up and locking the wardrobe closet.

"Come to my place for dinner."

She didn't answer right away, but didn't have to give it much thought before saying, "What time?"

"How about now? You can help me cook."

THE SINGLE-STORY Spanish-style bungalow located in the Belmont Shore area of Long Beach was as perfect as Josie remembered it from her visits last year. She'd gone to call on Richards after he'd justifiably shot a corrupt cop and then had to survive the awful aftermath. It was where she first met his teenage daughter, Beth, and heard about the death of his wife. The house was small but charming with a vintage kitchen, glassed-in front porch and french doors off the dining room and bedrooms leading to a brick patio surrounded by high walls covered with scenic paintings.

All the decorating and the paintings had been done by Richards's wife, and although they never met, Josie had a strange feeling she and the dead woman would've been friends if they had.

It took them an hour to get to Long Beach from Hollywood, and they arrived at almost the same time. The house was within walking distance of the ocean so street parking was nonexistent. Richards parked in the one-car garage, and she put her car in the driveway under a narrow carport. Unlike her Pasadena house, his home was welcoming and lived in. Potted plants were set outside by the front door and inside it looked as if someone actually enjoyed spending time there, with books and magazines open on the coffee table and an afghan thrown carelessly over the back of the couch.

He went through every room opening windows and the french doors. Within minutes the ocean breeze coming from just blocks away cooled down the interior to a bearable temperature. She stood under the awning on the patio and breathed in the strong scent of night-blooming jasmine that covered the side gate. In this weather, the patio became an outdoor room, in many cases the only place it was bearable to eat or sleep.

She could see into the kitchen from where she stood and watched him pulling things out of the refrigerator and then opening a bottle of red wine. He poured two glasses and brought them out to her.

"Pinot Noir from Napa, okay?" he asked, handing her a glass. "I'm pretty much a whiskey guy so I'm winging it."

She took a sip. It was wonderful. "Perfect. Can I help?" she asked.

"I have some homemade manicotti from two nights ago . . . thought I'd heat it up and make a salad."

"Let's relax awhile," she said, sitting at the rusted bistro table. "And talk."

He put his glass on the table and sat on a small bench covered with a padded cushion near the wall. "I don't talk about dead Hollywood drag queens at home," he said.

"Me neither. Truthfully, I'm not that hungry either."

"It's a rare occasion when Josie Corsino isn't hungry."

"I want to talk about us."

"I don't."

"What?" she blurted out.

"I'm tired of talking. I know everything I need to know about you. I'll learn the rest as we go along."

"Question is, do I know everything I should about you?"

"Probably not. My life's been complicated, but you do know I care about you."

"You have no idea what you're getting yourself into. I'm a workaholic; I'd rather work than eat. It's who I am . . . hate housecleaning . . . actually I'm a slob."

"I'm not looking for a maid, Corsino. Besides if it gets too bad you can always stay in the garage," he said, grinning.

She put her glass down and sat on the bench beside him. He put his hands on either side of her face and kissed her, a long passionate kiss. She couldn't remember her first kiss with Jake, but doubted she liked it this much. He stood and helped her up. He put his arms around her, before he took her by the hand and led her to his bedroom.

They made love. There was no hesitation or overthinking for a change on her part. She wanted him and over the next hour eagerly gave herself. Jake had been a good lover and knew how to satisfy her, but it was better with Kyle; he gave her pleasure and tenderness.

Later, a warm breeze blew through the open french doors and over the bed as they lay naked on top of the sweat-dampened sheets. His arm was resting on her chest as he snored softly into the pillow. She was awake and felt happy and pleased with herself, but a little disappointed, too, when she finally admitted that a false sense of loyalty to a bad marriage had kept her away from something genuine and wonderful. All those emotions she'd bottled up the last few months surged through her veins like the best illegal stimulant and sleep was impossible.

For a long time she watched him and felt guilty because she couldn't help comparing him to her husband. He was handsome, but unlike Jake didn't seem to care. His clothes were simple—Levi's and boots, not four-hundred-dollar suits. Tonight he had a day-old beard that rubbed against her face; she liked it. She rarely saw Jake unshaven. Kyle was athletic and firm, a warrior's body. Her husband had a tennis-playing lawyer's body—tan and fit on the outside, but not intended for heavy lifting. She must've snickered a little out loud, thinking about it.

"What are you laughing about," Richards asked, his eyes still closed. "I wasn't that bad."

"You are definitely a keeper. I'm starving."

"That's the Corsino I know," he whispered, rolling over to give her a kiss.

It was midnight, but he put on his bathrobe, and found one of his old ones for Josie, and they went into the kitchen, ate manicotti and finished the bottle of wine. They filled the dishwasher, sat out on the patio and talked, made love again on the living room couch and finally went to bed where Josie slept soundly.

Richards was still asleep when she woke the next morning. The house was cool and comfortable. All the windows were open, and she worried that he'd forgotten to lock the front door since the patio doors were wide open. Her .45 semiauto was on the nightstand nearby and she glanced over to his side of the bed and saw a Colt 1911 on that nightstand. She stopped worrying and pitied the burglar unlucky enough to pick this house.

By the time she showered and dressed, he was awake and had made coffee.

"Get whatever you want," he said, handing her a mug of coffee.

Josie smiled. No complaints, no recriminations, no attempt to control her, this was so much better.

She arrived at Hollywood station before her adjutant and, for the first time in months, realized she wasn't pissed off before the day started. Even the message on her desk from Commander Perry wanting what seemed like the hundredth update this week on Kessler didn't seem to annoy her this morning.

Richards got there a few minutes after her and went directly to the detective squad room where he and Behan were preparing to interview the sergeant from Personnel Division. Sergeant Castro was the logical link to Henry Trumbo, and after Ann Martin's softball interview in Josie's office, he probably wasn't anticipating the interrogation he was about to walk into this morning.

There was one matter Josie wanted to handle before the day's events distracted or sidetracked her. Unfortunately, after more than two decades in law enforcement where she'd encountered hundreds of attorneys, she couldn't come up with the name of anybody she trusted enough to handle her divorce. She called Gaby Johnston for a referral and got several names that Gaby swore were decent and fair. She wasn't angry with Jake any longer and just wanted a clean break. Gaby offered her condolences on the divorce and suggested an after-work drink or two to commiserate. Josie assured her the condolences weren't necessary, but they should definitely get together for the drinks.

"How's the hunt for drag queen killer coming," Gaby asked, after finding all the phone numbers for the lawyers.

"Not much happening on that front," Josie said, wondering if Marge had been talking too much again.

"It's fascinating to us lay people how you guys put a case like this together. Maybe we can chat more about it when we have that drink," Gaby said.

Josie knew this sort of investigation had a lot of prurient interest but she wasn't about to discuss it with anyone outside her division and would make a point of reminding Marge again that Gaby shouldn't be privy to information in any criminal case.

It took a single phone call to one of Gaby's attorneys to start the paperwork rolling and set up a meeting where Jake and his lawyer would attend. There was nothing Josie wanted except half the proceeds from the sale of the house if she couldn't keep it and any furnishings Jake didn't want. No custody issues for an underage kid or pedigree dog were looming, so she figured it should be pretty straightforward and fast.

After spending more than half her life with someone in such an intimate way, Josie thought she might've felt some regret about this separation, but she didn't. Jake's behavior had absolved her not only of guilt, but eliminated the possibility of second thoughts, and even if she and Kyle Richards didn't stay together another day, what they had now for as long as it lasted was better than what she'd left behind.

SERGEANT CASTRO came to her office for his interview and was surprised to find Josie sitting at her desk signing paperwork with Maki.

"Detective Behan is waiting for you in the detectives' squad room," Josie said, when Castro seemed immobilized in the middle of the room. He wasn't a big man, pale and thin and a bit too jittery for any supervisor Josie might have faith in.

"Thank you ma'am," he said, not moving. "I just assumed it would be here again. Sorry to disturb you."

"No problem, but I think they're waiting for you. Do you know where Detective Behan's desk is?" she asked, attempting to dislodge him.

"Yes ma'am, I'm certain I can find it."

Maki groaned just loud enough for Josie to hear and got up. "I can show you, sir," she said, walking past him. "Sir," she repeated when he didn't follow right away.

"Oh . . . sorry again, ma'am," he said and finally left.

What a strange little man, Josie thought, and decided she'd wait long enough for them to get into an interrogation room and then go back and watch the video feed. She'd never met a uniformed supervisor who seemed so unhinged by simple conversation and wondered how he had handled a patrol assignment or if he had actually ever done that.

Some supervisors got promoted because they passed the test, but if everyone knew they'd be dangerous on the street, a place would be made for them in some office downtown where damage control was easy, mistakes fixable, and nobody died or got injured because of their poor judgment. She suspected Castro might be one of those supervisors.

Richards had just finished reading the administrative rights when Josie got to the video room. The sergeant sat with his hands folded on the table staring intently at Richards who had to ask him twice if he understood his rights.

"I'd like a league rep and my lawyer," Castro mumbled, and began nervously scribbling notes on a yellow legal tablet he'd brought with him. Josie wondered what he was writing since they hadn't actually begun.

"Don't you want to know what I'm going to ask first?" Richards asked.

"No," he said, still writing.

"Make your calls and we'll come back on tape in half an hour," Behan said.

The interview was stopped to allow Castro time to contact his lawyer and a league representative. Behan and Richards left him and walked around the corner into the video room where Josie was waiting.

"That guy's got to be on some kind of medication," Behan said, sitting beside Josie.

"He's barely able to concentrate . . . looks sick," Richards said. He took a chair, turned it around, and sat facing them resting his elbows over the back. "I think there's something seriously wrong with him."

"I doubt his rep's going to let him be interviewed today," she said.

"Why's that?" Behan asked.

"It's the template they follow. The union wants to give them time to get their story straight and settle down. Watch, they'll claim he's feeling sick or faint or some other off-the-wall excuse nobody believes but there's nothing we can do about it," she said matter-of-factly.

"That's pretty cynical," Behan said.

"No it's not. I've been CO long enough to understand how the game is played. His rep should make him sit down and tell the truth, but that's not going to happen."

There was a light knock on the door and it opened before anyone could respond. The burglary supervisor peeked in, looked around and finally stepped into the room when she saw Behan.

"Red, that sergeant you were interviewing next door just left. He wanted me to tell you he was sick and was going home."

"I'll call his captain at personnel and have him secure Castro's locker and desk," Josie said, following the burglary supervisor out of the room. "You two get over there and search before he gets a chance to take anything." She suspected Castro was panicking and most likely wouldn't respond to calls, but she'd tell his captain to try and contact him or leave messages advising him he had the right

~ 147 ~

to be present while his department property was being searched.

Ann Martin was coming in the back door of the station as Josie left the squad room.

"Are you working?" Josie asked.

"Yes ma'am," she said, but didn't sound pleased about it.

Josie explained what had happened with Sergeant Castro and finished by saying, "I want you to take Trumbo's police ID out of property and take it to personnel. While Behan and Richards search Castro's locker, you find out who ordered and processed that ID, then pull Castro's and Trumbo's packages and find a connection."

"I already did that. There's nothing connecting them."

"Do it again and tell Behan so he knows what you're doing."

Martin nodded and walked slowly down the hall toward the property room. Her shoulders were slumped and she looked as if every step was the last she'd ever take. It was tempting for Josie to run up and kick the woman in the butt. Marge was right. Martin needed to get over herself and do what she was getting paid to do.

Josie went back to her office and called Gaby again.

"Did you just get a call from Sergeant Castro? He's assigned to personnel," Josie said. "Do you know if he's contacted a union rep?"

"Nope, why? Should he?"

"Behan was questioning him here at Hollywood a few minutes ago, and he bolted."

"If it's the guy I'm thinking of, he has requested counseling in the past . . . but ethically speaking I shouldn't be talking to you about that."

"Did he ever mention an association with Henry Trumbo?" Josie asked, ignoring the disclaimer. It got very quiet on the other end of the line. "Gaby, are you still there?"

"I'm thinking, Captain. You've presented me with a dilemma. Tell you what, I'll give you a tiny bit of inappropriate data if you reciprocate and feed my curiosity about your drag queens," she said with a low snicker.

"Done," Josie lied. She had no intention of revealing anything, but needed to know what was going on between Trumbo and Castro.

"You realize you can never use any of this or tell anybody where you got it."

"Of course."

"Sergeant Castro did admit to me he had a relationship with Trumbo. He wouldn't say how, but apparently he helped him get into the police academy despite shall we say Mr. Trumbo's shady character and intellectual shortcomings, but as soon as he had the job, apparently the ingrate wouldn't return Castro's calls. The academy had fired Trumbo by the time I found out so I didn't pursue it . . . figured no harm had been done."

"Why would Castro admit all that to you?" Josie asked, but didn't say what she was thinking. Sergeant Castro should've gotten a personnel complaint and lost his stripes over what he'd done. Gaby wasn't a sworn officer but she worked for the Protective League and should've told someone about the misconduct. She was a police counselor not a priest.

"Same reason most cops tell me stuff. There's nobody else they can talk to, and they know I'll keep it confidential." She hesitated and added, "Usually."

"Did he say anything else?"

"He mentioned that Trumbo lived with him for a short time after he got fired, but Castro said he had to ask him to leave when he started making crazy demands."

"What sort of crazy demands?"

"Don't know, but it wasn't sex. The sex was incidental. Castro found out something that scared him."

"Scared him enough to kill?"

"Do you think he killed Trumbo?" Gaby asked. "It wouldn't surprise me."

"Why do you say that?"

"He told me he was desperate and would do anything to get Trumbo out of his life . . . and he's certainly emotionally unstable enough to do it."

"I'm curious," Josie said. "Did you tell anybody at the league about Castro? Obviously, he isn't someone who should have a badge and gun."

"Nope, not my thing. I know you've got rigid standards and you're not going to like this, but if I start snitching on these guys, word will get out around the department and nobody will trust me. I'll be out of a job . . . I happen to think my particular skills are needed and valuable."

"Did Trumbo mention Castro when you met with him?"

"No, and I didn't tell him I knew what Castro had done for him. He was terminated and wouldn't be back, so what was the point."

Josie had a feeling arguing was pointless so she let it go, but she was seeing Gaby Johnston in a whole new light and wasn't liking it.

She'd never had any tolerance for corrupt cops and didn't believe there was a shield of confidentiality or rules of engagement when it came to exposing and firing them. Police officers had the power to take away another person's freedom or life. Absolute integrity was essential—no lying, stealing or other criminal behavior was ever acceptable. Protecting your job wasn't a good reason to allow someone like Sergeant Castro to continue carrying an LAPD badge.

Their conversation ended without Gaby asking for information about the drag queen homicides, but Josie figured that marker would be called in eventually. She didn't give it much thought because she didn't intend to reveal anything. If Gaby was curious about the sordid details of that particular lifestyle, she'd have to do her own research.

It was several hours before Behan and Richards got back from downtown, but Josie had a rash of emergencies and meetings and didn't have an opportunity to get together with them until the following week. Richards would dedicate most of that night and the next few days to searching for Castro, so she reluctantly resigned herself to speaking with him on the telephone and sleeping alone in Pasadena until the sergeant was found.

Toward the end of the week, she was returning from a Hollywood Chamber of Commerce meeting when she saw Richards headed upstairs in the direction of the coffee room. He noticed her too and came back down.

"You okay? You look tired," Richards said.

"What's new? I've been tired since the day they gave me these captain bars. Get anything interesting at personnel? Did Castro ever show?" she asked, attempting to suppress a smile. She'd never had an urge to kiss one of her sergeants. It was weird.

"What's so amusing?" he asked.

"Nothing," she said, shaking her head. "I'm seeing you in a whole new way . . . it takes some getting used to."

"Good," he said, but she could sense he wasn't all that comfortable either in acting as if all they had was a professional relationship. They both had been around the department long enough to understand that while he was working for her, even though it was temporary, there couldn't be any public display of affection. Everyone got pretty uptight in a police station when the boss had a favorite among them, worse yet, a lover. Once he went back to RHD, it would be different.

"So, I'm guessing you didn't find Castro, but was there anything in his locker?" she asked.

"Not really, but we found copies of paperwork signed by him in his desk requesting Trumbo's phony sergeant ID. He initiated the process and most likely stole the badge too. It belonged to a retiree who turned it in to personnel the same week Trumbo got fired. There's no real inventory of older badges, so taking it would've been easy."

Josie reminded him what Gaby had revealed to her the previous week and said, "The question is how Trumbo scared or bullied Castro bad enough to make him hand over that ID and badge."

"From what I've seen, it probably doesn't take much to frighten Sergeant Castro."

"But was he frightened enough to kill Trumbo?"

"I doubt it," Richards said. "I'm betting it took a lot more man than Castro to slit that guy's throat." He looked around to make certain no one was within earshot and whispered, "Come back to Long Beach after work, doesn't matter what time."

"Okay," she said, and added quickly, "So, will you keep looking for Castro today?"

"Martin and Behan are checking all his associates and relatives we didn't get to last night. I've got to track down Rago, my gangbanger informant. He still hasn't produced any info on the woman he allegedly saw take the Kessler murder weapon."

"I've gotten so wrapped up in Trumbo . . . haven't thought much about Kessler."

"That's all Seymour Kessler thinks about and he's pestering my captain and your commander and the chief of police every day. Which means all of them ask me every day why I haven't made an arrest yet. Lately, they don't seem satisfied with 'I'm working on it,'" Richards said.

"Have you considered bringing in Flowers's secretary . . . what's her name?

"Miss Mabry."

"Why not drag her ass in here again and pressure her?" Josie asked. "Seems to me she's in the middle of all the main players . . . she probably knows why Flowers tried to pass off that fake office as Patrick Kessler's, and what Susan Kessler was really looking for in her husband's briefcase."

"Maybe you're right. Other than Rago, we've got no other leads," he said and took his beeping cell phone out of his shirt pocket. He answered, listened for several seconds before saying, "Be there in twenty," and turning it off.

"What's up?"

"They found Castro. He's dead."

TEN

The Ocean Park Motel on Sepulveda Boulevard in El Segundo was five minutes from the Los Angeles International Airport but an hour or more from Hollywood in rush hour traffic. Richards managed to get them there in less than thirty minutes. After years of working surveillance assignments, he'd accumulated invaluable knowledge of every shortcut and alley in southern California. He drove through places Josie guessed rarely saw vehicular traffic and stayed off the busy streets and freeways.

The motel was a one-story ugly orange stucco building with all its doors facing the gravel parking lot. There were security bars and closed curtains on every window. A plastic swimming pool under a torn beach umbrella was on a patch of grass near the lobby door at the other end of the building. A garden hose was on the ground and the running water had created a mudhole near the pool where a couple of three- or four-year-old boys in their underwear were standing ankle deep in the gooey mess watching the activity. An older dark-skinned woman in a bright green strapless sundress sat in a lawn chair nearby drinking something out of a paper bag. Not the sort of place Josie expected to find the nervous LAPD sergeant, dead or alive.

Behan in his shirtsleeves with his tie loosened was waiting by an open door at the other end of the building. He was leaning against the wall drinking a bottle of cola and watching Richards's car kick up a dust storm in the lot. Massive perspiration stains under both arms were proof he'd tried to keep his jacket on as long as possible.

"Looks like suicide or accidental," Behan said, when Josie got close enough to the doorway to get a whiff of the unforgettable stench of putrefying flesh on a very hot day.

She felt bad because her first thought was, "I hope that's just cola Red's drinking."

"What do you mean looks like?" she asked, stepping around Behan and into the room. She'd gotten close but didn't detect any odor of alcohol on him.

"Look for yourself," he said, flinging the empty plastic bottle into his open car window.

Although a ceiling fan had been turned up to the highest speed, it was barely moving and air in the room was still muggy, hot and smelly. Josie and Richards stood over the bed where Sergeant John Castro lay dressed only in his white briefs with his hands by his sides, a picture of serenity if he didn't have that belt strapped around his skinny inner thigh and a syringe stuck in his vein.

Josie had been a narcotics detective for years and immediately recognized the track marks of a dedicated heroin addict on Castro's leg, hardened veins from hundreds of intravenous injections left his skin looking as if someone had drawn erratic silver lines from his groin to his knee. There was a little white residue left in the spoon he'd used to prepare the drug. Most of the heroin she'd seen lately had been tar or the brown stuff referred to as Mexican mud.

The coroner's investigator arrived a few minutes after Josie. He talked to Behan and immediately began examining the deceased. He couldn't establish when Castro had died or how long it had been after he'd bolted from the Hollywood interview. The extreme heat had accelerated both decomposition and rigor mortis, so it was difficult to be certain.

Detective Martin had been interviewing the manager in the motel office and came back while the coroner's investigator was taking the body temperature. She gave Behan a copy of the search warrant she'd obtained telephonically. Even he would have to admit she was quick and efficient at getting warrants and doing the administrative work.

She was briefing Behan but Josie and Richards moved closer to listen. Martin's lethargic posturing from the day before had disappeared and Josie was relieved to see her energy and enthusiasm had returned and thought it was amazing how a dead body could wipe away so much of the petty stuff.

"The manager is saying someone in sweatpants and a hoodie went into Castro's room yesterday, late afternoon, stayed five, maybe ten minutes and left. She didn't get a good look at him but was pretty sure he was a tall, light-skinned guy with a backpack," Martin said. "Castro had checked into the room about an hour before the sweatpants guy got there."

"No security cameras?" Josie asked.

"Yes, but they don't turn them on until later when it gets dark. The manager only noticed the guy because he was wearing all those heavy clothes in this heat."

"Red, come here a minute," the coroner said. He was standing over Castro's body staring at his head. "See that," he said, pointing at the dead man's neck.

Behan got on one knee and leaned closer. "I missed it."

"His skin's just dark enough to camouflage the injuries. We would've picked it up in the post when I looked closer," he said. "It's on the other side too."

Josie looked at Richards and he shrugged and said, "I don't see anything."

"Light scratching on both sides of his larynx," Behan said and put both hands up to his throat to demonstrate. "When there's something around your neck and you can't breathe, it's a natural reflex. You grab with both hands to try to pull it away. Sometimes the nails scratch the skin, but I don't see any bruising or cuts from a ligature."

"I used to see this injury all the time years ago when I worked at Central Receiving," the coroner said. "Recruits at the police academy practiced the carotid and bar-arm choke holds on each other before the police commission banned them. If some kid stayed out too long, they'd take them to Central to get checked out. They all had these same marks right there on the larynx. It's the place you stick your fingers in to pull the arm away on a carotid hold."

"The good old days when you could put your arm around an asshole's neck and put him to sleep . . . no fighting, no shooting, beating with batons, torn uniforms, just 'night-night' asshole and off to jail," Behan said.

Although the department didn't teach the carotid choke hold any longer, Josie had an uneasy feeling. Most cops knew how to use it and she was certain a few of the older ones still did use it out of habit. She had been hoping Castro was Trumbo's last tie to the department, but at the moment she wasn't so certain.

"I think his shoulder's dislocated too," the coroner said. "It might've been an old injury that popped out again in a struggle, but it's definitely out."

"Can somebody do that?" Martin asked. "Grab you hard enough to pull your arm out of the socket?"

"Serious dislocations reoccur if there's sufficient damage the first time. It'll pop out repeatedly until it's sur-gically repaired," the coroner said as he and his assistant turned the body.

"Once he's unconscious and his shoulder is out, he'd be easy prey if someone wanted to inject heroin and make it look like an overdose," Josie said, gently touching the silver tracks on his leg. She knew these marks were very old. He hadn't used those veins for a long time and even if he were still using heroin, he probably wouldn't shoot up there.

"Castro might've tried getting Trumbo out of his life," Richards said. "But I'm guessing he knew Trumbo's business and that's what got him killed."

"He had to know. The same way Kessler did. Now they're both dead, but then so is Trumbo," Josie said, shaking her head. "So where does that leave us?"

"You might be on to something with Mabry. If you're done here, do you want to go with me to her place and try talking to her again?" Richards asked.

They were standing outside the room watching the coroner load Castro's body into the van. Before Josie could respond, Commander Perry's new black Ford drove into the parking lot kicking up enough gravel and dust to chase the kids out of the mudhole and send them ducking for cover. Josie had called him as soon as she received news of the police sergeant's death but never expected him to show up. There wasn't any reason to show support and respect for a cop as marginal as Castro.

After Behan finished briefing him, Perry turned to Richards and asked, "Do you have any real evidence this is connected to your Kessler investigation?"

"Maybe," Richards said, not backing down.

"If you're not certain, why are you wasting time here?" He was talking to Richards but glanced at Josie to let her know he wasn't pleased with her either.

"There aren't a lot of leads in Kessler's murder, but it's looking like we might have a connection to Trumbo and now Castro," Richards said without emotion. Josie admired the way he held his ground. She would've done the same, but would've made certain Commander Perry knew she was pissed about his interference.

"Your people have until the end of the month to come up with a suspect on Kessler," Perry said to Josie. "If you can't, the chief will hand it over to another team. I suggest you stop wasting time."

"My people don't have the Kessler investigation, sir, RHD does. We're assisting Detective Richards."

"With all due respect, Captain, we both know that's a load of bullshit. I've allowed you to play this little game of who's really got the case, but not much longer. Solve it or give it up," Perry said, and leaned over to whisper in her ear: "Find Patrick Kessler's damn killer before I'm forced to shoot his pain-in-the-ass father."

They left Commander Perry with Behan and Martin finishing up at the motel after the body had been taken to the morgue. Josie would've preferred someone else went with Richards to talk to Mabry, but it was a long drive back to Hollywood to drop her off and then go out to the Valley, so she agreed to do it.

Besides, she enjoyed working with Richards or maybe it was just being with him. They would've been excellent partners even if they hadn't slept together. It was difficult in the police world to find a person you trusted who matched your personality, work ethic, and instinctively knew how you would react. Before Richards, Behan had been the only one who did.

The home address Richards had for Mabry was only minutes from Councilman Flowers's district office. It was an apartment building with locked glass doors leading to a courtyard with an enormous Art Deco flamingo fountain, definitely fifties décor. Richards pushed the buzzer under her apartment number, and the glass door lock immediately clicked open.

Miss Mabry intercepted them before they reached the stairs leading to her apartment. There was no doubt she was expecting to rendezvous with someone in her courtyard but it clearly was not the police. She was wearing a low-cut, sleeveless, black dress and an annoyed expression when she realized who was waiting for her.

"Captain Corsino . . . what are you doing here?" she blurted out, after nearly bumping into Josie.

Josie introduced Richards and said, "We've come to ask you a few more questions about Patrick Kessler's murder."

Mabry sidestepped nervously. She obviously didn't want to deal with their questions at that moment and kept looking past them at the glass doors.

"You can see I'm just leaving. Can't we do this tomorrow during business hours . . . at the office?"

"We're here and police work doesn't really have business hours. It will only take a few minutes. I'm sure your friend will understand. We can wait here and ask if you like," Josie said, and noticed the color drain from the woman's cheeks.

"No," Mabry said quickly.

"Do you want to go back up to your apartment to talk?" Richards asked.

"No," she said again, more emphatically. She touched her forehead with two fingers as if she were getting a headache and said, "Come with me. We can go to the garden room. It's usually empty this time of night, but I can't stay long. This really isn't right. The councilman is going to hear about it."

Josie caught one more furtive glance at the glass doors before Mabry led them around the fountain to a screened-in patio area with wrought iron tables and chairs. It was clean and well-maintained with ceiling fans, a brick floor and lots of potted plants. The string of decorative lights hung across the ceiling put out barely more than a candle glow, but the low light made it seem cooler. A misting system was spraying the plants, giving the room a tropical forest ambience and providing a welcome refuge from the Valley heat. Mabry sat at a table in the corner where it was impossible to see the fountain or any other part of the courtyard.

"Do you need to call your friend?" Josie asked, noticing the woman check her watch.

"I'll just text if you don't mind," she said, taking her phone out of her purse and quickly typing a short message. "Now what is it you want?"

"Why wouldn't you show me Patrick Kessler's office?" Josie asked.

Mabry shook her head and started to speak but Josie interrupted and said, "Don't bother lying. I know that wasn't his office. What are you and Flowers hiding?"

"The councilman has nothing to hide," she said, defiantly. "I resent . . ." she started to say, but Josie cut her off again.

"Resent all you like. It doesn't alter the fact you lied to the police."

"You have no right to go through Patrick's personal things," she said.

Josie could sense Mabry didn't like her, and was determined to win the argument even at the cost of admitting she'd lied. Richards's instincts were good, so he didn't say a word. He understood anything he interjected now could change the chemistry of Josie's interrogation and the woman might stop talking.

"There shouldn't be anything that personal in the workplace," Josie said.

"Patrick was a very private man. He wouldn't have wanted anyone, even the police, going through his things."

"What things?" Josie said with as much sarcasm as she could muster which was plenty. "Pens, pencils, paper clips . . . what could he possibly keep in his office that was so personal?"

Mabry was stumped. She stared hard at Josie. There was no doubt about it; she hated her a lot. Finally, she cleared her throat and said softly, "The councilman thought it was best."

"Detective Behan and I will be there at eight A.M. tomorrow with a search warrant for Kessler's office," Richards said. "How long did Kessler work there?"

Miss Mabry looked confused for a few seconds and then mumbled, "Two years, I think . . . why?"

"I'm expecting his office to look as if he worked there that long or you're going to jail for obstruction," Richards said.

Josie sat back. Richards had inserted himself at the right moment. A hard-boiled detective had just replaced the object of the woman's loathing. Fear was always a lot trickier to deal with than hate.

"Fine, are we done here?" she asked with whispered bravado. She looked as if she wanted to run away but Linda Mabry had given them ample hints that she was not the sort of woman who had the fortitude to stand up to anyone.

"No," Richards said.

The woman's shoulders slumped and she sighed. "This is too much. I have plans this evening. I just don't understand . . ." Her voice trailed off. She leaned back and folded her arms.

"What did Mrs. Kessler think was in her husband's briefcase?" he asked.

"Insurance documents . . . I've already told you."

"But you lied, just like you lied about the office," Richards said. He was calm and matter of fact. Even Josie thought he sounded as if he actually had proof she wasn't telling the truth.

"That's what she told me."

"Why did you go to Nicola's?"

"Susan asked me; she didn't want to go alone. That's a terrible place."

"What was in the briefcase?"

"Papers."

"But not insurance papers."

"Susan thought he might've taken documents from work."

"What documents?"

"She said she didn't know . . . wanted me to look at them, but the briefcase was gone."

"Why did Mrs. Kessler think it would be at Nicola's?"

"She knew Patrick went there every night . . . we all knew, and she'd looked everywhere else."

"Are there documents missing from your office?" he asked, and waited a few seconds but she didn't respond. "Linda?"

"No," she whispered.

"Then why did you go with her if nothing was missing?"

"I don't know. We're friends . . . she asked me. I don't feel well. May I go now?" she asked, standing.

Josie thought she did look pale. Perspiration had left dark spots under the arms of her nice dress and tiny beads of sweat spotted her bare arms and neck. The garden room was pleasant and relatively comfortable compared to the temperature outside, but Linda Mabry looked as if she'd been sitting in a sauna.

Richards agreed to stop the interview but warned her that tomorrow morning she'd better take inventory and be able to tell him what documents were missing. She scurried away from them. Her hasty departure reminded Josie of a scared little animal released from a cage.

They got up, followed her out to the courtyard and watched her go back upstairs to her apartment.

"You pretty much ruined her evening," Josie said.

"Me? I believe that was a team effort."

"You do realize that any chance of her searching for documents evaporates as soon as she talks to Flowers, don't you?" Josie asked when they were back in the car.

"True, but they will have to show us the office . . . or what's left of it."

He turned the corner, drove about a quarter of a mile and came back down the street parking between two cars, almost three blocks from Mabry's apartment. From their position, they could barely see the driveway.

"Think her date is still coming?" Josie asked.

"We'll see. She's had a chance to call by now. Can you stay here a few minutes or do you have to get back? By the way, I was really looking forward to a quiet night at home with you . . . good dinner, good sex."

"Warned you life with me would be difficult," she said as a black Cadillac pulled up in front of the apartment house. Mabry, now wearing a light blue dress, hurried out to the car and got into the passenger seat. "I've got time. Let's ID the mystery guest."

The car turned onto the first major street before Richards pulled out of the parking space. Josie had worked a surveillance squad and had to admire how easily he followed the Cadillac using traffic and distance as cover, but always keeping the car in view. Normally, it required at least five or six vehicles to do what he was doing. He got close enough one time for Josie to write down the license plate number. She ran it through DMV, but it came back to a new lease without identifying information.

Traffic was especially bad in LA's San Fernando Valley, but Richards managed to keep the Cadillac in sight for several miles until it entered the covered driveway of a place called the Ringside Tavern on San Fernando Road. Valet parking attendants opened the doors, but Richards couldn't get his car positioned fast enough before whoever was driving the Cadillac disappeared inside the tavern. There was, however, only one way in or out of that parking lot so he found a spot down the street in front of a liquor store where they had an unobstructed view.

"We need to be inside," Josie said, after they sat in the car a few seconds.

"Mabry isn't the sharpest pencil in the drawer but even she would recognize us from less than an hour ago. Maybe Marge has someone we could borrow for a few hours."

"I'll see if she can do it herself. I don't want some baby police officer blabbing about following Councilman Flowers's secretary . . . or worse yet, the councilman himself, if that's him driving the Cadillac."

Marge Bailey was tapping on the rear passenger window of Richards's car less than thirty minutes after Josie called her. Somehow, Josie immediately recognized her coming down the sidewalk toward their car despite the fact she looked completely different.

"Don't shoot. I'm a friendly," Marge said, sliding into the back seat.

She was wearing a red wig cut to fall just below her ears. It was sexy and stylish. Her green sleeveless dress wasn't too short. Josie always admired how savvy Marge was about fitting in undercover. She looked great but wouldn't be the center of attention.

"You look terrific as a redhead. How'd you find the wig so fast?" Josie asked.

"Took it off Petroski," she said and laughed at Josie's disgusted reaction. "Just fucking with you . . . it's not really drag queen fashion. It's mine from another life."

Josie gave her a brief explanation of what they had seen and learned from Mabry's interview. Five minutes later, Marge walked into the Ringside Tavern on a mission to identify the driver of the black Cadillac.

Richards had just put his seat back to settle in for a long night when Josie's cell phone rang.

"You're not gonna fucking believe this," Marge said on the other end. "Your mystery man is Sergeant Doug Miller."

"Doug Miller from the Protective League?" Josie asked.

"The very same dumb ass," Marge said. "Can't keep his chubby hands off that poor woman. I think the asshole's married and got young kids, too."

"Any chance he'll recognize you?" Josie asked.

"Not hardly, he's never done a day's worth of police work, and I don't fraternize with union slugs. Besides this place is really dark and smells like stale beer . . . not exactly where I'd expect to see these two."

"Are they alone?"

"So far, but they keep looking around like they might be waiting for somebody. I'll hang out until they leave if you want."

Josie and Richards agreed they would wait, but it only took a few minutes for Marge's next report. Councilman Flowers and Susan Kessler had joined the party a few minutes after the first call.

"Didn't take the widow long to get back in the saddle, did it?" Marge said and told Josie she was sitting on a barstool not too far from the table where the two couples were drinking. "Must be some serious shit . . . they're on the third round and still arguing. Everybody's pissed at the Mabry woman."

"She might've told us more than she should have," Josie said, grinning at Richards.

There weren't any further updates. About an hour later, Marge came out the front door, walked back down the sidewalk to Richards's car and got into the rear seat again.

"Well, that was damned enlightening," she said, pulling off the wig and vigorously scratching her head. "Bunch of ancient chubby fuckers playing grab-ass in the dark under the tables all night . . . Miller's car should be coming out any minute. Councilman Flowers and Mrs. Kessler are in separate cars, but they're definitely a couple. His tongue was in her mouth more than her gin and tonic."

Even after Marge left, Richards didn't make any effort to start the engine. He and Josie had already decided the surveillance was over, but they sat quietly for several minutes. Josie knew he was probably pondering the same thing she was—did tonight's events mean anything? Flowers wouldn't kill Patrick Kessler just to cheat with the guy's wife. Patrick was ready to dump his wife anyway. Besides, they were probably having sex long before he got killed, which would explain why Flowers was so adamant about keeping her out of the investigation. Josie figured Doug Miller was just a scumbag who left his wife and kids at home while he wined and dined another woman probably on the union's credit card . . . but . . . and it was a troublesome but . . . what were they hiding?

There was something Patrick Kessler had and probably gave to Trumbo in that briefcase. Councilman Flowers, his secretary, Mrs. Kessler and now Doug Miller seemed to have a problem with the police knowing what it was. Very curious, she thought, but was any of it a motive for murder.

Richards reached over, touched her face, startling her, and she jumped.

"Sorry," he said. "Didn't realize you were that deep in thought. I'm taking you back to the station to get your car. Probably not a good idea for your officers to see me bring you to work in the morning wearing the same clothes."

"Okay, then follow me to my place. Nobody's there; you can spend the night . . . that's if my kid left any furniture."

ELEVEN

The Pasadena house was dark and stifling hot when Josie arrived. She immediately turned the air conditioner to the coldest setting and put the fan on high. It didn't take long to bring the temperature down to where it would support human life. Richards had stopped at the grocery store to pick up fresh fruit and eggs for the morning. After everything was put away, neither of them was hungry. Josie had completely lost her appetite when she realized the breakfast table and chairs were gone. A more thorough search revealed the toaster oven, juicer and some of the better pots and pans were missing too.

"Well, I did tell him to take what he wanted," she said, peeking into the dining room and holding her breath until she saw the table and china cabinet were still there. "I'm hoping they left the crystal and good silverware," she said before looking in the top drawer at the flatware.

She went upstairs and stopped in the doorway of the empty piano room. Indentations in the carpet were the only sign that the baby grand had once occupied that space. David had taken everything connected to his music—books, shelves, trunks full of sheet music, pictures of him at different competitions—every trace of him and his wonderful talent was gone.

His bedroom was empty, too. Bare walls, an empty closet, and dirty carpet were all that remained. She thought about the condition of her bedroom and realized the two men who had shared this home with her for so many years had removed every hint of their lives as thoroughly as locusts might wipe out a wheat field.

"What are you doing up there?" Richards shouted from the bottom of the stairs.

"Feeling sorry for myself."

"Sounds depressing."

"I've got expensive Tennessee whiskey."

By the time Richards found the den on the second landing, Josie had poured two glasses of Jack Daniel's and set them on the wet bar. The couch and coffee table were gone but her two loungers had been spared and were still in place separated by the small antique oak table. An old brass Tiffany lamp had fit perfectly on that table, but it was gone.

"It's easy to see where all your furniture used to be," he said, looking around the room. "Did he take anything you wanted to keep?"

Josie thought for a moment and was surprised when she realized that, other than the piano, there was nothing in the house that had much value for her now.

They sat in the loungers, drank and talked until after midnight. He listened mostly and seemed to know she needed to work some things out.

"What would you think about moving in with me?" Richards asked when she got up to fill their glasses again. "Take what you want from here and sell the rest or put it in my storage unit."

She didn't answer right away, but not because she didn't like the idea. There was no way she could separate her job from her personal life. As a captain she couldn't live with a man who worked for her. Even if he were her husband she wouldn't want Kyle taking orders from her every day. It was complicated on a lot of levels and she wasn't certain she could explain her feelings, but until he went back to his division or someplace other than Hollywood, living together wasn't a real possibility.

"I get it," he said, after she tried to make her feelings clear. "I guess I wouldn't like it either if our positions were reversed." He took the last swallow of his drink, got up and stood in front of her lounger. He reached out and helped her stand. "On the other hand, I have no problem temporarily taking orders from a woman I've made love to, but we should find out if you still have a bed."

The bed was there in her room, and thanks to her one-day cleaning spree it had fresh sheets. They made love, and Josie didn't remember falling asleep but woke early the next morning completely rested and starving. She checked her phone for messages because she'd slept so soundly she was afraid she wouldn't have heard a call from the watch commander at Hollywood station. There were three missed calls but they were all from David. She felt guilty because she had intended to call him back yesterday, but as usual got busy.

Richards was still sleeping, soundly. When he was home, Jake never moved in his sleep and his side of the bed always looked as if he hadn't been there. This morning all the blankets were on the floor and the remaining sheet barely covered Richards. Watching him, she had an urge to get back into bed and snuggle, but knew that wasn't going to happen. She wanted to talk to Behan about what had happened last night. The fact that work was her priority wasn't a surprise. The shocker was that for a moment she actually considered not leaving.

She took a shower, dressed and went downstairs to make coffee. It felt weird not having a table in the kitchen so she dragged the card table out of the garage and set it up with the four folding chairs. David knew his mother well enough not to take her favorite coffeemaker. She made a full pot of coffee, filled a mug and drank it while searching the kitchen for a decent pan to make an omelet.

She was sitting on the floor pulling an old frying pan out of the cupboard when the door that led from the garage into the kitchen creaked and opened slowly behind her. As she turned, her hand instinctively slid down over the grip of the holstered .45 semiauto. Her husband peered into the kitchen from the outside stair; she let go of the gun, grabbed the pan again and got up.

"Morning," he said, stepping into the kitchen. "You're up."

"What are you doing here, Jake?"

"I wanted to talk . . . thought I'd take you to breakfast."

"I'm in a hurry. Why don't you call me later?"

"I can make us breakfast here," he said and added with that irresistible smile, "just like old times."

"Sit down," she ordered and dropped the frying pan on the stove.

"Where's our table . . . and chairs?" he asked, holding up one of the folding chairs.

"I gave them to David. I don't want to have breakfast with you or relive the good old times. There's someone upstairs. I'm making breakfast for him."

"You slept with someone . . . in our bed?"

She watched his smile morph from hurt feelings into devastation. A few weeks ago that might've been enough to make her feel bad, not this morning.

"Buck up, Jake, I'm selling the bed after the divorce so it really doesn't matter. You've opted out of my life so I'm asking you to respect my privacy. Sorry if my having a relationship hurts your feelings."

"Morning," Richards said, from the dining room doorway. He still had a day-old beard but had showered and his salt and pepper hair wasn't completely dry. Josie figured he'd heard them from upstairs and was curious. His lanky frame filled the space, which was impressive since every doorway in the house had been heightened to accommodate the unusually tall Corsino clan. His Colt .45

was holstered on his belt with his badge and the cowboy boots added at least two inches to his already over-six-foot height making him an imposing figure.

Josie had been concentrating on Jake and didn't notice him right away. Jake apparently hadn't seen him either and got twisted up in the folding chair trying to get up and put some distance between himself and Richards.

"Sorry," Jake said. "You startled me. I'm . . . Josie's husband."

Even he has a hard time saying that these days, she thought, enjoying the moment.

"Kyle Richards," he said, staring stone-faced at Jake.

After a few seconds of uncomfortable silence, Jake said, "I'll have my lawyer call you later," and left the same way he came.

"What did he want?" Richards asked when they were alone.

"To annoy me and ruin my day."

"Did he?"

"No," she said, shaking her head and was surprised because she meant it.

After breakfast, Josie left for Hollywood station and Richards told her he was going to stop by St. Margaret Mary's to see if Father O'Reilly knew where he could locate Rago. The deadline had passed but the gangbanger hadn't called Richards about the woman he allegedly saw at the Kessler murder. It was beginning to look as if the young man might've been lying so Richards was about to keep his promise and find him.

Traffic was bad so Josie used her Bluetooth to call her son while she waited in the bumper-to-bumper mess. He sounded groggy as if he'd been sleeping. It was nearly ten A.M. David had taken after her and wasn't an early riser unless he had to get up.

"Sorry," she said. "I thought you'd be getting ready for work."

"The restaurant doesn't do breakfast."

"Saw your calls last night. Sorry I didn't get back to you. What's up?" she asked.

"Kizzie and I wanted to thank you and let you know what I took from the house."

"Not necessary."

"Dad already called me this morning . . . your friend freaked him out."

"Are you two settled in?" she asked. She wasn't going to talk to her son about her love life.

"Okay . . . but go easy on dad. I think it's finally dawned on him how badly he fucked up everything. Do I get to meet him? Dad said he's a cop."

Josie lied about having to get out of the car and hurriedly ended their conversation. She was still sitting in traffic on the freeway, but didn't want to talk about her relationship with Richards yet. It was too soon. At some point, she'd introduce him to David and give them an opportunity to get to know each other. She wanted Kyle in her life, but had to be certain he wanted her in his life before she could expect him to deal with all her complicated attachments.

This might've been the hottest day of the summer. The soaring temperature hit her like a furnace blast as soon as she opened the car door. Shimmering waves of heat bounced off the black hoods of police cars parked in a line behind the station waiting for change of watch. She caught one of the probationary uniformed officers not wearing his protective vest and made him go back and put it on before he started his patrol shift. She understood it was tempting not to add another heavy layer under the uniform but better to be miserable than dead.

The Hollywood Community Police Advisory Board made up of local community leaders had delivered several cases of bottled water for the officers and donated a freezer filled with different kinds of ice cream. She didn't expect much police work to get done in this weather and didn't blame officers for not wanting to get out of their air-conditioned cars, but this was the life they had chosen—work on Christmas, miss your kid's birthday party, get shot at, and go out in weather even postal workers avoided.

Of course the air conditioning had gone out completely in the station; it was an unavoidable summer occurrence in the old Hollywood building. Josie attributed it to the city's business model of going with the lowest bidder who'd contributed the most to reelection campaigns and was willing to adhere to the city council's affirmative action, global warming, and human rights edicts. Competence was never a requirement.

Electric fans were set up in every office. Detectives had a dozen operating in their squad room and several of the tables had individual fans as well. Josie anticipated the ensuing power outage would hit around lunchtime. Security measures were nonexistent with all the station doors wide open, but she didn't worry about it since several hundred people carrying lethal weapons should be a trespassing deterrent to all but the very stupid.

There was a fan sitting on Behan's desk too but he wasn't there. Josie located him upstairs in the vice office huddled in a corner with Marge and having a very intense conversation. They stopped as soon as they saw her, but it wasn't an argument. They were sharing something that seemed to please both of them.

"I told Red what happened last night," Marge said, giving Josie a look that said: I'll explain what you just saw, later.

"Kyle's on his way. We're going to look at Patrick Kessler's real office this time, at least what's still there, and pick up Mabry. I want her statements on record," Behan said. "We're not expecting much but you never know."

"I should go with you in case Flowers tries to interfere," Josie said.

"That's not a bad idea. You can keep him occupied while we work on Mabry."

"Do you know if Richards found Rago this morning?" she asked.

"No, he left a message with Father O'Reilly to tell the little thug he'd better show his ugly face this afternoon or be prepared to be hunted down."

Marge gave her a puzzled look and then a smirk.

"What's the matter?" Josie asked.

"Nothing."

Behan told her they'd leave as soon as Richards got there, and he went downstairs to finish reports.

"What were you two whispering about?" Josie asked as soon as he was gone.

"Miss Vicky threw his ass out last night. He's staying with me. How did you know Kyle had gone to the church this morning?"

"He must've told me. Are you sure that's a good idea? You're barely over the last time you and Red did this."

"I'm sure. Are you sleeping with him?"

"None of your business," Josie said, walking away.

She reached the hallway before she heard Marge shout, "About fucking time!"

WHEN THEY got to Councilman Flowers's district office, Mabry was at her desk but her expression made it clear she'd rather be anywhere else. The coldness she'd exhibited during their first visit was replaced by nervous twitching. Flowers popped out of his private office within seconds of their arrival and looked prepared to do battle. Josie immediately began her charm offensive, smiling and shaking hands, thanking him profusely for his cooperation and complimenting him on his willingness to help in their investigation.

"If you don't mind, could we talk a minute while Miss Mabry shows my detectives Kessler's office?" Josie asked, moving in the direction of his open door and almost forcing him to follow as soon as he realized she was going in there with or without him. "There are a few details I think only you can clear up and it's better if we do it in private," she said, closing his door behind them.

During the ride from Hollywood, Behan had asked her to talk to Flowers about his relationship with Mrs. Kessler and Sergeant Doug Miller. It wouldn't be a formal interview, but they both knew Josie had a way of getting people to say things they'd never admit in an interrogation. Flowers wasn't a suspect in Kessler's murder, but he might know the killer's motive. They all agreed the motive probably wasn't Mrs. Kessler since it seemed her husband would've been happy for someone to take her off his hands.

"We know you've been seeing Mrs. Kessler," Josie said and stopped him when he started to protest. "Don't bother denying it. No one would blame her for wanting a real relationship since her husband had . . . other interests."

He seemed to relax and said, "She's a very attractive, intelligent woman. Her marriage to Patrick was a sham and mine is virtually over, so I won't deny it."

Josie wondered if "virtually over" meant his wife didn't have a clue he was cheating, but she asked, "What would Patrick Kessler take from your office?"

"I have no idea."

"Then why did you tell Mrs. Kessler to search Patrick's briefcase?" she asked, not knowing if he had told Mrs. Kessler to do anything, but hoping the question would elicit the truth.

"Did she say that?" he asked. "I'm certain that isn't what she meant," he added with a nervous laugh.

"Miss Mabry said she went with her to Nicola's to search the briefcase for documents taken from your office. Was she mistaken too?"

"Look I have no idea what Susan . . . Mrs. Kessler and Miss Mabry are doing. It has nothing to do with me or my office." He stood, started to go toward the bar, but changed his mind and came back saying, "I should see if Miss Mabry or your detectives need anything."

"I'm sure they're fine," Josie said and quickly asked, "What can you tell me about Sergeant Doug Miller?"

He stopped and asked, "What do you mean?"

"I know he works with your office on union matters."

"Of course," he said and sat on the couch across from her. "The council works very closely with the Protective League on a number of issues concerning the police department and its personnel."

"Did you know he's dating your secretary?"

"Miss Mabry? No, but I don't see how that's anyone's business."

Josie had to stop herself from smiling. He lied. Marge had seen all of them together last night and Miller couldn't keep his hands off the woman. Flowers was attempting to keep some distance between himself and Sergeant Miller.

Behan knocked as he was opening the door and said, "We're done if you're ready to go. Miss Mabry's coming with us. I'll have one of my guys drive her back."

"Is that really necessary?" Flowers asked.

"Afraid so," Josie said.

"You realize this is police harassment. You badgered the poor woman last night. She said you barged into her home."

"Not exactly," Richards said. "And I need a formal interview." He was behind Behan standing next to Mabry who was clutching her purse with both arms, behaving more like a prisoner than a reluctant witness.

"This is ridiculous, Captain," Flowers said. His pink face and balding head grew a shade redder. He got up and pointed at Josie. "You can't treat people this way."

"One of your employees has been murdered, councilman," Josie said, standing a few feet from him. "I'd like to tell Commander Perry and the chief I have your full cooperation in finding his killer."

"Don't think this is the end of it," Flowers ṣaid, following them out of the office into the lobby. He was sweaty and flushed and looked as if he was having trouble catching his breath as he stood in the doorway. He didn't step outside, but watched until they reached Behan's car.

Behan slammed the car door shut after Mabry was in the back seat. He turned to Josie and with a serious expression said, "Stop grinning Corsino, or that sorry excuse for a man will think you don't respect him."

ANY GOOD detective would acknowledge that solving a murder required a combination of determination, expertise and a lot of good old-fashioned luck. Josie knew her team had an abundance of the first two, but the third one had evaded them. She told Behan to press Mabry on exactly what Sergeant Miller's role was in the city councilman's office. Gaby had told her at their first meeting that Miller was angling for a job with the councilman after retirement and eventually intended to move on with Flowers if he reached higher office. So why would Flowers be reluctant to admit there was a close relationship or deny he knew his secretary was dating the sergeant. It wasn't much, but Josie had learned to respect her deception detector. If someone lied, especially when the truth seemed harmless enough, there was usually a reason. In this case, she guessed Flowers wanted distance . . . but why? What was going on between them that he would rather not talk about?

As the interview with Mabry was about to begin, the desk officer knocked on the door and told Richards that a guy named Rago was in the lobby saying he needed to talk with him. Another interrogation room was empty, so Behan asked Martin to sit in his interview with Mabry, and Richards took Rago into the other room.

Josie wanted to hear Behan's interrogation but knew she had better get back to her real job. After Flowers's warning, it was predictable that Commander Perry would call, and she wanted to be available. What she didn't expect was to find Perry in her office with Seymour Kessler. Maki had intercepted her in the hallway so it wasn't a complete surprise, but nevertheless unpleasant.

After she listened to both men complain for ten minutes about the unbearable heat and stuffiness in her office, Commander Perry gave her his public servant lecture on how he believed captains were the face of the LAPD in their divisions. Seymour Kessler sat quietly wiping his sweaty face with a handkerchief while Josie's boss pontificated on the crucial role of public relations, political correctness and the finer points of command. Perry would never berate her in front of anyone, especially a civilian, but he was doing just enough to let Kessler know he wasn't happy with her performance.

"Have you arrested my son's killer?" Kessler asked, interrupting Perry.

"No," Josie said.

"Are you close?"

"Not really."

"Why are you wasting my time?" Kessler said, turning to Perry. "Find someone competent. I want the coward that murdered my son."

She noticed Perry straighten up as if he'd just been stabbed in the back.

"Detective Behan is one of the best homicide detectives in the city," Perry said.

"I'm not talking about him. I mean her. Put a man in charge who knows what he's doing."

Perry clasped his hands and glanced up at the ceiling before looking at Josie. She cocked her head and stared back at him but had already decided she wasn't going to say a word. The commander would have to do his job. If he thought she was screwing up, then take the case away; if not, defend her and tell this powerful pest to shut up and let her run her case.

"In this instance, sir," Perry said, clearing his throat, "the best man for the job happens to be a woman. Captain Corsino will remain in charge."

"Then you're a fool too," Kessler said, slowly getting up. "I need to get out of this oven. Turn on the damn air conditioning. Why do I pay taxes if you won't use the damn thing?" He was standing by the door and when Perry didn't move fast enough, demanded, "Take me home. I've got calls to make."

Perry escorted the older man out to his car and instructed his driver to take Kessler home. He was back in the station within five minutes. He wasn't done with Josie.

"You could've made some effort to appease him," Perry said, pacing in front of her coffee table. "Don't you understand this guy can ruin your career? Stubborn and inflexible are not the smart way to go here, Corsino."

She leaned back in her chair and folded her arms. He stopped moving. "Thanks for supporting me," she said and added under her breath, "it took you long enough."

"I give up," Perry said and dropped onto her couch. "I hope you'll be happy working communications with civilians who sue if they don't get enough potty breaks because that's where you're going when the chief gets tired of hearing complaints about you."

"Want an update on the investigation?" she asked. She knew the chief of police. He was happy with the way she ran Hollywood, and she was certain Seymour Kessler wouldn't intimidate him either.

"Why not," he said. "Then I'll have something to tell the chief when he's done yelling at me."

She reviewed everything they'd learned in the last few days. Although they weren't any closer to identifying the killer, she told him they might be establishing a motive for Kessler's murder and that could eventually lead to a suspect.

"So, you think whatever he had in that briefcase might've been the reason he was killed?"

"Yes," Josie said. "We have a witness who says Kessler gave it to Trumbo the night he died, and in less than twenty-four hours, Trumbo's dead too and the briefcase is gone."

"So, what was in it?" he asked.

"I think it's something he took from Flowers's office. Mabry's the weak link . . . more likely to talk than her boss or Sergeant Miller or even Mrs. Kessler, but I'd bet a year's salary they all know what it is."

Commander Perry became less agitated as Josie talked. He was a good cop who still wanted to catch the bad guy and she was painting a picture that made sense to him. She was relieved he didn't press her on the Trumbo investigation. Her detectives believed the ex-cop was connected to Kessler's murder but other than uncovering his relationship with Sergeant Castro and finding his badge and ID in Marvin Beaumont's office, the case on Trumbo was going nowhere.

Josie never thought she'd be grateful for the lack of air conditioning until Perry complained he couldn't take the heat any longer and left. She called Marge as soon as he was gone and asked her to come downstairs. The vice lieutenant had become very close with Gaby Johnston at the league and Josie wanted to take advantage of that friendship.

"Can you get Gaby to do some snooping at the Protective League without telling her too much?" Josie asked.

"Depends," Marge said, sitting on the couch and resting her feet on the coffee table. "What are we looking for?"

"Anything we can find on Doug Miller, what he does, his connection to Flowers or any other council person."

"Are you hungry?" Marge asked, sitting up.

"What about Gaby?"

"No problem, she'll do it. She doesn't like the shithead."

"But don't give her any more information on the investigation."

Marge got up and glared at Josie. "I fucked up; I'm sorry. I said I wouldn't do it again and I won't."

"I know, but she's a very persuasive lady. I like her too, but she's at the league and we don't know what she might inadvertently say to the wrong person."

"Trust me on this one boss, that woman is not going to screw up. She's about two steps ahead of the rest of us mortals."

"Good, use her, but keep her out of the loop," Josie said.

"Can we eat now?" Marge asked, walking out to the admin office.

Josie should've known her friend had an ulterior motive. They sat in the bar at Nora's and Marge immediately started asking questions about Richards, but Josie refused to discuss him. They ate their hamburgers and finished a bottle of wine in silence.

"I'm the one that encouraged you to be with the sonnofabitch," Marge said, in one last attempt before they paid the bill. "The least you can do is let me know what's going on."

"I'm divorcing Jake and I'll most likely have to sell the house."

"Sorry . . . about the house, that is."

"I'm not. I wanted everything to stay the same, grow old with Jake, spoil David's kids, but none of that's going to happen. So, I'll sell it if I have to and start again."

Josie heard herself say the words as if she'd accepted her fate and was willing and able to move on, but saying it out loud made everything sound so wrong. Dismissing her past meant losing a future. She'd do it because she had no other choice, but she was damned pissed off and would never pretend to be okay with the way things had turned out. If Jake expected her to remain his girl buddy and have one of those friendly divorce experiences, he had a huge surprise coming.

They returned to the station and found Richards and Rago standing by the back door. The usually cocky gang-banger was subdued and quietly listening to Richards explain why he was going to jail for violating his probation.

"I don't give a shit about your probation, but you're lying to me," Richards said, grabbing the smaller man's arm to escort him down the hall to be booked.

"What the fuck, you fuckin' with me, man," Rago said, stopping and staring into the detectives' squad room. "Jackin' me and you got the bitch."

"What're you talking about?" Richards asked, tightening his grip when Rago tried to pull away.

Rago refused to move and pointed toward the squad room. "That's the bitch," he said, in an excited squeaky whisper.

Josie moved around them to see where he was pointing. There wasn't any woman in view except Detective Martin.

"Her?" Josie asked indicating Martin.

"Fuck no, the other one . . . the old one," he said.

Miss Mabry was standing outside the interrogation room talking to Behan and wasn't paying any attention to what was going on in the hallway or she might've realized an eyewitness had just identified her as the person who ran away from Patrick Kessler's bloody body carrying the murder weapon.

TWELVE

They regrouped in a holding cell down the hall, Josie, Richards, Marge and Rago. It was a small padded room used to temporarily keep arrestees when they were out of control, drunk or crazy enough to bounce off the walls. Orderlies hosed it out every morning but the lingering odors of vomit and unbathed bodies embedded in the walls and rubber-coated concrete floor became so much worse when the air wasn't circulating.

"What's that bitch doin' here, anyways?" Rago asked, when Richards pressed him on his accusation.

"Looks to me like you picked the first woman you saw and identified her just to stay out of jail," Richards said.

"I fuckin' swear on my mother's grave. She's the one I seen."

"Your mother's alive in prison asshole," Marge said.

"What was she wearing that night?" Josie asked. She'd make him get specific. If he was lying, they'd know right away.

"Black," Rago said, immediately. "Ah . . . tight black thing, nothing on the arms . . . could see too much of them ugly tits."

"Low cut sleeveless black dress," Josie said.

"Yeah, shit . . . fuckin' old bitch arms, fat hangin' . . . gross." He shook his head at the unpleasant memory.

Josie looked at Richards. Rago had described a dress similar to the one Miss Mabry was wearing the night they interviewed her at the apartment.

~ 184 ~

"Where did she go after she picked up the knife?" Richards asked.

"Told you she run past the hotel . . . I got the fuck outta there . . . didn't wanna be around when the cops come."

They left Rago in the holding cell and went to Josie's office. The gangbanger didn't protest his confinement because he was probably smart enough to realize that although he wasn't free, he hadn't been booked either.

"This is a shitty predicament," Marge said, sitting at the worktable. "Rago's not what you would call a reliable witness if it's his word against Mabry's."

"She's shaky," Josie said, as she dialed Behan's extension. "Maybe Red can get to her."

A few minutes later, the big redhead was there listening to Richards recount what had happened.

"He's worthless in court. Nobody's gonna believe him," Behan said. "Maybe I can get her to break down, but if she lawyer's up we're done."

"Don't Mirandize her. She's a witness, not a suspect," Marge said.

"Yeah, right, that's gonna fly . . . weren't you told Miss Mabry was seen running from the scene carrying the murder weapon, Detective Behan, and you still didn't think she was a suspect when you questioned her?"

"You believe she killed Kessler?" Josie asked.

"Don't know. It fits. He knew her and she could get close without him suspecting anything was wrong," Behan said. "Rago didn't see her drop it, but that doesn't mean it didn't happen."

"Look at her. She's practically a goddamn grandmother. You fuckin' believe she could stab a guy Kessler's size . . . three times?" Marge asked.

"After the first one, the next two would be easy if he's surprised or in shock," Richards said.

"Not buying it," Marge insisted. "I think asshole's lying."

"Then tell me why he picked out Mabry?" Richards asked. "Don't you think it's peculiar that she's the only woman in the station connected to Kessler's murder who isn't a cop and Rago points right at her?" Richards asked.

"Shithead's lucky," Marge said.

"I'd question her, but unless she's a moron, as soon as I mention her rights, she'll have an attorney and won't open her mouth again," Behan said.

"What do you want to do?" Josie asked.

"Nothing right now . . . We'll get Rago's statement and keep him in custody. Martin can drive Mabry back to the Valley. We don't have enough to charge her and I'm not ready to tell her what we do have."

"Has she said where she was the night of the murder?" Richards asked.

"Home alone . . . went to bed early."

They all agreed the first step was to prove Mabry wasn't at home that night and had lied in her statement. Richards would go back to her apartment building, interview the other tenants, and try to find someone who might've seen her coming or going the night of the murder.

A couple of hours after everyone had left her office, Josie finished sorting through her paperwork with Maki. Her adjutant wanted to stay and finish up a few more projects but Josie was tired and sent her home to enjoy her weekend. Josie intended to work on Saturday and knew she could finish everything tomorrow when the office was quiet and the phones weren't ringing. Richards hadn't come back from Mabry's apartment building, and she didn't expect to see him for hours, if at all tonight. She was really hungry and called the vice office to ask Marge if she was available to go to Nora's for a late dinner. The vice lieutenant told her to stay put and she'd be downstairs in a minute. They needed to talk.

It hadn't taken much persuading to convince Gaby Johnston to dig into Doug Miller's activities at the Protective

League. She had called Marge back a few minutes before Josie's call with a complete rundown on everything Miller had done or was about to do for the police union which was easy because it turned out he didn't have a lot of responsibilities. Gaby faxed copies of anything she could find related to his position and duties and apparently he did embarrassingly little for a man who was still getting paid a sergeant's salary.

"She says there's something sensitive she needs to tell me in person," Marge said.

"Does that mean you don't have time to eat?" Josie asked, as her stomach rumbled.

"Have you ever known me not to eat, Corsino? It means I want you to come with me and we'll eat with Gaby, but we need to find a place cops won't go."

"Why?"

"How the fuck should I know. That's what she said."

Josie thought for a second and said, "I know a place just north of downtown; it's Italian but too pricey for most cops."

"Perfect, I've got Secret Service money to spend before the end of the month. Give me an address; we'll meet her there."

"Is that the extra money I got from the bureau?" Josie asked.

"Yep, if I don't spend it today, they'll take it back Monday."

Josie wasn't looking forward to Perry's monthly budget meeting where she'd be expected to justify Marge's vice expenditures including hundred-dollar door charges at a drag queen club and dinner at a five-star restaurant.

The Italian restaurant Il Piacere was on north Broadway close to downtown LA, but it catered to lawyers and corporation CEOs. They might run into someone in the income bracket of Seymour Kessler, but no cops. Josie,

however, knew the chef. David's new job was at that restaurant, and lucky for them he was working tonight. Her
son promised he'd have a table for his mother and her
friends anytime she wanted to come. She called him, and
he sounded excited like when he was a little boy and
found out she'd come to his first baseball game and had
watched him make an impossible catch. Her being there
was special for him, and she felt guilty because she was
using him.

David met them in the lobby wearing his apron and
chef's hat and after introductions personally escorted
the three women to a table on the enclosed patio. Their
entrance created quite a stir and Josie could see Gaby was
nervous with all the attention, but it probably wasn't just
David's presence that had created the buzz. Marge and
Gaby were two tall beautiful blondes; Josie was taller, and
knew she was attractive too, but she was wedged between
gorgeous bookends that didn't go anywhere unnoticed.

The waiter brought a bottle of expensive wine to the
table, compliments of the chef, and filled their glasses.

"To safe sex," Marge said, as they clinked the rims
together.

"Your son's handsome," Gaby said, almost emptying
her glass. "Is he married?"

"Not if my luck's holding out," Josie mumbled. "Marge
said you found something about Miller you wanted to tell
us in person." She changed the subject because she didn't
want to dwell on the subject of David's love life. Her disappointment frequently led to more alcohol.

The waiter brought several plates of appetizers and
salads and the subject changed immediately to food, spices
and sauces. They emptied the plates in a few minutes and
finished the wine. Josie ordered a bottle of cheaper Chianti that she really liked. Without anyone placing an order,
three entrees appeared within minutes. David had decided
for them. The veal Marsala was wonderful, and Josie had

to admit she was proud of her son. It wasn't the career she wanted for him, but he was surprisingly good at it.

It wasn't until the coffee was poured that Gaby was ready to talk about what she'd discovered in the Protective League office.

"I went through the books, and I think Doug Miller is taking money from our legal accounts," Gaby said.

"How much money are we talking about?" Josie asked.

"Who knows? The city council gives us thousands of dollars to hire representation for officers, not just criminal cases, but anytime they need a lawyer. No one ever audits those funds or how they're spent. We give the city a Mickey Mouse accounting, but there's never any independent review."

"What makes you think numb nuts stole the money?" Marge asked, ignoring the coffee and pouring another glass of Chianti.

"I know how many requests for representation we get from officers. I'm involved in every single case. The books are cooked. Names, cases I never heard of. I'm telling you to find a way to audit those books. He's taking money, a lot of money."

"But Marge is right, how do you know it was him?" Josie asked.

"He keeps the checkbook . . . besides . . ." She stopped.

"What?" Josie asked.

"I've got a buddy at B of A. He said not one of those phony checks Miller signed was ever cashed. The money was electronically transferred out of the league's account."

"Where'd it go?"

Gaby shook her head. "Don't know, but I'm sure you guys have people who can track it."

"Roughly how much cash are we talking about?" Marge asked.

"At least a hundred thousand . . . it's a lot, but the city will never question it. They're afraid of the league's influence, so we never get audited unless it's a superficial handjob," Gaby said and slumped back on her chair. "You can't tell anybody where you got this. I'll lose my job."

David came out again before they left. He was busy but wanted to be certain everything had been perfect and told them dinner was his treat. They were grateful but put a hundred dollars on the table to cover tips and the extra wine. Josie hugged and thanked him for a wonderful meal. For the first time in years, her son looked really happy and probably wanted her approval. He was waiting for her to tell him this was all right. It wasn't, but she told him the truth, that he was a talented chef who had a remarkable gift. She'd do whatever she could to support him but couldn't help hoping at some point he'd change his mind and a concert hall, not a gourmet kitchen, would be his dream too.

The restaurant was nearly empty by the time they left. Richards had called Josie and said he would be at Mabry's apartment house until late so she'd better go to Pasadena, and he'd see her in the morning. He also promised to give her a key to his Long Beach house the next day so they wouldn't have this problem again. She was disappointed, but knew their life together was going to be like this. The next time it would probably be her making the call.

While they waited with Gaby for valet parking to retrieve her car, she talked to them about her house in Manhattan Beach on the strand. She wrote her home address on her business card and invited them to a barbeque on Sunday.

"Bring whomever you want," Gaby said, giving five dollars to the skinny illegal immigrant in a red jacket who opened the door to her Lexus. "We'll swim, eat, drink too much Sangria and enjoy the ocean breeze," she said, before driving out of the lot.

Josie waited until she and Marge were alone on the way back to the station before saying, "I'll bet you ten bucks we find that money in an account tied to Flowers or Mabry. They're joined at the hip with Miller."

"I'll bet you, me and knucklehead Behan won't find a damn thing," Marge said. "We need someone who understands financial stuff. I've seen your checkbook, Corsino; it's definitely not you."

They talked about giving the information to the department's financial crimes unit and working with one of their detectives.

"Yeah, but do you trust those pointy-headed squints not to blab to the league or the media?" Marge asked.

Josie knew some young cops had blind loyalty to the union, but the financial unit had older more savvy detectives; besides, she wasn't certain there was a choice. If Miller had transferred the money to an offshore account or some other techie scheme, they'd never find it. If it had gone to Flowers, she didn't believe the councilman would be stupid enough to make it easy for them to find it.

Her mind was racing with possibilities and more questions now. If Patrick Kessler could prove his boss had been taking money from Miller, and he threatened to expose them, it was a great motive for murder, but that was a huge "if," a theory with no proof. The bigger question in Josie's mind was why, if Kessler had that information, he'd share it with a man like Henry Trumbo.

The detective squad room was empty, but they found Behan in one of the interrogation rooms finishing reports on Sergeant Castro's death. He told them some of the toxicology reports had come back and Castro had died from an overdose of pure China white heroin. The coroner was right about the scratches on his neck. He found skin under Castro's fingernails and a dislocated right shoulder. Someone else had stuck that syringe in the man's thigh and it looked as if the strange little sergeant had fought hard to stay alive.

"Seems to me he was a Trumbo loose end that got taken care of for whatever reason," Behan said. "Where have you two been?"

Josie let Marge tell him what they had learned from Gaby. He listened while he organized the reports and had everything in a neat pile by the time she finished.

"So Patrick Kessler, Mabry, Flowers . . . they're all in that council office. Kessler might've stumbled on to something or he might've been a party to it and took a share of the money from Miller until he got cold feet."

"Maybe, but we can't prove anything. How are we going to get the city to do an audit? At least we can nail Miller's ass and see where that takes us," Marge said.

"Let me talk to Commander Perry," Josie said. "Should I bring in the financial unit and try to find any hidden bank accounts?"

"Don't need to," Behan said. "Martin can do it."

"Really," Josie said.

"Yes really, you ought to read personnel packages when you hire these people, boss," he said, giving her a dose of Corsino sarcasm.

"I read them. That doesn't mean I have to remember . . . smartass. Don't," she said turning to Marge who was about to say something.

"Martin's a CPA. She was with the FBI for two years before she decided to do real police work," he said, looking way too pleased with himself.

"Great, then let her run with it," Josie said and got up. "I'm going home." She saw Behan give Marge a quick smile as she and Josie walked out together. "You never learn do you?" Josie asked as soon as they were in the hallway.

"What?"

"Tell him to go back to his rich wife."

"Not this time," Marge said. "Woman had her chance. I'm keeping his sorry ass."

THE COMBINATION of too much wine and food had completely relaxed Josie and she had a difficult time staying awake on the ride home. All she thought about was crawling into bed and passing out until morning.

She should've known her life couldn't be that simple. Jake's Porsche was parked in the driveway. It was tempting to keep driving past the house and wait on Kyle's patio until he got home. It would be more pleasant to sleep on the outdoor bench than deal with her cynical soon-to-be ex-husband, but she wasn't sure she could stay awake long enough to get to Long Beach.

The garage door was open so she drove in and parked. The kitchen door was unlocked and all the lights were on downstairs. She knew it was probably him, but couldn't turn off being cautious. Her hand stayed on the grip of her gun until she saw him sitting at the card table with a bottle of wine and two glasses. The bottle was half empty so he'd been waiting awhile.

"Sorry to be here so late, but I really wanted to talk to you alone," Jake said. He stood and she could see he wasn't steady on his feet.

"I'm really tired. We can talk tomorrow," she said and noticed that all the drawers had been opened in the kitchen and dining room. There was a box by the door with things he'd collected, mostly cooking utensils, but there were glasses wrapped in paper towels too, so she suspected the Waterford crystal no longer occupied space in the wet bar cabinet upstairs. She didn't care. It was a small price if he'd go home and let her get some sleep.

"I've got to explain . . . before we do something really stupid that we'll both regret."

She pulled out one of the folding chairs and sat. There was something different about the way he was behaving. When Jake was drunk, he usually got sleepy and stupid. Tonight he was agitated and looked angry.

"Explain," she said.

He poured another glass of wine and put it in front of her then refilled his glass and took a drink. Josie left hers. The last thing she wanted was more wine. Two bottles was her limit on a work night.

"I think we should try again."

"Good night Jake," she said getting up. "Lock the door when you leave."

"No, wait . . . I admit I acted like a real jerk, but I think we should try to fix this don't you?" he asked, grabbing her arm to keep her from leaving.

"No," she said calmly, peeling his fingers away.

"We've got twenty-four years of our lives invested in this marriage . . . a son, a house. Aren't those good reasons not to give up on me?"

"They might've been six months ago, not now. You can't love someone and behave the way you did."

He stared at her for a few seconds and didn't speak. She saw something new in his eyes. It wasn't disappointment or remorse. The man she'd loved for nearly a quarter of a century hated her guts.

"Don't expect any financial support," he said coldly and poured the last of the wine, drinking it in one swallow. "The investments are mine. I've set them up . . . you won't get a penny of that money."

She laughed. It was an involuntary reaction. "There goes my last good reason not to give up on you," she said, walking away.

This time he didn't attempt to stop her. She heard him kicking at the chairs as she went upstairs. There was a lot of banging and swearing and Josie suspected the card table and folding chairs and maybe even the dining room furniture wouldn't survive his rampage. Her first thought was "too bad David didn't take the china cabinet." The noise stopped after twenty minutes and it got very quiet, but she wasn't worried. Even drunk Jake wasn't stupid enough to come after her. A woman with a gun who knew how to use it was way out of his league. He would get his revenge the only way he could—in a courtroom.

THIRTEEN

On Saturdays, Josie allowed herself the luxury of sleeping in, but this morning she was awake early and eager to get out of the house and back to work. She took a shower and hadn't thought about her encounter with Jake until she went into the kitchen and saw her card table and chairs had been converted to kindling. The dining room had been spared, but the expensive silver flatware was missing as well as a beautiful crystal vase Jake's parents had given them as a wedding gift.

She cleaned up the kitchen and ate breakfast in the dining room. Her cheap coffeemaker had escaped both David and Jake's attention so she got her regular dose of caffeine, an egg and toast. Before leaving, she retrieved a small overnight case from the garage and packed a few necessary toiletries and a change of clothes. There wasn't a doubt in her mind she'd be staying in Long Beach tonight.

The shooting range at the old police academy in Elysian Park was open, so she stopped there on the way to Hollywood station. No one was on the course, but she found one of the instructors and got a hundred rounds of .45 reloads to practice on the combat range. The distances were shorter here than the qualification range. She'd already qualified for the month, but liked to practice shooting the shorter distances on this range. Statistics showed most police shootings took place within a few feet of an assailant, and it was scary how many shots got fired by officers who didn't hit anything except the neighbor's car, house or each other. She stayed seven yards from the target, practiced drawing from the holster, reloading, malfunction drills, standing, kneeling, and from behind the barrier, shooting until the ammo container was empty and her trigger finger was sore.

The target was full of holes, mostly where she'd wanted them, so she considered it a successful practice. She picked up an empty brass bucket and started collecting casings that had bounced off the concrete and scattered everywhere. After a few minutes, a couple of young instructors came out onto the range and helped. Josie thanked them and smiled when they asked what specialized unit she worked before noticing the captain badge on her belt.

"Sorry ma'am, no disrespect intended," the shorter one said. "Don't see many bars and stars out on a Saturday."

"Thanks for the help," she said, tossing the last casing into the can.

"Yes ma'am," he said with a grin and added, "From what I saw you won't be needing much help."

She walked back to her car parked down by the café. Damn I love this job, she thought. There was no way to explain how good it felt knowing she was among an elite few who woke up every morning and got paid to strap on a gun and go look for trouble. She liked helping people too but had to admit, without the dangerous, adrenaline-pumping aspects of this job, it would be social work and she'd be doing something else.

The station parking lot was nearly empty on a Saturday morning. Admin staff, most civilians, and detectives didn't come in on the weekends unless there was something unusual happening.

Josie wasn't surprised to see Behan and Ann Martin in the detective squad room already working when she got there. They had the Kessler murder book open with pages spread out covering one end of the homicide detectives' table. Martin was sitting at the other end completing the rough draft of a flowchart.

She had expected to see Richards, too. He'd texted her as she was leaving the shooting range and said he was headed toward Hollywood.

"Richards is upstairs in vice," Behan said, as if he were reading her mind. "He and Marge are doing backgrounds on a couple of wits he tracked down last night."

"Did he find somebody who saw Mabry leave her apartment?" Josie asked.

"To be exact, two somebodies," he said.

Josie was looking over Martin's shoulder as the detective drew lines connecting events and people that had anything to do with the Kessler and Trumbo homicides—Nicola's, Susan Kessler, Seymour Kessler, Mabry, Miller, Flowers, Castro, etc.—the lines resembled a crazed spider's web, crossing erratically back and forth across the paper.

"Does this help?" Josie asked. The jumbled mass of lines was giving her a headache.

"Actually it does," Martin said. "Do you notice the most common point of contact in this matrix?"

"Not really."

"Susan Kessler . . . she knows both victims and is connected to most of the other players in some way."

"So?" Josie asked. She still didn't understand why that was valuable information.

Martin stopped writing and looked up. "Motive . . . husband wants out of the marriage; she gets Trumbo to kill him; she has reason to kill Trumbo."

"Is that what you think, Red?" Josie asked, knowing she'd had a similar scenario running through her mind not too long ago, but she couldn't seriously consider Susan Kessler a strong suspect in Trumbo's death.

"No, but it's another plausible theory I guess, especially if Mabry snatched the murder weapon. Susan and Mabry are friends."

"Sergeant Miller and Mabry are probably lovers. That trumps friends any day. Have you started doing the financial checks?" Josie asked.

"I'll get to it in a few minutes," Martin said. "I'm almost done here."

"Miller and Flowers are still my prime suspects," Behan said, probably catching Josie's annoyed expression and most likely thinking the same thing she did that flowcharts didn't catch murderers. "Have you talked to Commander Perry about doing the audit?" he asked.

"Not yet, I'll try calling him this morning. He hates being bothered on the weekends," she said, with a smirk.

She wanted to see Richards before going to her office and facing the tedious ordeal of reasoning with her boss. She found him talking with Marge in the vice office.

"Morning," Richards said, getting up when he saw her. Josie could tell he wanted to touch her, but he backed away and looked confused.

"That was fucking smooth, Kyle," Marge said. "There's nobody around. Just kiss the woman before you give yourself a goddamn hernia."

Josie gave him a quick kiss. "Morning," she said. "I understand you got something last night." He looked tired. His eyes were bloodshot and he hadn't shaved.

He scratched at his beard and said, "Found two people who saw Mabry. A waitress who lives in a second floor apartment saw her car coming into the underground parking close to three A.M. She was on her way to work an early morning shift at a twenty-four-hour coffee shop and waved, but Mabry acted as if she didn't see her."

"Who's the other one?"

"Maintenance guy had to turn off the water leaking in one of the apartments; he passed Mabry in the hallway about three A.M. She was opening the door to her apartment. He remembered because her hair was a mess, mascara smeared and her black dress looked dirty. He stopped to ask if she was okay, and she told him to mind his own business."

"Photo IDs?" Josie asked.

"Didn't hesitate . . . both of them picked her out of a six-pack. We have their statements, and neither has had prior encounters with Mabry."

"Great, I'll call Perry and get the ball rolling to audit the legal fund."

"Martin better get her CPA ass in gear and find where they stashed that money before Miller figures out we're on to him," Marge said.

Josie and Richards exchanged a look. They were probably thinking the same thing. She would talk to Perry about using the Internal Affairs surveillance team to watch Sergeant Miller. If he decided to take the money and run, they would know. Surveillance was Richards's area of expertise, so he could supervise the IA squad and still help Red with the homicide investigation.

THE WATCH commander had taken all the fans from the admin office for the front desk and the jail. None of her staff would be working today so Josie told him to keep them until Monday morning. She found one small fan in her office on top of the wardrobe that somehow had escaped notice. She put it on the worktable, turned it on full blast until the motor started to overheat, then lowered the speed and pointed it directly at her desk.

When she couldn't stall any longer, she sat behind the desk, took a deep breath and dialed Commander Perry's Blackberry. He didn't pretend to be pleased to hear from her.

"You must need something, Corsino. We both know you'd never call for my advice."

She told him everything they had learned from Gaby and Rago and how Mabry had lied to them.

"Actually sir, I do need some direction from you. It's no secret the city council and the union have each other's backs. We need an audit of the money the council gives them for their legal fund. Does the chief of police have the authority to order that kind of audit?" Josie asked. She knew what had to be done, but needed Perry's support so she'd let him come up with the plan—with her calculated prodding of course.

"Probably not unless there's a crime, like a credible allegation of theft, which you seem to have. Let me talk to the old man, see if he'd be willing to ask the mayor for his blessing . . . see if we can do it without stepping on too many toes, especially if we don't come up with anything."

"We should have a shot since police union funds went to the mayor's opponent in the last election," Josie said.

"True, but the league has spread enough money around to his favorite liberal causes to make amends by now. The mayor is basically honest. I think we can get the audit, but then we have to find somebody we trust to do it."

"I have somebody," she said. "Detective Martin is a CPA who worked with the FBI. We can keep it in-house. If there's nothing wrong, Sergeant Miller's reputation remains intact. Nobody ever needs to know there was a suspicion he was dishonest."

"Do you have any proof Miller has the money besides this paralegal's word?"

"Not yet," Josie said. "But we're working on it."

"I can't make any promises, but I'll call the old man. It would help if you found money Miller can't account for."

"We will," Josie said, trying to convince herself as much as him, then added, "It's critical Councilman Flowers isn't privy to any of this. Actually, it's best if none of the city council is involved, but I know that's not possible."

Perry seemed confused so she repeated the evidence they'd uncovered of a connection among Flowers and

Miller and Mabry. He still seemed a little puzzled but promised not to include Councilman Flowers in discussions and said he'd advise the chief to try dealing directly with the mayor as much as possible.

Josie asked him if he thought they should have Richards and an internal surveillance squad watch Miller in case he somehow found out what they were up to and decided to flee before the audit was done. He told her to do it. She thanked him, knowing Richards had already called and made the arrangements, but it was much better if her boss thought the idea came from him. Surveillance was expensive, and this way the bureau couldn't complain about overtime costs.

She didn't like having to deceive and manipulate Perry but running her police station was a lot like playing chess, and she'd learned over the years to get what she wanted by staying several moves ahead of the bureaucracy. Otherwise, the many levels of administration constantly looking over her shoulder would eventually bring any semblance of innovative police work to a grinding halt.

Richards came into her office just before she'd finished talking to Perry. He sat at the table and let the fan blow on him while he waited. She was listening to her boss but watching him. There was no denying he was already a significant part of her life, not just the physical attraction but she knew they had a connection. She'd let him get into her head in a way only one other man had ever done. It was scary because she knew how that relationship ended . . . in nasty recriminations and a kitchen furniture massacre.

As soon as she hung up the phone, Richards got up and closed her office door. He walked back to her desk and kissed her, a long, I've-really-missed-you kiss. Then, he stepped back and said, "There, that's better. Good morning." He opened the door again and sat at the table.

"Were you talking to Commander Perry, Captain?" he asked, as if nothing had happened.

She stopped thinking about Jake.

"He's going to meet with the chief, but Martin needs to get busy looking for that money, and you should probably start watching Miller right away. This is a lot like making a meal come together. Everything has to be ready to go at the same time."

He took a house key out of his pocket and put it in her hand.

"See you tonight," he said. "Let's hope Sergeant Miller goes to bed early."

Josie went back to detectives to tell Behan about the audit, but got sidetracked at Martin's desk, watching as she accessed different computer programs that allowed her to collect information and create a financial profile on their main suspects. Josie didn't know what or how she was doing it, but in a few hours Martin had eliminated Mabry as a suspect who had large deposits of cash hidden anywhere. She had a checking account and small money market accounts and, like many civil service employees, owed too much money for car payments and credit cards.

Miller and Flowers were another story. The detective worked another couple of hours on each of them but couldn't find anything significant. Josie was sitting near Behan's desk with him and Marge and could hear the frustrated mumbling as Martin went in and out of different programs, made phone calls and finally sat back, groaned and covered her face with both hands.

"Is it a bust?" Behan asked.

"No, I've got to make some more phone calls . . . but not until Monday. The people I know who specialize in this kind of work don't do weekends," Martin said, rubbing her neck. She got up and stretched. "I'll give them credit. If they've got that money, it's buried really well . . . there are a few more things I can try," she said turning off her computer. "But not today, my eyes are crossed from staring at that screen." She looked at their faces and had to sense the disappointment.

"Don't worry," she said. "If it's there, I'll find it. I've been told I can be a stubborn pain in the ass when I put my mind to it."

Even Behan had to smile a little at that one.

Josie went back to her office to finish reviewing a personnel complaint that Marge had written for one of her wayward police officers, made a few notes and left it locked in her desk. She was tired and knew Marge had a prostitution task force that night and wouldn't be able to get away for a while. The detective squad room was empty when she looked in. There was no sign of Behan, Martin or her manic flowchart, and the murder book had been reassembled and put back on the shelf.

She didn't want to dwell on where Behan might've gone, but had a strong suspicion he was sitting at his favorite bar with a single malt whiskey waiting for Marge to call it a night. She went upstairs to the break room and dropped all the change she had into the vending machine and was about to choose something disgusting and full of all those trans fats everyone warns you not to eat when Officer Hoffman came in wearing civilian clothes and carrying her uniform in a plastic, dry-cleaning bag.

The final probationary ratings had come out yesterday. Hoffman squeaked by and, primarily through the generosity of her training officer, would become a full-fledged cop. Josie didn't question or second-guess his assessment because she trusted him and knew he wouldn't allow her to get off probation unless he believed she could eventually do the job. The young woman had the heart of a fighter but her size and strength were still worrisome.

"Good morning, ma'am," Hoffman said and added quickly, "Guess I've got my days and nights mixed up."

Josie empathized. She could never work through the night. It was fine until about four in the morning when her eyes would automatically close. Even during the riots, she'd excuse herself at four A.M. to take a twenty-minute nap. The only good part was she ate breakfast, her favorite meal, three times a day.

"Congratulations," she said, getting a cup of coffee to go with her candy bar. "I read your ratings. You're really working hard."

"Thank you, ma'am," she said, as she waited by the coffee machine for her cup to fill. Her back was to Josie but she could sense there was something the young officer wanted to say.

"Is everything all right, Hoffman?"

"Yes ma'am . . . it's just," she turned around but hesitated.

"Are you having a problem with someone on the watch?"

"No, ma'am, it's nothing like that. It's just there's something I should've told Detective Martin, but I forgot and afterward I was afraid you'd think I was trying to hide something so I kept quiet because I didn't want to mess up my rating."

"Call me captain or boss. Ma'am makes me feel like we're at a really bad boarding school. What didn't you tell her?"

"I did see Henry Trumbo with somebody besides Sergeant Castro. It was a lady. They were in the academy café."

"Did you know her?"

"No, she was tall, blonde, and very pretty. She looked a lot like Lieutenant Bailey but dressed really classy."

Josie gave her a detailed description of Gaby Johnston and the officer agreed that could've been the woman.

"Miss Johnston was representing Trumbo in a discrimination suit after he got fired."

"But I saw them before he got fired."

"She's a sort of an ombudsman for the union so it was probably connected to his job performance. Detective Martin can follow up but I appreciate you telling me."

Hoffman tossed her empty cup into the trash and picked up her uniform. "Sorry it took so long. Guess I'd better get changed for roll call." She stopped in the doorway and said, "I know I'm gonna get wheeled to a new division next deployment but I wanted to let you know I really enjoy working for you and I'd like to come back to Hollywood."

Police officers were in and out of Hollywood all the time. Josie wanted them to be comfortable and never interfered with their choice of divisions, but she had a feeling if Hoffman stayed in patrol, something bad was going to happen to her or her partner. Josie thought one of the specialized divisions might give her an opportunity to work out of uniform. Because of her size, she'd be perfect in juvenile narcotics or DARE working in the schools. Josie knew the captain at Juvenile Division and would make a phone call on Monday.

She wasn't surprised that Gaby had met with Trumbo. It was the paralegal's job to represent union members in legal matters. Trumbo probably had a suspicion the academy staff was planning to drop him from his class and was laying the groundwork for his lawsuit. It wasn't an unusual pattern for below-par performers since it was well known that the city of LA would rather pay than litigate.

The invitation to Gaby's barbecue at the beach had almost slipped her mind. It was going to be a girls' thing because Richards couldn't go and she doubted Behan would show up. She would rather spend Sunday alone with Kyle but that wasn't going to happen. The surveillance squad had to be there when Miller woke up and put him to bed every night. The captain in her understood that, but she was a woman too and wanted to be with him.

They were just getting to know each other, but, as usual, work had a way of complicating her life.

It was late, but Josie wasn't tired and wanted a glass of wine before facing the drive to Long Beach. She was trying to reach Marge on the police radio and ask if she was almost done for the night when Richards called. He told her his squad had followed Sergeant Miller to a bar where he met Mabry, and it looked as if they intended to be there awhile. She was disappointed but not surprised.

"Stay with them. If I fall asleep before you get home, wake me when you get there," she said and felt bipolar talking like his captain and a disappointed lover at the same time. But there was no doubt in her mind she needed him to keep tabs on Miller more than she needed him in her bed and that caused a familiar red flag to pop up in her brain.

"So what?" Marge asked. It was almost an hour later, and they were sitting in Nora's finishing a bottle of wine and a basket of greasy onion rings.

Josie had tried to describe her apprehension at not feeling worse about keeping Richards out all night. She regretted broaching the subject almost as soon as she brought it up because her friend wasn't someone who had the temperament to navigate subtleties in life, but there wasn't anyone else she trusted enough to talk about this.

"Maybe Jake was right . . . I've got some abnormal attachment to my work."

"Your only abnormal attachment was that fucking ass-hole you married."

"Can't really argue with that one," she said and sighed. "I've got to stop thinking so much. I'm not gonna change who I am so what's the point? Where's Red? Why aren't you with him?"

Marge put down her glass. "Good questions."

"Did you check his regular spots?"

"Yep, nobody's seen him, fucker's not answering his phone," Marge said and recited the litany of a dozen familiar bars she'd called.

"Want me to call Miss Vicky?" Josie asked, knowing the last thing she wanted to do was talk to Mrs. Behan about her wayward husband.

"No, he's not there."

"You called."

"Had to know if he went home or it was another lost weekend."

"Another?"

"He'll come to my place Sunday night and be at work Monday, but the rest of the weekend is a fucking mystery to both of us."

"I'm not sure I can put him into another detox program without Perry forcing him to retire or making him face discipline," Josie said, but knew she didn't want to do anything yet for another selfish reason. She needed him.

"He won't go anyway until this Kessler thing is wrapped up and maybe not even then," Marge said. "It's not the work. He needs to work. He just can't give up his damn booze . . ." She looked as if she wanted to say more but didn't.

"Did you try the Dugout?" Josie asked.

"He doesn't drink in that shithole," Marge said, then asked, "Does he?"

"I've seen his car parked there a few times. He'd fit right in. It's full of drunk cops. He's on his own time, but I'll go there and threaten him if you want."

"No, I can make him come with me. It's finding him that's the hard part."

They finished the wine and Marge left to pick up Behan. Josie knew it was a temporary fix. He wasn't going to stop drinking. He'd been through enough detox programs for her to say that with some confidence, but if he lost his job, she was certain the drinking would accelerate and he'd drown himself in a bottle even faster.

She needed his expertise, but in a strange way, he needed to do the work that very likely had caused him to start drinking. A number of the best homicide detectives she knew drank too much, but then what normal person wouldn't need something to help forget years of sorting out the horrible and often disgusting havoc human beings could inflict on one another. She knew she was justifying something that made her uncomfortable, but then like always she would do whatever she thought was best for Hollywood. At the moment, that was keeping her homicide supervisor at work and sober. Besides, rationalizing was one of the things she did best. It kept her sane in the crazy world she inhabited.

THE LONG BEACH neighborhood was in a lot of ways similar to the area around her home in Old Pasadena, not as many tourists but when the weather was hot, people stayed outdoors and walked the streets. Here, they went to the ocean and walked along the coast. In Pasadena they browsed the shops and ate at a variety of nice restaurants.

Josie hadn't been there long when Richards arrived. She was drinking the last of a Pinot they had opened and knew he wouldn't mind. He was a whiskey drinker and admitted to putting wine in the same category as canned soda. She had opened all the windows and french doors in the house and was out on the patio enjoying the thin breath of an ocean breeze that barely moved the dainty glass chimes. Car lights flashing off the garage roof told her he was there and a few seconds later he joined her holding a glass of whiskey.

He dropped onto the cushioned chair beside her, then leaned forward and gave her a kiss. Three candles in glass holders were the only light other than a full moon, but Josie could see his eyes looked glassy and tired.

"You might have to order out for a lover tonight, I'm finished," he said, touching her face.

"I'm just getting used to you. I think I'll wait."

He told her what Miller and Mabry had done all night and that his squad had left them at her apartment when the lights went out.

"One of my guys got close to them earlier at the bar and heard them talking about plane tickets and hotel reservations, so we'd better not drag our feet or they're gone," Richards said, finishing his drink and leaving for a minute to get the bottle.

"No meeting with Flowers or Mrs. Kessler," Josie said.

"No, but they were both on their cell phones all night."

"Hopefully, Martin's contacts can find something Monday and we'll get the green light on that audit."

"How does Red see us doing this?"

"What do you mean?" Josie asked.

"I know you and Red think Miller took money from the union and somehow that's the motive for Kessler's murder. Even if we prove he took the money, we still can't prove he killed Kessler."

"Behan's always got a plan."

He drained his glass and rubbed his face, pulled at the beginnings of a scruffy beard. "I know you put a lot of trust in Red. I do too, but maybe you need to rely less on him and give Martin more responsibility."

"Why would I do that, Kyle?" she asked and knew her tone was too confrontational for the moment.

"Never mind, forget I mentioned it," he said, filling his glass.

"No, tell me what you're thinking," she demanded.

Richards stared at her for several seconds as if he were trying to decide how to say something. He put his glass down and said, "I know you and Red are friends, but

I think that guy's on the edge. I've seen it before, but you know him better than me, so if you say he's okay, I won't bring it up again."

"He's okay," she said, coldly.

He finished his drink in silence.

"I'm done talking about work," he said, turning the empty glass upside down.

"Sorry," she said, but wasn't. Behan was her problem. She knew Kyle was trying to help but he needed to trust her to do her job.

"Don't be," he said.

"He's my friend. I'll take care of him."

They stopped discussing Behan but stayed up talking until the early morning hours. He spoke guardedly about growing up in Texas, his parents and a younger brother who had been killed during the war in Afghanistan. Although he gave details without much emotional attachment, that peek into his life was a catalyst to share more of her feelings about her husband and son; how the disintegration of her family had been devastating. They fell asleep on the couch in the living room and the last thing she remembered thinking before drifting off wrapped in his arms was, even though being with him felt so right, like everything else in her complex life, this wasn't going to be easy.

The next morning she'd slept so deeply that she woke confused and disoriented. Where was she and where should she be? What day was it? Was she late for work? It took a few seconds to clear her head and remember the chronology of events that left her in this place, lying on this couch Sunday morning. Kyle was gone. She looked at her watch and knew he would already be in his car watching Mabry's apartment.

There was a note stuck to her holstered gun on the coffee table. It told her to go to the kitchen and turn on the coffee machine, and "like magic your caffeine will appear." She had slept in her panties and tank top, leaving her jeans on a kitchen chair with her boots nearby. The windows at the back of the house were open, but it was already starting to get hot so she opened the doors to the secluded patio and had her coffee outside in her underwear.

Before making breakfast, she called Marge to see if Behan had been located and put to bed for the rest of the weekend.

"He's okay," Marge said, after thanking Josie for directing her to the bar. "He wasn't as fucked up as I thought he'd be, but he's tired, so I'm gonna let him sleep all day unless there's another dead body."

"I'll tell the watch commander to call Martin and another team first. She can supervise and handle the preliminary stuff then catch him up on Monday."

"He's not gonna like that," Marge said.

"Too bad, we'll argue about it on Monday after he's had some sleep."

"Are you going to Gaby's place?" Marge asked.

"Might as well, I've got nothing else to do today. You should come, just let him rest," Josie said, guessing that Behan would probably stay passed out if no one disturbed him.

"I'd planned on it. I'm not gonna babysit the fucker."

They agreed to meet at Gaby's in a couple of hours. Josie wanted to make breakfast and take a shower. She had shorts, sandals and a tank top in her overnight bag but didn't have a swimsuit. Swimming in the ocean wasn't her favorite activity so it wasn't a problem.

She was surprised when she got to Manhattan Beach and saw the house. Gaby had warned them that it was on a walk street, so there was nowhere to park unless they used her driveway on the alley side. The house wasn't big but stood only a few yards away from stairs that led down to the beach. The ocean view was spectacular.

Facing a public sidewalk, Gaby's patio was enclosed with a three-foot wall. The house lacked privacy but that was more than compensated for by the location.

"How the hell can you afford this on a paralegal's salary?" Marge asked, as soon as Gaby had finished giving them a tour of the expensive bungalow.

"I can't. My aunt left it to me after she died last year. I got it with all the furnishings, a cool dune buggy and no mortgage," Gaby said and grinned. "I was always her favorite."

"Fuckin' amazing. My relatives leave me sick dogs and their unpaid bills."

Josie was listening to them as she looked at an antique curio filled with porcelain figurines. Delicate features and flawless workmanship told her they had probably cost more than she'd be willing to spend for anything that looked so fragile.

"My aunt was a bit eccentric, but she was very good to me when I went through a rough spell," Gaby said, carrying a pitcher of Sangria and glasses and leading them out to the Spanish-tiled patio.

They sat and drank as the locals passed by stopping to lean on the wall and share gossip with Gaby.

"This is great," Josie said. "I'm not sure I could convince myself to leave home every morning if I lived here."

"Trust me I wouldn't either except somebody's got to pay the taxes and insurance."

"Poor fucking baby, get to live in paradise for the price of taxes. I'd trade places," Marge said.

"Would you? I wonder," Gaby said with a weird expression and went back inside to retrieve a plate of bacon-wrapped cheese and liver.

Josie and Marge exchanged a look, shrugged and let it pass. It was too hot to delve deeper into what she meant. They finished the Sangria and appetizers then walked down to the beach. Gaby wore a long-sleeved tee shirt over her bathing suit, with a Hawaiian wrap around her waist covering her legs down to her ankles. They strolled on the bike path for a while, watched the volleyball, and returned to the patio where Gaby started the barbeque. Marge and Josie had each brought a bottle of wine, and Josie had picked up a half gallon of chocolate gelato for dessert.

The wine was open on the outdoor table and the three women drank, ate more appetizers, joked and told stories until Gaby brought out a platter with chicken, sausage and vegetables and put everything on the grate. Standing near the grill, she rested her foot on the edge of a colorful pot in front of the wall.

"Aren't you melting in that outfit?" Marge asked. "It's too hot to be wearing so many clothes."

"It's embarrassing, but I'm a Manhattan Beach dweller who can't tolerate the sun," Gaby said.

"Why's that?" Josie asked.

"Sounds like the makings of a good lawyer joke to me," Marge said and ducked the ice cubes thrown at her by Gaby.

"Besides my legs are ugly."

It wasn't until they finished eating that Gaby brought up the audit on the Protective League's legal fund. Josie told her the truth. They were still trying to get permission.

"I feel guilty snitching on him," Gaby said. "I know it was the right thing to do, but I'm certain he can see it in my face every time we talk. It's like I've violated some trust."

"He's a thief, you don't owe him squat," Marge said.

"You're right, of course. It's just . . . forget it." She started gathering the empty paper plates and asked, "Anything new on the murders?"

"No," Josie said, before Marge could answer.

"Why do you suppose that is?" Gaby asked.

"This sort of investigation is always tough."

"Do you still think it's a serial killer? Seems strange there haven't been any more victims," Gaby said, reaching over the wall and throwing the dirty paper plates into a dumpster on the other side.

"Suspect might've moved on to another area or maybe he got arrested for another crime and is sitting in jail," Josie said, not wanting to talk about it, but knowing Gaby would persist unless she fed her a little information.

"As an almost lawyer, I'm curious," Gaby said, sitting at the table again. "What happens to these drag queens when they get arrested? Do you put them in a men's or women's prison?"

"Men's usually, but isolated. I think if they're full-blown transgender they'd go into a women's prison."

"Why so curious? You thinking of specializing in drag queen law when you get your license?" Marge asked.

"I'm thinking of making a lot of money which means practicing anything but criminal law. Family law . . . I've heard divorces are the way to get rich."

"Wish you could handle mine. The guy you recommended is okay, but sometimes I get the feeling he'd rather be representing Jake."

"That's because you won't let him go after your husband's assets. He wants to make a killing and you're stifling his natural greediness."

"I don't hate Jake, and I don't want his money. I just want him officially out of my life . . . and I want to keep my house."

"Sorry, hold off for a couple more months and I'd be happy to do it for you."

"No, I need to get this done."

"Corsino has seen the light," Marge said, grinning.

"How's the Martin situation?" Gaby asked. "I haven't heard from her, so I assumed she's worked something out with Behan."

"At the moment they're too busy to fight," Josie said. "I almost forgot I wanted to ask you something about Henry Trumbo."

"What's that?" Gaby asked with a faint smile.

"How many times did you meet with him?"

"Once, I think."

"Was that in your office?"

"Yes . . . I think we did talk one time at the police academy too . . . maybe before he got fired. It's difficult to remember. I see so many of these guys. Why?"

"No reason, I was hoping you'd recall something. We're at a dead end with his investigation."

"Sorry, I just don't remember that much about him. Do you believe the same person killed him and Kessler?"

"It's a good possibility," Josie said. Actually, she didn't really think so, but the cautionary voice of experience told her not to admit that outside the confines of Hollywood's detective squad room. Marge went along with her, and they managed to shift the conversation to something else before their curious friend could pry more details out of them.

Josie stayed longer than she intended, but the day had been relaxing. The weather at the beach was pleasant, and she enjoyed the company of two smart women. It was nearly seven when Marge said she wanted to get home and check up on Behan. Although Josie hadn't heard from Richards, she knew he'd be working until Sergeant Miller went to bed. She was tired and the wine had mellowed her almost to the point of wanting to curl up and take a nap, but she needed to go to her house, shower and change clothes before driving to Long Beach for the night. She and Marge left the Manhattan Beach bungalow together with a standing invitation from Gaby to do the same thing every weekend if they felt the need to unwind.

She managed to get to Pasadena without running into anything or hitting stray dogs. Although it wasn't the first time she'd had too much to drink and had driven the city car, her tolerance for alcohol was usually much higher. She figured it had to be the combination of wine, excessive heat and weekend exhaustion.

Although her plan had been to be waiting seductively in Kyle's bed when he got home, that wasn't going to happen. The trek upstairs to the third floor bedroom was grueling on her rubbery legs, and she declared it the end of her day, dropped onto the bed face first and fell into a deep sleep.

The annoying ring of her bedside phone woke Josie the next morning. Her adjutant had a message from Commander Perry. He wanted her and Behan to meet with him and the chief at the police administration building at 1300 hours. When Josie's eyes finally focused and she could make out the numbers on the alarm clock, she was relieved to see there was plenty of time for a handful of Advil and black coffee. Even though Maki also advised her Behan was already at the station waiting for her.

After twenty minutes, she convinced herself to sit up in bed and was surprised the aftereffects weren't worse. Her head felt reasonably clear and her stomach needed food but wasn't nauseous. She found her cell phone in her purse and checked messages. Kyle left one saying he'd talked to Marge last night when he couldn't reach her and was told she probably wouldn't be going to Long Beach. He said he'd see her or talk to her sometime that day with interesting news.

The shower felt good but by the time she was dressed, Josie's stomach felt better and she was really hungry. Unfortunately, David and Kizzie, during their brief stay, had wiped out most of the eggs, bread and other healthy foods she'd stocked in her kitchen. They did leave behind a bag of Veggie chips that Josie tossed in the garbage as soon as she discovered them. She decided her only recourse was to stop in Starbucks, so she arrived at Hollywood station feeling rested, clean, and on a sugar-caffeine high.

Her office door was closed and Maki told her Behan and Martin were in there working. They were sitting at her round table going over printouts Martin had accumulated during her early morning search of Miller's and Flowers's bank and portfolio assets.

"This is really genius," Behan said, waving a sheet of paper at her.

Josie, still wearing her sunglasses, tossed her purse and briefcase onto the floor of the wardrobe, then looked over the rims to give Behan a look that clearly said, "Don't ask."

"Have a good time yesterday?" he asked, trying not to smile.

"What have you got?" she asked, ignoring him. Once again, Marge had blabbed too much and told him about their wine fest at Gaby's.

"She found this and more through her sources," Behan said, indicating Martin and handing Josie a page copied from a ledger. "We were looking for places they stashed money and she found it right under our noses."

Josie examined the page but it was just numbers.

"Explain," she said. "This doesn't mean anything to me."

Martin described how she had located Flowers's campaign finances through public records and then followed the pattern of donations into that fund. The Protective League had been a faithful and big donor for each of the councilman's reelections. But, during the last year, there were additional donations from the union and each one appeared after the city council made large deposits into the league's legal fund.

"Can you guess which city councilman made the motion to increase the allotment to the league's legal fund?" Martin asked.

"Jeff Flowers . . . no brainer," Josie said.

"Immediately after the union got the money, there was a deposit in Flowers's campaign account," Behan said.

"Flowers has accumulated nearly two million dollars for his mayoral run in less than a year. At least a third of it came from the union," Martin said.

"Gaby told you the league's books show money going for nonexistent legal expenditures, but I'm betting Miller transferred that money right back into Flowers's chubby hands," Behan said.

"We know how much Flowers got, but I'm certain when they look into the league's account books, they'll be able to see how much Miller kept off the top," Martin added.

"So they're ripping off the city and officers who need legal help," Josie said. "If Kessler was part of their scheme or found out about it and was going to spill his guts, Flowers and Miller both had something to lose."

"More so Sergeant Miller," Martin said. "Flowers can always plead ignorance and say he thought it was a legitimate donation."

"We need to get the league's books audited," Behan said. "I'm hoping none of the other directors had a clue they were sending that much money to Flowers."

"We're late for our meeting," Josie said, getting up. "Bring this with you." She pushed the printouts toward Behan. "You come too, Ann. By the way, good work. Is Richards still watching Miller and Mabry?" she asked, and Behan nodded.

"Good, keep him out there until the chief okays the audit. When do you intend to pick up Miller?"

"As soon as we can verify what Gaby told you. If Miller signed those bogus checks and that money really went to Flowers, we've got him . . . at least on the fraud. The plan is to bring him and Mabry in and make one of them turn on the other."

THE OFFICE of the chief of police was on the top floor of the new police administration building, PAB, on First Street in downtown LA. Josie called the building a gerbil run since it lacked any real architectural character and every floor and every office looked very similar with dark impersonal hallways leading to more depressing hallways. The former PAB on Los Angeles Street was gone, but Josie remembered the run-down, structurally unsafe building fondly for its unique openness, spirit and personality. The ghosts and stories of an LAPD she loved and admired had occupied that structure and they had clearly refused to inhabit the sterile corridors of this one.

The chief's office was the rare exception to the dullness factor in the rest of the building. It was spacious, bright, and had a huge balcony that looked out over much of the downtown area. The current chief was Behan's classmate. Behan never talked about him, but Josie suspected that until Chief Powell began his climb up the promotion ladder, the two men had been friends.

Commander Perry was waiting in the office talking to one of the chief's drivers when they arrived.

"You're late," Perry said. "But he's not here either. A special Police Commission meeting is running long."

Josie quickly explained what Martin had found and added, "We need to get this done today before Miller figures out we're on to him and those ledgers disappear or get altered."

"Not to mention this surveillance is costing a fortune," Perry said.

The chief arrived a few minutes later and listened intently as Behan and Martin explained what they had uncovered.

"Do you realize what you've got here, Captain?" Chief Powell asked, looking very uncomfortable. "A city councilman and a director from the union stealing money from the city . . . this should've been handled with oversight from this office not by area detectives."

Powell was a thin, nervous man with one eye that was slightly out of alignment with the other and a thick mustache. He squinted a lot and that gave him a shifty, sinister appearance. He reminded Josie of those Saturday morning television villains in Gene Autry westerns who stayed in the background and got shot first in every showdown. No one would argue with his incredible intelligence, but he leaned toward social engineering more often than hardcore policing.

"It's more than that, sir," Josie said. "Patrick Kessler, our first murder victim, was Flowers's chief of staff. If Kessler threatened to expose him and Miller, there's a good motive for murder."

"I know Doug Miller. He wasn't a great field sergeant, but he's no murderer," Powell said.

"Maybe," Josie said, ignoring Perry's stern expression. "But Miller's girlfriend was seen removing the murder weapon from the scene immediately after Kessler was killed. She hasn't got the size or strength to have killed him, but Miller does, and he's got a good reason."

"What is it you want from me?" Powell asked, scratching his neck under his uniform collar.

"Ask the mayor to order the city council to audit the money they gave to the Protective League's legal fund," Josie said. "They'll find a lot of checks written to phony police officer clients. We can trace that money back to Councilman Flowers's campaign fund and probably put some of it in Sergeant Miller's pocket."

Powell shook his head. "This is a quagmire, and you're asking me to step right in the middle of it. What if you're wrong and those checks aren't there? We'll destroy our relationship not only with the union but with the city council . . . for what . . . a hunch based on what someone has told you."

"Our informant is inside the union office . . . confidential but reliable," Josie insisted.

"I think they've established sufficient probable cause to believe city money is being misused," Perry said, holding up the ledger sheet.

"Still conjecture at this point . . . the mayor will never agree to it before the election," Powell said. "He's hand-picked Flowers to succeed him. This investigation would taint the man but can't prove he did anything wrong. You've admitted as much. Maybe we'd get Sergeant Miller, but at what cost?"

"Can't we do the audit and just go after Miller?" Perry asked.

"No," Josie said. "Flowers knew; he's a party to this."

"I'm sorry," Powell said. "You're going to have to find another way. I can't lose face with the mayor, city council and the union all at once. Forget about the money for now and concentrate on who killed Seymour Kessler's son. I'll have the financial unit follow up on what you've done and if there's actually something there, it's more appropriate they handle it."

"With all due respect, sir, that money may very well be the reason Kessler's son is dead," Martin blurted out and blushed when she realized she was a very tiny animal who'd just stepped in the middle of battling elephants. "Sorry," she said.

"Don't be. You're right," Josie said, having new admiration for her quirky detective. But it didn't matter. The chief had made up his mind. There wasn't going to be an audit.

THEY LEFT Perry in the chief's office and took the elevator down to the first floor. Behan had parked in the underground lot but Josie wanted to stop by the police memorial sculpture and garden area on the top tier plaza adjacent to the headquarters. It was a simple wall of staggered brass plaques, each with the name of an officer who had given his or her life in the line of duty. It was a quiet place to sit on the steps and regroup.

"Can we get a warrant?" Martin asked, moving to sit in a shaded area of the steps beside Behan.

"Doubt it," Josie said. "Same reason the city is skittish about auditing those books . . . there're attorney-client privacy issues, but they could do an audit because tax money's involved."

"So maybe we pick up Mabry and threaten to charge her with murder," Behan said.

"Maybe," Josie said. "But if she holds her ground, it's her word against Rago's. We're looking pretty weak there."

"Except she lied about not leaving her apartment that night," Martin said and groaned. "This really sucks."

Behan got up and brushed off his pants. "Okay partner, guess we start from scratch. We'll go over every inch of the Regency again inside and out and that alley. Mabry didn't take the bloody knife home with her so she dumped it somewhere. We'll look again at every item we removed from Trumbo's murder scene, too."

Before following him back to the car, Martin leaned over and whispered to Josie, "Did you hear what he called me?"

Josie cringed thinking Behan had said something inappropriate. At a time they should be concentrating on this case, she'd be handling another personnel complaint. What the hell is wrong with that man, she thought, but asked tentatively, "No, what?"

"He called me partner. I've conquered the big red mountain."

FOURTEEN

Behan had made up his mind by late the next morning to bring in Mabry and confront her with Rago's eyewitness statement as well as the inconsistencies in her alibi. He and Martin had gone over every report and each piece of evidence in both homicides and it seemed like the next and only logical step. He also intended to use the information they had uncovered about the union's legal fund and try to make her believe they knew more than they did. Flowers's secretary was the weak link between the councilman and Sergeant Miller. Behan was convinced if he piled enough accusations on her, she would break and turn on both of them, maybe give them a killer.

He asked Richards to arrest Mabry at work, hoping her boss would be there to see her taken away in handcuffs. Flowers was a politician so he most likely didn't bluff easily, but if he had any role in Kessler's death he'd have to be wondering how much his secretary knew and what she'd be willing to say.

Jail was a poor substitute for living happily ever after, and Josie agreed with Behan that, faced with the reality of serving the better part of her remaining years in prison, Mabry might reconsider any loyalty she had to her boss or her lover.

Another possibility was the knife was in her hand because Mabry had killed Kessler, dropped it and picked it up again, but they needed to confront her and see what happened.

Josie agreed with Behan's decision because she couldn't see another direction now that the audit was off the table. She was becoming frustrated by the lack of solid clues in this investigation. Rago wasn't the sort of reliable witness any detective wanted in a murder case, but the gangbanger was better than nothing and that's pretty much what they had without him.

Josie was finishing the last stack of projects she and Maki had worked on all morning and was feeling pretty good about catching up on all the administrative work she'd let slide while spending too much time outside the office indulging her inner detective. She didn't notice when Behan came in and jumped a little when he spoke.

"Bad news, boss," Behan said. He was standing in front of her desk and looked tired, disappointed, no worse. "Mabry wasn't at work . . . didn't call in sick, just didn't show. Flowers says he doesn't know where she is."

"Did Richards check her apartment?"

"He got a key from the manager. She wasn't there, but her place had been trashed. I've got a couple detectives watching it in case she comes back."

"Great," Josie said, disgusted, and threw her pen on the desk.

"Richards's squad still has a tail on Sergeant Miller. If Mabry's alive, we're hoping he'll take us to her," Behan said.

"Where's Martin?"

"She's watching the Kessler house in case Mabry hooks up with Mrs. Kessler again," Behan said and sat in the chair near her desk. "I screwed up . . . should've pulled her in days ago . . . got bogged down in that stupid audit shit." He ran his fingers through his thick red hair several times, and then stood. "Damn it."

"Richards will find her," Josie said, trying to calm him but not believing it. If Mabry wasn't the killer, having been at the murder scene she had to be a liability to whoever was. Before Behan could respond, his cell phone rang. He talked for a few minutes, mostly listened and hung up. He stared at the floor long enough for Josie to call his name thinking something was terribly wrong.

"Yes," Behan whispered with a fist pump. "Can't talk anymore, boss, gotta write a search warrant."

"For what?"

"Mabry's apartment. Richards has a feeling we might find the murder weapon there."

Josie didn't ask if he had enough for a warrant because one way or another Behan always had enough. She also knew without having to ask that Richards already had searched the apartment and found the knife. The stupid woman had taken it home.

It took the homicide supervisor less than an hour and a half to write the warrant and find a judge to sign it. Josie stayed at the station, and when he was done, they drove to Mabry's residence together. Richards was still there waiting alone in the hallway outside the empty apartment. He'd sent the two Hollywood detectives back to their car to keep a lookout for Mabry should she return.

They complied with the required legal procedure of knock and notice and then opened the unlocked door and walked in.

"Holy shit," Behan said, when he saw the piles of debris scattered around the living room. "Somebody was search-ing for something . . . unless she keeps house like you, Corsino."

When Behan went into the bedroom, Richards touched her face and said, "Missed you, pretty lady. Did Red tell you what we caught early this morning?"

"No, is that the interesting thing you were going to tell me?"

"Turns out we weren't the only ones following Miller. My guys snatched a PI hiding in the bushes outside Miller's house. He won't tell us who he's working for so they're booking him at Hollywood jail for prowling and anything else they can think of. I'm going to let him stew in a cell a while then talk to him again when we get back."

"When this case is over, we really need to get away for a few days."

"We will," he said, and shouted behind her, "Red, come into the kitchen."

All the cupboards in the kitchen were open and the counters were covered with torn or emptied containers, a mix of contents scattered everywhere including in the sink and on the floor. Richards ignored the mess and went directly to one of the drawers. It was open, but he pulled it out a little more and there in the back buried under dozens of different-sized knives and wrapped in a single paper towel was a nasty looking folding knife, open with traces of what appeared to be dried blood.

"Hidden in plain sight," Richards said. "Whoever it was looked in the drawer but didn't pull it out all the way. Looking and seeing aren't the same thing."

"Maybe they weren't looking for a knife," Josie said.

"Maybe . . ." Behan said, but she could tell he agreed with Richards. He took a pair of latex gloves out of his pocket, put them on and picked up the knife to examine it closer. "Doesn't look like anyone even tried to wipe it clean . . . almost as if she saved it for some reason."

"Blackmail?" Josie asked.

"Or protection," Behan said.

"Or she killed him and she's an idiot," Richards added.

After securing the knife, they looked around the rest of the apartment and found a lot of empty hangers in the closet. Josie searched for the black dress Mabry had worn the night they interviewed her but it wasn't there. The contents of the dresser drawers had been dumped on the bedroom floor, but either she didn't have much in the way of lingerie or items were missing from there too.

"Looks like she packed a bag in a hurry and split," Richards said.

Behan was already on his cell phone talking to Marge. He asked her to do a background on Linda Mabry to find a relative or some location where the woman had lived or worked in the past where she might feel safe hiding.

They locked up and left the apartment, but Behan asked the two Hollywood detectives to stay and make certain Mabry didn't return or someone else didn't come looking for her. They were outside talking near the gate to the underground parking when Richards's surveillance team contacted him on the police radio to tell him Sergeant Miller was moving, driving away from the union office downtown, and they'd seen what looked like an overnight bag in the back seat of his car.

"Did you want to take my ride and go back to Hollywood, boss? I'm gonna stay with surveillance and see where dipshit takes them," Behan said.

"Think I'll stay too," Josie said. She liked the idea of spending more time with Kyle but her real motivation was the same as Behan's, a strong feeling that Sergeant Miller was about to take them to Mabry.

The surveillance squad radioed they were twenty minutes from downtown Los Angeles headed south on Interstate 5. It didn't take Richards long to catch up. He darted in and out of carpool and emergency lanes on the freeways and, when those backed up, he transitioned onto the side streets. Although Behan didn't have the same driving skills, he managed to keep up in traffic without killing himself or Josie. They reached the rest of the squad before Miller had led them out of Los Angeles County.

Almost two hours later they were entering San Diego County and Josie worried they were headed for the Mexican border. Her cops had no jurisdiction in Mexico and, in fact, couldn't cross the border to follow Miller. They'd have to ask the Mexican authorities for help and she knew that would be a complicated expensive enterprise.

Sergeant Miller stopped in Carlsbad to get gas and use the restroom. He left the Mobil station and drove slowly up the main thoroughfare as if he were looking for something. The squad played a game of leapfrog staying out of sight watching him from nearby parking lots or side streets then moving a block or two to stay ahead of his car. Josie was impressed how seamless their movements were. He would never know they were there, and yet they saw everything he did and knew everywhere he went. Finally he parked in front of a Mexican restaurant and went inside. One of the squad's female detectives followed him and sat at the counter where she could see his table. He ate alone, made one phone call and left about an hour later.

From there, he drove directly to downtown San Diego and parked behind a small motel in one of the seedier looking areas near Old Town. Richards located Mabry's car parked in the lot near the motel.

Members of the squad were out of their cars as soon as Miller turned off the engine and one of them followed him into the motel. They broadcast that he bypassed the front desk and knocked on a door at the end of a dimly lit hallway. Someone let him into the room. Richards positioned the remainder of his squad outside the motel to cover the windows and prevent a hasty escape.

"Wait for them to come out or go in and get them?" Richards asked, as he, Josie and Behan stood behind his car in the parking lot of a liquor store half a block away.

"One of them is possibly a murderer. If it's Miller, the odds of Miss Mabry surviving until morning don't look good to me. I'm thinking we've got some exigency here and we bust in," Behan said. "What do you say, boss?"

Josie didn't need to think about it. "We have to go in," she said.

"Okay," Richards said, pulling back the slide on his .45 and doing a chamber check. "I'll knock; you ID yourself Captain, and we'll see if they open the door. If not, I'll kick it. Behan goes first, me, then you."

"There's no dope involved, Corsino, so be careful," Behan warned, handing her a protective vest and a raid jacket from the trunk of his car.

Richards looked puzzled but Josie knew what Behan meant. When they worked narcotics together, she never allowed suspects to flush dope and ran straight to the bathroom when they broke down a door to serve a warrant. Behan thought she was reckless and always worried her tunnel vision would one day get her killed. It didn't and she never lost a gram of stash to a toilet, but this was different. Miller was an armed cop with a lot to lose. She wouldn't be charging into the room.

They entered the motel and moved quietly down the hall. Her two detectives positioned themselves on either side of the door, and Josie stood where anyone looking out the peephole would see her. She was hoping her presence would have a calming effect on both occupants, especially Miss Mabry.

"Open the door, Linda. It's Captain Corsino," Josie shouted after Richards pounded on it with his fist.

"What do you want? Why are you here?" Mabry's timid voice said from the other side.

"I'm arresting you for the murder of Patrick Kessler. Open the door."

"What?" Mabry said, barely audible.

"Open it," a male voice ordered from inside the room.

As the door opened, Josie moved aside. Behan and Richards, with guns drawn, stepped in front of her to clear the room. Sergeant Miller and Mabry stood in the center of the room frozen in place, her hands covering her mouth, his arm around her shoulder.

The space was dingy and small with a single bed, cramped bathroom and kitchenette. There was no place to hide and they couldn't escape; the only window had been painted shut.

"I didn't kill Patrick," Mabry whispered, sitting on the bed.

"Why are you running away?" Josie asked.

"I'm not . . . everything got so . . ." She bowed her head and was quiet.

Behan told her what they'd found in her apartment. She wasn't surprised about the knife but claimed she didn't know her home had been trashed. She'd been gone most of the weekend.

Before Richards let Miller sit beside Mabry, he searched the sergeant for weapons but couldn't find anything.

"Where's your piece?" Richards asked. "Is it in your car?"

"I'm not carrying," Miller said.

Josie shook her head—a police sergeant who didn't carry a gun. She knew why. The last thing a guy like Sergeant Miller wanted was to get involved in stopping crime. If something happened, he didn't want to be armed because then he'd be expected to take action the way any self-respecting cop would.

"You've been out of the field too long, Miller," she mumbled.

"I'm on my own time," he said, sitting beside Mabry.

"I'll bet you got that get-outa-jail-free police ID in your wallet right next to your driver's license though, don't you?" Behan asked, then turned to Mabry and said, "We're taking you back to Hollywood as a suspect in Kessler's homicide."

"I didn't kill him. I tried to help . . ." She stopped and looked at Miller.

"We've got a witness who puts you at the scene with the murder weapon in your hand. We recovered a knife from your apartment," Behan said. "I'm betting the blood on it matches our victim."

Josie knew what Behan was doing. He hadn't Mirandized Mabry, but he wasn't asking any questions either. He was throwing out enough information to get her to talk without the benefit of a lawyer. If her boyfriend Miller had a clue about police work, he'd tell her to shut up until she had an attorney.

"I picked it up off the ground. I would never hurt Patrick. He was my friend."

"Maybe, but we figure he was about to blow the whistle on your scam with your boyfriend here," Behan said.

"How did you . . ." Miller started to ask but didn't finish and put his head back as if he realized he had very stupidly just admitted something.

"How did we know about the money you took from the legal fund?" Behan asked, finishing his question.

Richards and Josie were side by side leaning against the wall. They knew Behan was on a roll and they weren't about to interfere.

"Can I please talk to her for a minute?" Miller asked, looking at Mabry whose complexion had turned pale and sickly and seemed to be getting worse.

"No," Behan said. "I think it's time you pack up your stuff. We're going back to Hollywood."

"No, wait," Miller said, squirming on the bed. "We can help each other, but I need to make a deal. I'm not going to jail."

Mabry's mouth opened, and she stared hard at her boyfriend.

"Stand-up guy," Behan said, picking up on her disdain.

"No, no, you know what I mean, Babe. We're in this together," Miller whined as Mabry pulled her hand away from his. "We'll tell you, both of us, what we know, but I want some guarantee of immunity or you'll get nothing."

"And if they get nothing, I go to jail for murder," Mabry said, in a stronger voice. Her demeanor had changed suddenly and Josie saw a different woman, a tough, determined survivor. "I'll tell you what I know. I don't care about the money. I didn't take it, and we certainly don't have any of it. Do we, Babe?" she asked, mimicking Miller.

It only took a few minutes to pack their belongings, but Linda Mabry made no attempt to talk to Sergeant Miller during that time. She stood near the bed and waited patiently until Behan directed her to get into the back seat of his car. Josie slid in beside her. Miller would ride with Richards, but before they left, he complained about leaving his personal car in such a rundown area.

"I can have it impounded," Richards offered.

"Never mind," Miller grumbled and sat quietly on the passenger seat.

The ride back to Los Angeles was intended to be uneventful. Behan didn't talk to Mabry and Josie followed his lead. The woman was obviously upset and angry, and Josie hoped she was seriously reconsidering her loyalty to Miller, who had shown his true nature and was clearly not thinking of her best interests.

It was becoming evident to Josie that neither of them seemed capable of killing Kessler. They were the original gang that couldn't shoot straight. Whatever they were up to, she seriously doubted it included murder.

Nevertheless, Mabry did know something. She was there when Kessler was killed and she picked up that knife for a reason. They would give her a couple of hours to stare out the car window and contemplate how foolish it might be to keep quiet and spend the rest of her life in jail for a murder she didn't commit, instead of confessing to whatever it was she and Miller did do.

Shortly after they transitioned onto the Hollywood Freeway, Mabry stopped looking out the window and turned to Josie.

"You said someone had been in my apartment?"

"It was pretty much trashed," Josie said.

"But the knife was there."

Josie nodded and Mabry turned back to the window. Up close and in the fading evening light, she looked so much older than the first time Josie had seen her. She was preoccupied with other things and had let herself go. There was no makeup to hide the aging skin and tiny lines around her eyes. Her auburn hair needed touching up where new growth was darker with strands of gray. The tight capri pants and sleeveless shirt didn't flatter her flabby body. She seemed to be an unhappy middle-aged woman trying to slow down the inevitable course of time . . . for what, to hold onto a worthless jerk like Doug Miller? Josie might've felt a little sorry for her if Mabry hadn't been up to her sagging neck in theft and murder.

As soon as they arrived at Hollywood station, Behan took Mabry inside and put her in one of the interrogation rooms. Richards got there a few minutes later and kept Miller out of her sight locked in another room. They agreed Miller should be interviewed last. Behan wanted him to sit alone for a while and worry what his girlfriend might be revealing. However, he also knew Miller had time during the drive back into town to think about his situation, and he was fairly certain the sergeant's first words would be to demand his lawyer and a union defense rep, so there was no hurry getting to him.

It was late enough in the day that the squad room was nearly empty. The night detective was talking on the phone and had taken off his jacket and tie in a futile attempt to get comfortable in the heat. The door to Mabry's closet-sized interview room was left ajar and a small fan had been turned on full blast and directed at her from a nearby file cabinet. Josie sat near Behan's desk and watched as she dabbed at her sweaty face with a tissue and tugged nervously at her tight clothes trying to get comfortable.

"Here, maybe this will help," Josie said, pouring a glass of cold water from the cooler nearby and putting it on the table in front of her. The last thing she wanted was for Mabry to faint and have a reason to delay the interview.

"Can I have more?" Mabry asked, after finishing the drink quickly and handing the glass back to Josie. Josie filled it again and was about to leave when Mabry asked, "Can you stay awhile?"

"For a minute," Josie said. "Detective Behan will be right in." There was no way she wanted to hold this woman's hand or make her feel better. She knew Linda Mabry needed to believe her world was coming to a terrible end and her only salvation was to tell the truth.

Apparently, all Mabry wanted was the proximity of another human being. She sipped at the water now and didn't attempt to converse, ask questions, or profess her innocence. She simply wanted someone else in the room.

Josie slipped out when Behan and Richards sat down to begin the interrogation. Her presence seemed to comfort the woman and that wasn't good, so she settled in the room next door where she could once again watch the video feed. If body language were any indicator, Mabry was defeated. She slumped in her chair and wrapped her hands around the glass of water on the table, not looking at them and answering questions in a soft monotone.

She immediately waived her rights and seemed eager to tell her story.

"I was there the night Patrick . . . it was so horrible."

"Why were you there?" Behan asked. They had decided he would ask the questions since Mabry seemed the most intimidated by him.

"I followed him from work. I saw him put our money in his briefcase and leave."

"Okay, let's start from the beginning. This is the same money you were taking from the police union."

In a surprisingly coherent and organized way, Mabry confirmed everything they had suspected. She claimed Flowers had convinced the city council to give the Protective League more money for their legal fund. Knowing the fund would never be audited, Sergeant Miller transferred a lot of that money back to Flowers's campaign fund through phony donations. He covered the transactions by issuing checks to nonexistent legal cases for police officers and lawyers who never received them. That way the other league directors would never know how much money was going to Flowers. As the councilman's chief of staff, Patrick Kessler was in a position to take thousands of dollars off the top of those donations, money that would go into his and Miller's pockets.

"We knew we couldn't spend all the money or deposit it anywhere right away without raising red flags, so Patrick kept the cash hidden in his office safe," Mabry admitted.

"And that's why you and Flowers didn't want us searching Patrick's office. You were afraid he'd left some evidence of what he was doing," Behan said.

Mabry didn't say anything, but her closed eyes and bowed head were confirmation.

"How much cash are we talking about?"

"It had to be close to a million dollars. Doug and I trusted him," she said, shaking her head. "His family is filthy rich. Why would he steal it, right?"

"You tell me why."

Mabry straightened up and took a deep breath. "He wanted to be a woman and his father would never pay for it. He needed the money—not just half, but all of it. It was expensive, not only the operations, but travel and living expenses in other countries."

"But, he gave it to Trumbo."

She nodded.

"Why?"

"He told me weeks ago Mr. Trumbo was supposed to arrange the contacts for his transformation, make some payments up front . . . for an outrageous fee, of course."

Mabry said when she realized Kessler had taken all their money out of his safe, she followed him from the district office, not wanting to let the briefcase out of her sight. He had changed into women's clothes and went directly to Nicola's. That's where she saw him meet with Trumbo, but lost sight of the briefcase.

She called Sergeant Miller and told him what had happened. He was angry and wanted her to continue watching Kessler, until he could get there and force Patrick to give the money back. She watched him go into St. Margaret Mary's church and was following behind him when he hurried down the block toward the Regency Arms.

"Do you know who killed him?" Behan asked.

"Yes . . . Susan."

"His wife?"

Mabry nodded. "He looked surprised to see her there. She got close like she was going to hug him . . . Patrick didn't try to stop her. He didn't scream or defend himself. She dropped the knife and disappeared. I don't know what I was thinking. It all happened so fast. I picked it up."

She wiped her face with the crumpled tissue again. Sweat was dripping onto the table from her chin. "I was angry with Patrick for taking the money, but when she hurt him like that, I don't know what happened. I was confused . . . I grabbed the knife and ran."

"How did you pick it up?" Behan asked.

"What?" she asked, looking puzzled by the question.

"Did you use your bare hand?"

"No . . . the blood . . . I couldn't. There was a tissue in my pocket," she said, holding up the one she had in her hand. "I wrapped it around the knife and ran."

"Did Mrs. Kessler see you?"

"No, I'm certain she didn't. She seemed almost dazed. I don't think she even realized she'd dropped it."

"Was Sergeant Miller there?"

For the first time, Mabry hesitated and didn't answer.

"This is an all-or-nothing proposition, Linda. You tell us the whole story or go to jail," Behan said.

"Yes, when I was running away Doug got there and saw the knife. He thought I killed Patrick. I was hysterical and wanted to go back, tell the police, but he said no. They would think I did it."

"But why keep the knife in your apartment?"

"At first I was afraid someone saw me and I thought Susan's fingerprints . . . They should be there right?"

"And afterward."

"We lost a lot of money. Patrick's family was rich. Doug said if Susan paid us what Patrick took we could promise to give the knife back to her," she said and shook her head. "I can see now it was wrong. I should've told the police . . . but . . . what a mess."

"Did Mrs. Kessler know about the stolen money?" Richards asked.

"She knew. Patrick told her. The poor dope told Susan everything."

Richards got up and moved away from the table. "I don't get it," he said. "How would his wife know he'd be anywhere near the Regency?"

"Patrick told her he was going there to meet the doctor who'd agreed to do his treatments and surgery for half what it should cost . . . for cash." She stopped and seemed distressed. "I warned him back-alley doctors are all butchers and crooks."

"Do you think that's why he didn't bring the money with him?" Behan asked.

"Maybe, but I guess Susan assumed he would and she was furious when we went to Nicola's and the coatroom man told her Patrick had given the briefcase to Trumbo."

"Did she kill Trumbo, too?" Richards asked.

"I don't know . . . but, I don't think so."

"Why?"

Mabry looked down at the table and really didn't want to answer but said, "When we tried to get money from Susan, she swore she didn't have any and her father-in-law wouldn't give her a penny. She said whoever killed Trumbo was probably living really well off our money."

"Councilman Flowers has been sleeping with Susan Kessler. How much of this does he know?"

Mabry sighed and said, "He has no idea what sort of monster she is. Mr. Flowers may not be a very ethical man, but he really liked Patrick."

"Yeah, that's why he was sleeping with his wife. Did Flowers know Sergeant Miller and Kessler were stealing union money?" Behan asked.

"You'll never prove it. He doesn't touch campaign money . . . he's too smart."

"Not that smart," Josie said out loud to an empty room. "He was sleeping with a cold-blooded killer."

Josie listened awhile longer, but left the video room before they finished. She'd heard enough. Susan Kessler had killed her husband for money she never found. Josie did agree that Trumbo's killer, whoever it was, had probably taken the briefcase and was living well off almost a million dollars in cash.

In a few hours, the interview was over and Mabry had signed her statement. The knife was at the lab, and by morning, they would know if Kessler's blood was on it and if any prints were lifted. As soon as it was confirmed, they would have a warrant ready to arrest Susan Kessler.

Martin was still watching the Kessler house and she confirmed that Susan was home with her father-in-law. Another detective went out to take her place and Martin came back to the station to help Behan interview Sergeant Miller, but, as Behan suspected, Miller wanted a defense rep and lawyer so his interview was delayed until the next day, but they booked him on the same charge as Mabry. If he bailed out, Richards's squad would watch him until his interview.

The private investigator was still in custody and Richards told Josie he wanted to talk to him before the man bailed out on the flimsy charges. Since everyone was tied up, he asked her if she would sit in, assuring her it would be a ten-minute interview in the holding cell.

Tired of being in a hot smelly cell, Andy Cohen readily admitted he had been hired as a private investigator by Seymour Kessler to find out who'd murdered his son. He was doing routine surveillance on Sergeant Miller when Richards's squad caught him hiding in the bushes.

Cohen was a six-foot barrel of a man dressed in khaki shorts, Hawaiian shirt and sandals. Josie figured from his white beard and gimpy knees he had to be getting social security and Medicare. His head was shaved, and she thought he looked like the house dick for the Happy Islands Rest Home and Sanitarium.

"I ain't really got a clue who it was killed that kid. Looks like a random thing to me, but old man Kessler he ain't buying it and he don't trust you guys to do nothing, so I'm going through the motions."

"Why do you think he isn't buying it?" Richards asked.

"Beats me . . . he's got some conspiracy crapola in his head, but the kid was a fruitcake, that's all. They get killed all the time in Hollywood."

"So you haven't uncovered anything," Richards said.

"Nope, I told him that but I'll take his money if the old goat tells me to keep looking. I'm his second PI, so this ain't his first time at the dance."

"What do you mean his second PI?" Josie asked.

"He had another guy before me that got croaked."

"You know his name?"

"Sure, Trumbo . . . worked for the old man before his kid got killed."

"How do you know that?"

"How'd you think? I investigate. That's what I do."

"Do you know why he hired Trumbo?"

"Yeah, same reason most of them rich guys do, to follow his kid's old lady."

"Was she cheating?" Richards asked, glancing at Josie. They both knew she was.

"Nope, clean as a newborn baby's bottom."

"Really," Josie said. "Trumbo never saw her with anyone."

"Nope, personally I figured her for the horny tramp type but Trumbo told the old man he never saw nothing."

When they were ready to leave and Richards was locking the door to Cohen's holding cell, he said, "Thanks for being so up front, Andy. Don't worry about bail. I'm gonna change the charge to trespassing and let you out on your own recognizance. Just be sure to show up in court."

"Point a interest, detective," Cohen said, holding onto the bars. "In case you was wondering, Sergeant Miller's the one turned over his girlfriend's apartment. Night before last, while she was gone, I saw him use his key, go inside her apartment and trash it while your guys were waiting in their cars outside. I ain't saying how I saw all this, but he didn't act like he got what he wanted."

"Thanks, we know what he was looking for," Richards said, and when they were out in the hallway he told Josie, "I'll make sure Mabry knows it was Miller that ransacked her place. I don't think we have to worry about her having any lingering feelings for that asshole."

"I'm going to tell Red to let the chief's financial unit handle Miller's investigation. It's their area of expertise, and we're giving them more than enough with Mabry's statements to audit the union's books and prosecute him," Josie said, then changed the subject because it was bothering her and she had to ask. "Do you think Susan Kessler killed Trumbo, too?"

She always hoped finding Patrick Kessler's killer would lead them to the person who murdered Trumbo, but she was having a hard time believing Susan Kessler was capable of killing a man like Trumbo.

"No," Richards said, quickly.

"Me neither. I guess she could've caught him off guard in the middle of sex or something and cut his throat, but Trumbo wasn't a pushover like her husband and the Regency isn't where someone like Susan Kessler goes for sex. I just don't see it."

Josie's cell phone rang and she answered it without looking which was always a big mistake, but it was David and he asked if she could come by the restaurant before she went home. He had good news for her. Her son didn't know that home tonight meant Richards's house in Long Beach, which was in the opposite direction, but she agreed because he sounded as if it was something important.

"What's the matter?" Richards asked when she put the phone back on her belt.

"My kid needs to talk to me."

"Tonight?"

"I'll take care of it and come to your place in a couple of hours."

"He works at a restaurant, doesn't he? Why don't I go with you and we can have dinner?"

"That's not a good idea," she said, starting to worry about what David had to tell her that couldn't wait until tomorrow. She imagined the worst possible news—he and Kizzie had gotten married.

"Okay," he said, but from his body language she could see it was anything but okay.

"It's not about you Kyle. Truth is, if he tells me what I'm afraid he's going to tell me, I'd rather you didn't see me in full-blown Sicilian-Irish mode before you get to know me a little better."

"That bad?"

"I don't know. I love my son, but he has a way of making me crazy. Maybe you should come so I don't do or say something stupid."

"I can wait at the bar until you two work out whatever it is. When you're done, we can eat there or go someplace else," Richards said.

By the time they got back to the squad room, Behan had booked Mabry and Miller as accessories to murder for removing the knife from the homicide scene. There would be other charges related to the money, but there was nothing they could do to keep them in jail if they were eligible for bail. Behan had Mabry's damaging statement, which should give her some protection. Susan Kessler wouldn't gain anything now by harassing Mabry, and after her arrest tomorrow morning, she wouldn't be in a position to harm anyone.

There was no reason to hang around the station any longer, and although Josie was tired, her son sounded as if he really wanted to talk, so she'd drive to Il Piacere and meet with him. Richards told her he'd get to the restaurant as soon as he finished his paperwork and helped Behan and Martin complete their reports.

Josie put her gun in her purse, closed up her office and left. She got to the restaurant just as they were locking the front door. It was early so she worried there was something really wrong. She pressed her police ID against the glass, and a skinny young man in a business suit opened the door and told her David was in the lounge area waiting for her. There were a few customers finishing their meals in the main dining room, but the manager told her the air conditioning and some of the kitchen appliances had gone out, and he had to close until they could get everything fixed the next morning.

It was easy to find David. She followed the sound of piano music. A sad blues number she'd heard him play hundreds of times but never knew the name. He was alone in the darkened stuffy room, hunched over the ivory keys, eyes closed, his thoughts lost in that place he went to when he played. She sat at a table nearby and listened. Josie had no doubt in her mind he knew she was there, but he wouldn't stop until he was done. After ten or fifteen minutes, he improvised an ending and swung his legs around the bench to face her.

"Hi mom, want a drink?"

"What's wrong?" Josie asked.

He got up, reached over the bar and pulled out a bottle of Cognac. He poured two glasses and gave her one.

"Nothing's wrong. I had some good news and I wanted to tell you," he said.

"Is everything okay with Kizzie?" she asked, trying to sound concerned.

"She's fine, loves the apartment . . . actually sold enough jewelry at the last craft show to buy a new couch so you can have yours back."

"So why did you need to talk to me?" Josie asked, noticing Richards had arrived and was outside in the lobby talking to the manager.

"Mr. Gianini, the owner of the restaurant, told me tonight he thinks I'm a great chef and he's going to let me help run Il Piacere. I get more money, and he'll let me do whatever I want with the menu. He promised that in a few years if I'm still doing well, he'll arrange a loan for me to buy it. I wanted you to be the first to know."

She sipped at the Cognac, letting the news sink in, but had to smile at his excitement. "I'm proud of you," she said and meant it. "I knew you'd be good at whatever you decided to do with your life. What does your dad think?"

"I don't know. I haven't called him yet. You've got a lot going on right now, and I wanted to put your mind at ease about your wayward son."

She got up and put the empty glass on the table.

"I'm happy for you and proud, but I'm not surprised."

"I've decided I'm not going to be like dad. He's scared about getting older, dying and leaving nothing permanent to remind the world that he was ever here. Il Piacere . . . maybe even a bigger better restaurant, will be my legacy."

"Does your dad remember he's got a son?" Josie asked. "You're a pretty great legacy."

"He knows Kizzie's probably not going to have kids, so that's the end of his line."

"I gave birth to you; I've done my bit for his immortality."

"I know you don't worry about that stuff. You're so much stronger than he is . . . tougher. Sometimes I don't think you need anyone."

"Well, you're wrong," she said.

"I know, but you've got to admit you're not the soft mushy type either. Dad's more girlish than you are. I don't think I've ever seen you cry. He blubbers if he gets a flat tire."

"Crying uncontrollably isn't girlish; it's childish."

Josie finished the second brandy. She was having trouble reconciling this man sitting across from her with the immature boy she thought had grown up under her sometimes inconsistent, but loving, care and guidance. He was completely off track about her; she didn't have that soggy core that a lot of people had, but being strong and competent didn't make her any less a woman. Her work admittedly came first, and she never thought of herself as anything more than an adequate mother, but there should be more than breast-feeding and keeping house on the scorecard—intelligence, competence, loyalty, love should matter. She didn't pursue the point because it was a sure path to Kizzie's shortcomings. She was tired and would rather not have that discussion again tonight.

She always knew, along with all her son's exceptional talents, he was a decent, thoughtful human being, but with

Jake as a role model and her lack of attention, she wasn't always certain how he got that way. She did appreciate the unique man he'd become, and to her surprise, she had actually come to grips with the idea that his skill in the kitchen was just another incredible gift, the one, it seems, that would finally provide him a good standard of living.

"There's somebody I want you to meet," she said, thinking this was as good a time as any to introduce him to Richards.

"Good enough," David said, standing and stretching. His fingertips could almost reach the ceiling. They walked into the lobby together, his arm around her shoulder, joking now about some of the odd behavior Jake had exhibited lately. Sarcasm was something her son had inherited from her, and despite his desire to protect his father, like Josie, he recognized the humor in a sixty-four-year-old man having avocado facials and mud baths to look younger.

The manager and Richards were sitting in the lobby's waiting area, drinking whiskey, smoking cigars and talking. They stood as soon as Josie came in and looked a little disappointed their conversation had been interrupted. Richards introduced the manager to Josie as someone who had been in the marine corps and served around the same time he had. They'd both been in the Middle East and apparently had been sharing war stories.

Josie introduced her son to Richards and they shook hands. It wasn't as awkward as she had anticipated, but she could almost get a whiff of testosterone in the air. With their words and body language, they did the human equivalent of puppy butt sniffing to establish the alpha male. Hands down it was Richards, and David eventually took the edge off his attitude. She knew her son loved her, but despite what he said, he was sensitive about his father being replaced.

"Sorry we had to close so early," the manager said. "You could've had one of David's special dishes."

"Maybe another time," Richards said, finishing his drink and putting the cigar in the ashtray. The manager shook his hand and invited Richards back anytime on the house. David did too, but the manager looked as if he meant it.

The men probably could've talked longer but she was tired and hungry and managed to get Richards away. They talked in the parking lot and she told him her son's good news. They decided to go to Long Beach, make something light to eat there and go to bed.

"Thank you," she said, getting into her car while he waited.

"For what?" Richards asked.

"Not choking out my boy."

"No problem, I'm sure there'll be other opportunities. Just kidding, see you at the house," he said, giving her a quick kiss and getting into his car.

"You have no idea," Josie whispered.

FIFTEEN

The alarm woke her out of a deep sleep the next morning. Josie reluctantly opened her eyes and turned onto her back to find the other side of the bed empty. Richards's gun wasn't on the nightstand and his Levi's were missing from the chair where he'd left them last night. It was too early. She lay on top of the sheets staring out the open doors at the perfect herringbone pattern of bricks in the courtyard patio. She should get up. Behan's briefing time was only two hours away, but her excitement over the prospect of arresting Patrick Kessler's killer was tempered by thoughts of being on her way to becoming a forty-something, single woman after she signed divorce papers this afternoon and seriously altered the only adult lifestyle she'd ever known. She looked around Richards's bedroom at the nice furniture, in a style she'd never buy, and knew she didn't want her life to become a series of mornings waking up in someone else's bed.

After a few minutes, she rolled off the mattress, took a shower and found his note by the coffee pot in the kitchen saying he'd set the alarm clock and left early to help Behan. They'd arrived home late last night, had a peanut butter and cracker snack with a whiskey chaser and made love before she passed out.

Her role as a captain didn't permit her to do all the prearrest odds and ends, logistics she enjoyed so much. So, she showed up at Hollywood station in time to call

Commander Perry, brief him and approve Behan's game plan, and then she watched with envy as the worker bees had all the fun. She sensed a blend of anxiety and anticipation had infected the detective squad room. Not only those officers associated with the homicide table, but everyone seemed engaged in activity with a new sense of purpose. An investigation was coming to a successful conclusion. The pieces of the puzzle had fit together and they were about to see the completed picture. Josie was someone who had worked many cases as a detective and had struggled through the disappointments and difficulties, so she could appreciate what it meant and how it felt when a crime was solved and the guilty person was going to jail.

The lab results were sitting on Behan's desk. She stopped to get a mug of coffee before reading them. It was all there—Patrick Kessler's blood type and a single identifiable fingerprint from Susan Kessler's index finger had been found on the knife. Copies of Susan Kessler's arrest and search warrants were attached to the lab report.

"Showtime," Behan said, striding toward her like Eisenhower on D-day, with Richards and Martin by his side. They were all wearing raid jackets. "You ready to go?" he asked, handing her one of the blue nylon jackets with the word "POLICE" in big white letters across the back and an LAPD badge stamped on the front.

Behan intended to treat Susan Kessler as if she were an ordinary murder suspect. He had officers surround the huge estate while he, Martin and Richards knocked on the front door. Josie stayed with his entry team knowing that no matter what happened there would be complaints. The Kesslers were wealthy, and it had been her experience that many rich people didn't do well with the intricacies of law enforcement. Whether it was a traffic ticket or felony arrest, they generally couldn't accept or understand the concept that laws applied equally to them regardless of where they lived, the car they drove or how much money they had invested in AT&T.

It must've been the housekeeper's day off. Just seconds after Richards rang the bell, Susan Kessler answered the door. She was dressed in a blue silk jumpsuit and a cloud of expensive perfume instantly descended over the porch. Her arrogant demeanor wilted as Behan told her why they were there. Martin had her handcuffed and moving toward Behan's car before she had an opportunity to protest. She shouted a high-pitched command at Josie to tell Marvin Beaumont she'd been arrested.

"You're allowed a phone call; tell him yourself," Josie said, calmly closing the car door.

Behan got into the driver's seat with Martin sitting in the back beside Susan Kessler, and he drove away.

It all happened so fast, Josie thought it looked more like a cartel kidnapping than an arrest, but that's the way Behan planned it. He didn't want Seymour Kessler interfering or getting the chief of police involved. Josie and Richards stayed behind to serve the search warrant and deal with the old man who didn't come downstairs until there wasn't a single police officer remaining on his property except the two of them.

"Where's Susan?" Kessler asked, looking around the room, confused and groggy. "What are you people doing in my house?"

He was unshaven and wore an open striped bathrobe over a white tee shirt and black pajama bottoms. His white hair was unkempt and flat on one side as if he'd just lifted his head off the pillow.

"She's been arrested for the murder of your son," Josie said and waited for a reaction that never came.

"Nonsense, what have you done with her?" Kessler asked, rubbing his bad hip.

Richards told him the story as briefly as he could, including details about the knife and the eyewitness account.

The old man's mouth tightened and his eyes narrowed as he listened quietly, slowly shaking his head. As soon as Richards stopped speaking, Kessler turned his back to them and stayed that way for several seconds. Finally, he turned around again and asked in a steady, cold voice, "Where have you taken her?"

"She's being booked," Josie said.

"I see," Kessler said, emotionless. "You're telling me I sheltered and comforted my son's killer in my home."

They didn't respond. The answer was obvious.

"Why did you lie about knowing Henry Trumbo?" Richards asked, after several seconds of silence.

"What?" Kessler asked and seemed confused they would be talking about anything except his daughter-in-law's treachery.

"You hired Trumbo to watch Susan, but you told us you didn't know him," Richards said.

"You tried to make us believe your son was afraid of Trumbo, and he was some mysterious stranger, when he had worked for you," Josie added.

"That's my business. It has nothing to do with this."

"It does now," Richards said. "Trumbo had a relationship with your daughter-in-law and we believe he got a lot of money from your son. We all know your son didn't kill him, but you and Susan are starting to look like good suspects."

"I don't kill people."

"The question is, did you have someone else kill Trumbo because you believed he murdered your son and slept with his wife?"

Kessler limped slowly into the spacious living room and with a groan dropped onto a large white couch.

"No Detective Richards, I did not. If I killed everyone Susan slept with I'd do little else in life. Patrick was naïve and believed whatever she told him. She's a whore. I've always known that, but she's also the mother of my grandchildren. I kept Patrick's family in this house to protect those children from their mother . . . and maybe their father."

"Then why lie about Trumbo?"

"I wanted you to look at him as a possible suspect. I found out he was a disreputable thug. Truth is, I had no confidence you'd find my son's killer on your own. I was trying to help. I even hired another private investigator," Kessler said, winced, and leaned back with his arm covering his eyes. "While the murderer was here under my nose. I'm such an old fool."

Richards handed him a copy of the search warrant for Susan's bedroom suite. Seymour voiced no objection and led them upstairs. When Josie briefed her boss that morning, Commander Perry had strongly suggested that she accompany her detectives and they keep any search of the house very low key to avoid Kessler's wrath, but by the time they mentioned it to the old man he was emotionally spent. He left them alone in that part of the house and swore whatever they didn't remove he intended to dump into the estate's incinerator before morning and burn it with all the other garbage. He would leave no reminder under his roof of that "evil woman."

The search was quick and predictably fruitless. Susan was smarter than Mabry, and they didn't really expect her to keep anything incriminating, but had to look. She did have a huge walk-in closet full of fur coats, designer dresses, shoes and purses. Josie was impressed with the collection, but hoped Patrick Kessler's spirit had a ringside seat near the incinerator that night for the bonfire.

When they left the house, Richards drove them back to Hollywood station. Josie tried to feel sorry for the nasty old man but she couldn't. She hadn't met Kessler's grandchildren but Seymour was patriarch of a family rampant with instability, thievery and murder. He had to bear some responsibility for that much human chaos.

The interrogation of Susan Kessler had already begun by the time Josie got back to the detective squad room. Marvin Beaumont had arrived just minutes before her, but he was already sitting in the interview room with his client.

All the formalities were complete, and Susan had apparently waived her right to remain silent because she was denying any part in her husband's murder at the very moment Josie sat in front of the video feed. She denied being on Santa Monica Boulevard the night her husband was killed and claimed she knew nothing about any money he might've had in his briefcase. She swore her life with Patrick was unusual, but stable and loving, and she and their children fully supported his needs, including dressing like and eventually becoming a woman. Josie figured if she was being anywhere near truthful, Ozzie and Harriet were pikers compared to the Kessler brood.

Mrs. Kessler had no explanation for her fingerprint being on a murder weapon she'd never seen, and she didn't understand why anyone would lie and say they saw her stab her husband. Beaumont was her attorney but he never interfered with the interrogation by Behan and Martin and made no effort to control his client or stop her incessant talking. He seemed to recognize that he'd been given a minor role in this event. Susan was in charge, and she had no intention of taking direction or advice from him or anyone else as she piloted her fate like a burning plane crashing nose first into the ground.

Given her bizarre marriage arrangement, Susan's alibi for the evening her husband died wouldn't be completely implausible to a jury. She swore she spent that whole night in her bedroom with Henry Trumbo. Her justification was simple. She'd accepted her husband's foibles; therefore, Patrick should've understood her need for male companionship. Of course, Trumbo was dead now and couldn't back up her story. Josie doubted Seymour Kessler, if he was home that night, would be willing to lie for the woman any longer.

Susan also denied killing Trumbo and professed her undying affection for him. Her attorney nodded in agreement as she recounted how difficult his death had been for her, apparently even more traumatic than her husband's. Her alibi for the night Trumbo was killed happened to be Councilman Flowers, her dead husband's boss. They had dinner together and afterward went to a Best Western hotel in the Valley, registered in her name, and spent the night. She gave Behan the names and locations of the hotel and restaurant.

Josie turned down the sound. The woman's endless detailed saga of middle-aged promiscuity was giving her a headache. She understood if the dinner and hotel information could be confirmed, Susan Kessler had to be eliminated as a suspect in Trumbo's death. They'd solved her husband's murder but were back to square one on her lover.

The interview seemed to deteriorate from that point. When Josie noticed Susan jump up and flap her arms like a bird, she raised the volume again in time to hear the agitated woman refuse to answer any more "ridiculous" questions and then deride Beaumont for his incompetence and swear he would never see a penny of his exorbitant attorney fees.

Behan's shallow well of patience had apparently dried up because he told Martin to "take the 5150 away" and get her booked at the LA County women's jail, and held until her arraignment. The California Welfare and Institutions Code, Section 5150, provided for an involuntary psychiatric hold, but 5150 had evolved into a cop code word for someone who exhibited loony behavior. Josie wouldn't disagree with Behan's assessment, but knew it wasn't unusual for a murder suspect to develop signs of incompetence as soon as it became clear her sanity needed to be jettisoned to stay off death row.

There wasn't a good reason to stay any longer, so Josie left the detective squad room and was talking to a group of patrol officers when Marvin Beaumont called out to her from the other end of the hallway near the watch commander's office. He was holding a large cardboard file box with his briefcase lying on top.

"My God, don't you have air conditioning in this building," he whined when she got closer. He was obviously struggling with the weight of the box and sweat was dripping down the sides of his face and neck staining what looked like an expensive shirt.

"Sometimes," Josie said, taking his briefcase to lighten the load. "Want to talk to me?" she asked, moving toward her office. He didn't answer but followed quietly and dropped the box on the coffee table as soon as they got there. She asked Maki to bring a couple of bottles of cold water.

After Beaumont quickly finished the first bottle, he removed his suit jacket and tie, throwing them on top of the box.

"Thank you," he said, sitting at her worktable and opening the second bottle.

"What can I do for you Mr. Beaumont?" she asked, still standing but leaning against her desk.

"There are things about Henry Trumbo . . . I don't think you know. To begin with, Mrs. Kessler isn't lying about her relationship with him or Councilman Flowers."

"I never thought she was," Josie said, wondering what he really wanted.

"I'll deny I ever said this, but we both know Susan killed her husband, but I'm certain Henry Trumbo put her up to it. She's greedy and simple and he excelled in manipulating that sort of person," Beaumont said and paused before adding, "I tried to tell him Seymour controlled the wealth, but Henry insisted Susan would have her own money. He was a terribly frightening man."

"If he was so terribly frightening, why did you hire him and give him office space in your building?"

"I hired him for protection, but after I realized what he was I bought a gun because I was so afraid of him . . . and I hate guns."

"He's dead, Marvin. What's your point?"

"I truly believe Henry Trumbo was a psychopath, but I know there was a man who had some sort of . . . hold on him. That's what I wanted to tell you."

"Who?"

"I don't know, but the day he died, Henry said he was going to put an end to it."

"What does that mean?"

"I don't know."

"Come on, Marvin, if you're going to tell me something, do it, or finish your drink and we'll call it a day."

"Henry's gun and badge were not in the file cabinet where you found them after he died. I saw him wearing the gun when he left for the Regency that night. Obviously, you didn't find it with his body either," Beaumont said. He hesitated then blurted out, "I lied to you."

"What a surprise," Josie said.

"I told you I didn't search Trumbo's office after he died, but I did. I had to be certain none of my case files were in there . . . high-profile clients who . . . never mind. The thing is, I looked in that drawer. It was empty. I'm no saint, but Trumbo was an addict, a thief and a liar, and I'm sorry I ever had anything to do with him, but I'm terrified that whoever killed him got into my building and left those things for a reason."

Josie sighed and sat at the table next to him. "I need more, Marvin. We can't do anything or help you with what you've given me. Did Trumbo tell you more about that man you mentioned?"

"No," he said and sighed. "It could've been some sort of lovers' quarrel. He had male lovers too."

"Maybe . . . but we need a place to start looking."

Beaumont wiped sweat from his face with the sleeve of his shirt and gathered his belongings.

"I'm not sorry he's dead, but you've got to find his killer so I can sleep again," Beaumont said, with as much dignity as he could muster on the way out.

Josie sat at her desk and stared at the empty doorway. "That's what I live for, Marvin. Every day I ask myself what I can do to make certain Marvin gets a good night's sleep."

"Who are you talking to?" Marge asked, walking in and looking around the empty office. "I was waiting for shithead to leave."

"What do you want? I'm busy," Josie said, knowing that sounded exactly how she felt . . . testy. The closer it got to signing divorce papers, the more irritable she got and didn't know why, because she definitely wanted it. The whole business was just distracting.

"Morning boss, nice to see you too," Marge said, with a fake smile. "I need to vent. Red is driving me batshit with his new best buddy. Martin is so smart. Martin is so organized. Did you see what Martin found?" she said, mimicking Behan.

"Aren't you happy they're getting along? He seems better . . . sober, and she isn't complaining all the time. I'm damn happy."

"Great," Marge said and opened the bottom cabinet drawer. She grabbed a handful of candy bars from Josie's stash, sat at the worktable, and started devouring them.

"Don't you have work to do?" Josie asked, taking the top file off a stack of papers.

"Red asked me to follow up on the hotel and restaurant where Susan Kessler said she and Flowers spent the night."

"Did you?"

"It checks out. She couldn't have killed Trumbo. I already told Red. You know a place called Thompson's in the Valley?" Marge asked, crumpling the candy wrappers into a ball and making a hook shot into the wastepaper basket.

"Nope."

Marge switched on the television on the wall above the table and put on a cable news program. It was loud.

"I'm trying to work here," Josie said, tossing her pen on the desk. "Turn that thing off and go away."

"You're busy?" Marge asked and Josie just stared at her. "Too bad, I was going to ask if you wanted to go to the Valley with me. Thompson's is a gun store. When I was checking Susan Kessler's Visa for the motel and restaurant, I found an item for sixty-eight dollars she bought two days before her husband was killed."

Josie closed the folder. "Definitely wasn't a gun, not for that amount of money."

"What else can you buy at gun stores? Really nice knives," Marge said, not waiting for her to answer.

Josie put the folder back on the stack. "Have you got an address?"

"Does a big-ass bull have hairy balls?"

"A yes or no would've been fine."

THEY LOCATED Thompson's on Van Nuys Boulevard in Pacoima, a low-income neighborhood in the San Fernando Valley. The shop was on the boulevard among other struggling small businesses. The front window was blacked out and covered with security bars. An antique store next door had a window display with funky bottles, ordinary glassware and cheap broken furniture, the sort of antiques Josie imagined could be found in any alley or dumpster in downtown LA.

The smell inside the gun store was reminiscent of her Italian grandmother's steamer trunk that hadn't been aired out for decades and was filled with musty old wedding clothes and frayed graying portraits. Billy Bob standing behind the counter was another story. He wore a tee shirt with an American flag pictured across the front and faded baggy jeans with suspenders. His long gray hair hung loose constrained only by a headband of braided leather. His gray beard reached the middle of his scrawny chest and was full enough to house a family of wrens.

They showed him their police IDs, and he had to lift his granny glasses to read them. He slowly chewed something while they talked. Josie was grateful the wad of brown stuff never left his mouth.

The shelves were cluttered with relics—old guns, Civil War and World War II replicas and pictures of anywhere a gun could or had been used to kill wild beautiful animals or other human beings. The display case in front of the counter was another matter. It contained a decent collection of knives, some of them rare and expensive. On the bottom of the case were two Smith & Wesson Black Swat Knives, identical to the one Richards found in Mabry's apartment. The price with tax would be sixty-eight dollars.

"We know one of these was purchased on the tenth of this month," Marge said, pointing at the knife.

Billy Bob leaned over the case to see. "Good blade," he said, grinning with tobacco-stained teeth. "Want one?"

"No, I want to see the sales receipt," Marge said.

"Don't you need to get yourself a warrant or something to do that?" Billy Bob asked.

"Not if you give it to me," Marge said.

"Maybe I would if you asked me nice."

Marge glanced at Josie, looking for permission, and Josie nodded.

"Maybe I'll just get that warrant, Billy Bob," Marge said, sweetly. "Course I'll have to lock up this shithole until I write it. You know, just to make sure you don't destroy evidence. Oh yeah, I write real slow, so it might take awhile before you can open up again. That's after I thoroughly examine every piece of crappy junk and sheet of paper you've got in this toilet and if anything is questionable I might have to confiscate it until I'm absolutely certain it's not stolen or borrowed by mistake." She stopped and grinned at him, "That fucking nice enough for you, Billy Bob?"

The man didn't move for a few seconds, but his smile faded. He turned to Josie and she shrugged. He took his glasses off and put them on the counter.

"Wait here," he said, opening the door behind him. Josie lifted the hinged counter gate and they followed him into the back room. He stopped for a second and looked as if he wanted to protest, but took a deep breath, blew it out and said, "No respect for a man's property no more."

"Just give me the fucking receipt," Marge said.

It was clear why he wasn't eager for anyone to rummage through his store. His back room looked like a hoarder's warehouse, full of garbage and stacked boxes. The desk where he retrieved a copy of the sales slip was piled with papers, but Billy Bob seemed to know right where to look.

Marge took the entire sales book and gave him a property receipt. She also wrote down all his personal information and advised him he'd probably be subpoenaed to testify at the trial if there was one.

They left him in the back room, but when they went out the front door, heard noises as if he were slamming heavy objects against the walls.

"That wasn't bad," Marge said, getting into the car and buckling her seat belt.

"Citizens working with the police, it's a beautiful thing," Josie said.

"I'm calculating Susan Kessler's signature on this sales slip will convince sleazebag Beaumont that getting her to plead to a lesser charge is the only way to keep her off death row . . . which granted in California is more like die-of-old-age row."

"You're probably right, but we still got zilch on Trumbo," Josie said. "Beaumont was telling me Trumbo had a run-in with some guy that might've been one of his lovers."

"Was there anybody this slut didn't sleep with?" Marge asked, with a raised eyebrow. "The late Sergeant Castro's a possibility."

"Maybe, but I can't see Trumbo worrying about a guy like Castro. Besides, I agree with Behan; Castro's death looked like the killer was cleaning up a loose end. Oh shit," Josie said, looking at her watch. "Can you run me downtown for about a half hour?"

"You bet, boss. What's up?"

"My attorney's got some papers for me to sign."

"Is this it?" Marge asked and Josie nodded. She must've looked as annoyed as she felt because Marge added, "Do I need to remind you why you're doing this?"

"Nope," Josie said. She knew why and had no intention of changing her mind, but terminating a marriage seemed like a lot of work for someone her age with so many other things to do.

"Just don't think too much, Corsino," Marge said, getting off the freeway on the Sixth Street ramp.

She drove into the underground parking of the office building at the corner of Seventh and Flower and they took the elevator up to the attorney's office on the eleventh floor. Marge sat in the reception area while Josie followed her attorney's junior partner back to their conference room.

The possibility that Jake might be there had never crossed her mind. She hadn't asked, but assumed it would just be her and her over-priced lawyer signing the final papers. All the details had been worked out to everyone's satisfaction, so why was he here, she wondered. When Josie walked in, Jake was standing by the window with his attorney, a very pretty, intelligent-looking young woman who glared at Josie. Josie did her best to ignore her, which intensified the fierce looks.

They signed the papers and, during the process, Josie made an effort to be nothing more than polite. She spoke directly to Jake in answering his pretty attorney's questions and that resulted in some unprofessional grumblings and more angry stares from the woman.

"Is there something wrong with you?" Josie finally asked when the behavior got annoying enough.

"I beg your pardon," the attorney said.

"You're behaving like a horse's ass. What's the problem? I'm divorcing him, not you."

"I can see everything Mr. Corsino has told me about you is accurate," she said, giving Jake a consoling, intimate look.

"I get it," Josie said, knowing exactly what that glance meant; Jake was flirting with his teenage-looking lawyer for her benefit. "Are we done here?" she asked.

"Just one minute, Hon. I have something for you," Jake said, reaching under the table and producing the crystal vase he'd taken from their dining room, the one his mother had given them for their wedding. "I'm sorry I took this. I was upset, but my mother always wanted you to have it. It's awfully valuable and I love it, but you were special to her. Please," he said, carefully handing it to Josie. His wimpy expression was a bad attempt at gracious humility, but she took it anyway even knowing his generosity was all a show for the gullible, pretty attorney.

"Thank you," Josie said, tucking the vase under her arm with copies of her divorce papers, and walking into the reception area. "Let's go," she said to Marge who jumped up and followed her into the lobby.

They didn't speak going down in the elevator. Marge's car was on the fourth level and Josie told her to drive slowly going up toward the exit. On the second level, she spotted Jake's silver Porsche and told Marge to stop.

"Open your trunk," Josie ordered.

"You're not gonna do something fucked up. Are you, boss?" Marge asked, but opened it.

Josie searched around and found a tire iron and put it on the ground. She also pulled out a shabby jail blanket Marge kept folded up in there for long surveillances. She wrapped the vase in the blanket and pounded on it several times with the tire iron.

"You have any of those clear plastic evidence bags?" Josie asked, slowly unfolding the blanket to find what remained of the pulverized crystal vase. Putting on Marge's leather gloves, she filled the plastic bag with the tiny pieces of glass and gently placed it on the hood of the Porsche with a note clipped to the bag that read, "Oops," then rolled up the blanket and threw it back in the trunk with the tire iron. "Better shake that out before you use it again," she told Marge before getting back in the car.

"Feel good?" Marge asked, driving out of the structure.

"What do you think?"

"I think the fucker's lucky he gave you that vase."

SIXTEEN

They stopped in the Valley to have dinner at an Italian restaurant where Marge claimed she'd eaten at least once a week when she was a patrol sergeant. It was a family-owned business, and the staff remembered the tall gorgeous blonde and were excited to see her again but even happier to feed a paisano with the surname Corsino. They ate big pasta meals and finished two baskets of garlic bread and half a bottle of Chianti, as well as every special sampling the chef wanted them to taste.

Both women had healthy appetites but had to admit they might've overdone it as they groaned getting into the car to drive back to Hollywood. When they arrived at the police station, Marge left Josie by the rear door saying she was going out again to supervise a special prostitution task force targeting Sunset Boulevard. She'd allowed her crew to start without her, but wanted to check on their progress. Knowing there was a logjam of paperwork sitting on her desk, Josie declined an invitation to join them, but told Marge she'd give Billy Bob's evidence to Behan and have him do the report.

There were still a handful of detectives working when Josie arrived. She couldn't find Behan, but Martin was at the homicide table putting copies of reports and warrants in Patrick Kessler's murder book.

"Lieutenant Bailey did some great follow-up work. It's the coup de grâce for Red's case," Martin said, taking the receipt book from Josie. She agreed to write the evidence report and would leave a copy for Behan who she said was out with Richards.

"Do you know where they've gone?" Josie asked.

"No, they wanted to check on something but didn't tell me what."

"So, everything's okay with you and Red now?" Josie asked.

"Great, but I don't think Lieutenant Bailey likes me too much," she said and Josie grimaced at the prospect of another intervention. "Oh no, ma'am, it's all right. I have no complaints. I talked to Gaby Johnston, and she said I have to confront people and fight my own battles."

"Good advice," Josie said, "but I'd go easy on that confronting thing with Marge. Just talk to her."

There was plenty of work waiting in her office and Maki had added a few new items while Josie was gone. It had to be done but Josie was tired and ready to go home. She had mixed feelings about where home might be tonight. She wanted to stay with Richards, but there was no telling when he and Red would get back from whatever they were doing. For some reason she didn't want to wait there alone, and felt like being in her own surroundings with what was left of familiar things.

She half expected to find a nasty message on her desk from Jake, but there was nothing. She always suspected her ex-husband was a little intimidated by her, and was fairly certain the broken crystal vase would've been enough to confirm his worst suspicions. Josie wondered what sort of things Jake and David said about her when they were together, especially now that Kizzie could add her two cents into the mix. It actually didn't matter anymore. She was a free woman and her kid was an adult living on his own. It was liberating, sort of.

It was easier to work on the stack of paperwork in front of her than to drive home so she dug into it and when

Richards called, one corner of her desk was nearly clean. He told her that he and Behan were doing a follow-up on Henry Trumbo's application with the police department to locate friends, family members, anyone who might've known him. They were contacting every reference he used.

"If you're done, why don't you go to my place, and I'll probably be there in a couple of hours," Richards said.

"I've got to pick up some things in Pasadena. Let me see if I'm up to the drive," Josie said. She did want to be with him but didn't want to be alone in his house tonight.

"You okay?" he asked and sounded tentative adding, "Papers signed?"

She assured him everything was done but decided not to mention the crystal vase incident, afraid it might sound as crazy as it was. There wasn't any way to keep it a secret for long because Marge knew. She would blab to Behan and he would immediately tell Richards. Josie laughed to herself and thought it was probably a good thing. The man should have some idea of what he was getting himself into before he made any serious commitments.

As soon as he hung up, Josie went back to work and in less than an hour had every piece of paper off the desk and was caught up on the computer. She downloaded her calendar for the next day and was locking the wardrobe when the watch commander knocked on her door.

"Sorry to bother you ma'am, do you have a minute?" the young lieutenant asked.

"You bet," Josie said, opening the wardrobe again and throwing her purse inside. "What's up?"

This lieutenant was usually the unflappable one but he seemed uncertain and hesitant to say what was on his mind.

"I'm not real sure how to handle this," he finally said, rubbing the back of his neck.

"Talk to me."

"I got a sergeant sitting at County hospital. He transported a drag queen that got stabbed tonight on Santa Monica."

"Easy one, give it to Marge Bailey, that's her territory."

"That's the problem. He wants to talk to you and doesn't want Lieutenant Bailey to know where he's at."

"What's this guy's name?" Josie asked.

The lieutenant looked at a message pad he was holding. "Petroski . . . Steven, but at first he tried to tell the emergency room nurse his legal name was Ramona."

"How bad is he?"

"Superficial cuts. He was hysterical, so they took him from Cedars-Sinai to County and they're probably going to admit him overnight."

"Has your sergeant talked to him?" Josie asked. She wasn't eager to have to deal with Ramona or Petroski, or whatever he called himself.

"No ma'am, Sarge says the victim will only talk to you, but if you don't want to waste your time with this guy, I can go to County and make him tell me what he wants."

"Thanks for the offer lieutenant, but I'll go. Unfortunately, I know him."

Josie wondered what Petroski was involved in this time. The man was an original drama queen with the emotional equivalency of superglue—once he got attached to you there was no prying him loose, so she was curious why he didn't want Marge to know where he was. He was Marge Bailey's snitch, and she'd always taken good care of him. She paid him so often and so well that Josie had complained to her the drag queen was practically on the city payroll.

County hospital was downtown, but it was in the same direction as Pasadena. Josie figured she could stop by and talk to Petroski on her way home. It was late enough that the traffic had thinned out and she got there quickly.

Sergeant Brown was waiting for her in the emergency room. She always hated the antiseptic smells and cold temperatures in this place, but tonight, compared to outside, this walk-in freezer was a welcome relief. The orderlies hadn't taken Petroski up to a room yet, but Josie knew exactly where to find him. His theatrical moans led her directly to the closed curtain in a corner of the room. The sergeant told her Petroski had superficial wounds but had to be given tranquilizers to stop his shaking and crying. Brown asked if Josie wanted him to wait until she finished talking to the distraught man, but she declined. She didn't intend to spend a lot of time holding his hand.

She pulled back the curtain and there he was lying on the gurney whimpering, with the back of his right hand resting on his forehead doing a pretty good impression of Sarah Bernhardt. The hospital gown was open in front and seductively draped off his bare left shoulder. He had two small bandages on that shoulder and what looked like a razor nick on his chin. His face had been scrubbed and not a trace of makeup, including his eyebrows, remained. She was surprised to see a somewhat vulnerable-looking person under all the fantasy, a middle-aged paunchy man with a double chin and fear in his eyes. His thinning hair was clean and combed straight back, but to Josie, he still seemed to be someone who'd fit better standing on a street corner in Hollywood than anywhere in this sterile hospital environment.

"Oh my God, it's you, your honor," Petroski said, finally noticing her and grimacing with real or imagined pain as he tried to straighten up on the gurney.

"Sit still, Steven," Josie ordered, moving closer. "What happened?"

"I've been assaulted, practically murdered," he whispered as if it were a secret. Josie guessed there wasn't anyone in the hospital within earshot who hadn't already heard what happened to him.

"Why didn't you let the sergeant call Lieutenant Bailey?"

"Oh no, no, no," he said, wrapping his gown tight around his shoulders and bringing both legs up until his knees were almost under his chin. He seemed genuinely terrified.

"Who did this to you?" Josie asked, adjusting the sheet to cover parts of him she'd rather not have seen.

"Her, that's what I'm telling you darling, it was her," he said, stretching out his legs and falling back on the pillows in childlike frustration. Josie shook her head and was losing patience. He sat up again and said, "My gorgeous sergeant."

"Are you accusing Lieutenant Bailey of attacking you?"

"No, I'm telling you the crazy bitch tried to kill me. I swear," he said, eyes wide open and holding up his shaky left hand as if he were taking an oath then making slashing knife movements. "Hacking at me like Jack the Ripper . . . she tried to hide her face, but it was her . . . it's a hundred degrees; she's covered from head to toe in a hoodie and sweatpants, but I still knew her," he said, emphasizing the last three words.

"When did this happen?"

Petroski produced a copy of the ambulance report from under his pillow. It showed the exact time paramedics got the call and when they arrived at his location on the boulevard. It was approximately the same time Josie and Marge were leaving the gun shop in Pacoima on their way back to Hollywood. It would've been impossible for Marge to have been anywhere near either Santa Monica Boulevard or this drag queen when he was attacked. Josie explained all that to Petroski and he looked confused.

"It was her or her evil twin," he insisted and added in a whisper. "It all happened so fast, but I know it was her."

"But it wasn't. She was with me."

"Does she have a twin?" he asked.

"No," Josie said, backing up against the curtain. She was getting a very bad feeling over a possible explanation taking shape in her head. She wanted to get back to Hollywood, but that wouldn't do any good tonight. Everyone had gone. She needed to talk to Behan or Richards or maybe it would be better to think about her suspicions overnight before mentioning something that sounded a little crazy even to her.

She left Petroski asleep and snoring on the gurney. His hysterics had worn him down and all those drugs the nurses kept feeding into his IV had finally started to do their magic, which was good for him because it would probably be breakfast before he saw anything but the emergency room's pale green walls. Beds were a commodity at County hospital, and anxiety attacks brought on by superficial wounds weren't high on the priority list for admission. He'd drifted off, still not completely convinced Marge hadn't tried to kill him. Josie was positive he was wrong, but her possible explanation was still disappointing.

THE PASADENA house looked deserted when she pulled into the garage. The porch lights were off and one of the nicer neighbors must've hidden the morning newspapers behind the patio chairs in an attempt to fool burglars into thinking someone actually lived there. It was a nice gesture, but anything worth stealing had already been taken by either Jake or David. The house was stifling hot inside and smelled like those rotten onions in the wire basket hanging over the sink.

She opened all the upstairs windows and those at the back of the house to get some fresh air circulating. The spoiled fruit and vegetables got tossed into a garbage bag with most of what was left in the refrigerator and dumped in the garbage container outside. When that was done, she opened a bottle of Cabernet she'd almost forgotten was stashed in the credenza. She sat at the dining room table with her feet resting on one of the chairs, poured a glass of wine and kept the bottle nearby intending to drink for as long as it took to get her thoughts organized and then get sleepy.

As a part of the settlement, Jake had agreed to let her keep the Pasadena house in exchange for her relinquishing all claims to his investment income. The house was nearly paid for and would bring between eight and nine hundred thousand on today's market, so Josie guessed he must've accumulated a few million in his portfolio. She didn't ask her lawyer and didn't care. The house meant something to her, and she was happy to keep it. He could have the money if that's all it took to satisfy him.

One of these days, she'd begin the process of planning how to make the place her own, starting with new locks on all the doors. She wasn't going to put her life on hold waiting to find out if Richards would become her permanent partner. If their relationship worked out, it would make her very happy, but until that happened, she needed a refuge filled with objects that pleased her.

She wondered what a home decorated with just her taste might look like since this house had been designed and furnished by family consensus with a definite male slant. Richards's wife had put her personality and creativity into every aspect of their Long Beach house. Josie got a real sense of who the woman had been from those rooms and she wanted to do the same thing here, create her little sanctuary.

She tried to keep her mind on decorating but it kept drifting back to Petroski's story and if what he told her might lead to solving Trumbo's murder . . . but at what cost, she wondered. It was nothing more than a hunch, but she'd learned not to ignore gut feelings.

Everyone who knew them said it was uncanny how much Marge and Gaby Johnston looked like sisters. From their first meeting, the similarity not only in their features, but in size, mannerisms, even the salty language they both used, was eerie. In the darkness, a frantic Petroski could easily have mistaken one for the other and no one would blame him.

The more she thought about it, Josie realized Gaby had been in the middle of everything connected to the homicides, especially that missing money. Gaby was on the police union's legal team, the source of the illicit money. She admitted to knowing both Trumbo and Castro, and she had personally delivered Sergeant Miller to Internal Affairs and the DA on a silver platter. Josie wondered now if Gaby always had access to those ledgers and just picked her time to implicate Miller.

All that money Miller and Kessler took from the city still hadn't been recovered. So, who had it? It wasn't Susan. It wasn't Mabry or Trumbo or Castro, and Councilman Flowers probably never had a clue they were skimming it off his dirty campaign donations.

Josie wanted to be wrong but her instincts were pointing steadfastly in Gaby's direction. It was intuitive, a sixth sense that didn't mean much in the greater crime-solving paradigm, but Josie trusted her instincts, and they were screaming at her that it was Gaby Johnston who'd attacked Petroski tonight. This latest stabbing was another half-hearted assault like the others on Santa Monica Boulevard that never got reported, but there was one big difference. Petroski recognized his assailant or thought he did and that might finally mean a break for Behan.

She guessed if Gaby had killed Trumbo maybe she wanted to send detectives on a wild goose chase looking for someone who was attacking transvestites in Hollywood. It might've been intended to be a diversion.

She tried calling Behan's cell phone, but he didn't answer and neither did Richards. Maybe it was best to go with her original plan, sleep on this and consider it again in the morning when she was rested and thinking more clearly. The problem was the wine bottle was almost empty, and she still wasn't tired. Her body was weary, but it would be difficult to sleep with the crossword puzzle she'd been constructing in her brain. She put the cork back in the wine, closed all the downstairs windows in the house but left lights on in the kitchen and on the front porch.

Marge's number was on her speed dial. She let it ring until her friend picked up and waited until the profane ranting subsided.

"Can you meet me at the station?" Josie asked.

"It's four A.M. Corsino, you fucked up the best REM sleep I've had in weeks."

"Is Behan with you?"

"Wait a minute," she said. After a few seconds, Marge came back on the line and said, "No . . . I guess not . . . fucking wasted somewhere."

"I can't get him or Richards to answer their phones," Josie said. Unlike Marge, she wasn't concerned that Behan had been drinking and was passed out drunk somewhere. She believed Richards was still with him and wouldn't allow him do that, but her sixth sense was working over-time tonight and warning her that something was very wrong.

SEVENTEEN

No one at Hollywood station had heard from Josie's two detectives. They didn't respond on the radio or their cell phones, but she would wait another couple of hours until their normal starting time before doing anything extraordinary to find them. Behan had left Martin on call for homicides, so he wasn't obligated to answer his phone. Josie was concerned but she knew Richards was most likely with him, and she was willing to wait and give them an opportunity to contact her. Besides, there was no indication that anything had happened and Richards was more than capable of taking care of himself and Behan.

Marge said she was starving and couldn't concentrate on what Josie wanted to tell her unless they found someplace to eat first. They walked around the corner on Sunset Boulevard to a twenty-four-hour diner. Breakfast was usually good there, but the clientele ranged from local prostitutes to a variety of grungy street people. Josie found a booth near the back wall and away from the front window. A couple of young men in cut-off jeans and open shirts, who looked as if they hadn't bathed for a while, were the only other customers, but they were sitting at the counter downwind from a large fan.

As soon as they ordered, Josie told Marge what had happened during her unexpected meeting with Petroski.

"That douche bag told you I tried to stab him?" Marge shouted, loud enough for the young men, waitresses and probably the cook in the back room to hear. "If I wanted the sonnofabitch dead, he'd be dead laying on a slab in the morgue not some hospital bed."

The men left their menus on the counter and slinked quietly away out to the sidewalk and crossed the street without looking back.

"You done?" Josie asked Marge, then shrugged at their waitress who had plates in her hand but seemed reluctant to come closer. "It's okay," she said showing the woman the badge on her belt. The waitress sprinted toward their table, dropped the plates in front of them, and was gone just as quickly.

"Sorry, more coffee please," Marge said sweetly to the woman's back and whispered to Josie, "What the fuck's wrong with that fat bastard."

"He honestly believed it was you," Josie said and then told Marge her theory about Gaby.

Marge listened without interrupting. She continued eating and drinking coffee while Josie methodically went through the reasons why she believed it was Gaby who had attacked Petroski and maybe killed Henry Trumbo. It was conjecture, somewhat logical but Josie knew there was nothing to prove or back up a word of what she was saying. She hadn't touched her food and waited patiently until Marge was done for some response.

"You might be right," Marge said, slouching against the back of the booth and crossing her arms. "Remember at Gaby's barbeque all the clothes she was wearing . . . bullshit story about staying out of the sun, but she's got a better tan than both of us."

"What about it?"

"The night Petroski took Martin and me around to talk to those queens, the ones who'd been attacked but didn't die . . . I know you remember I mentioned it to Gaby at lunch that one of them tried to kick the asshole in the balls, but stuck his leg with a spiked heel. When Gaby was barbequing, her wrap opened a little and I saw a scar on her leg in just about the right spot. I didn't think anything about it but with all the other crap you're telling me, I think she was hiding that injury and you might be right."

They paid the bill and walked back to the station discussing what the next move should be. There were still more questions now than answers. Did Gaby know Trumbo before he was fired from the police department? What was their relationship? Did Gaby take the missing money? Was it she who put Trumbo's gun and police ID back in Beaumont's building, and if she did, why?

The murder weapon was a dead end. The bloody butcher knife had been left at the scene near Trumbo's body, but wiped clean of fingerprints, or the murderer had worn gloves. Even worse, it was one of a rusty set found in the apartment, so whoever killed Trumbo either hadn't planned it or knew it was available. Either way, it wouldn't lead to the killer like it had in Kessler's murder.

They agreed the first order of business had to be a thorough background check on Gaby. Computer searches were Marge's specialty so she went upstairs to the vice office to get started. The admin staff had arrived by the time Josie returned. Along with a pile of work, her adjutant delivered a message from Behan that he and Richards would be late and had a lot to tell her.

Josie was exhausted to the point of not thinking clearly, so she closed her office door and catnapped on the couch for what seemed like ten minutes before Marge barged in and turned on the lights.

"Wake up, boss," she said, gently pushing Josie's legs off the couch to make room. "Gaby went to some barely accredited law school in San Francisco and graduated last year. No record of her taking or passing the bar."

"So, another lie. I wonder why the league hired her?"

"The union hired her right after graduation. I couldn't find much on her before that so I worked on property records for her place in Manhattan Beach. It was owned by a Caroline Johnston, but she didn't have any nieces," Marge said, shuffling through her notes.

"Is Caroline dead?"

"Yes, but she left the house to her only relative, a brother, James Johnston, who still has title. Apparently their parents owned it and left it to Caroline who left it in a trust to her brother when she died."

"So, how did Gaby get there and where's James?"

"Good question. He apparently allows her to stay there, but she definitely hasn't got title. She was feeding us a pile of bullshit about an aunt leaving it to her."

"What's Gaby's relationship to James?" Josie asked. "Maybe they were married."

"Don't think so. There're no county records here or up north of a marriage or divorce . . . no death certificate for him."

"Maybe she's his daughter."

"Can't be," Marge said. "They're about the same age. Maybe they were lovers or roomies or who knows."

"Is Behan back yet? His message said he found something."

"I don't know," Marge said, just as Josie glanced up and saw Richards and Behan coming down the hallway toward them. Marge must've noticed her expression and turned around. "Where the hell have you been?" she asked, looking directly at Behan.

Josie thought both men looked exhausted and understood why when Richards explained they had just returned from San Francisco, a six-hour drive each way they'd accomplished in less than two days. They had traced Trumbo to San Francisco where he'd lived about a year before he'd joined the police department.

"Henry had an interesting background," Richards said, dropping onto the couch beside Josie.

"He lived in the tenderloin with his lover, some other guy, according to the landlady. That's a relevant fact that never came out when Trumbo applied to the department because it turns out his background investigator was the prematurely departed addict, Sergeant John Castro."

"I'm pretty certain that wouldn't have disqualified him these days," Josie said.

"It would if they were prostitutes and small-time hustlers," Behan said, and added, "which they were, according to the local cops."

"Arrest records, booking photos?" Josie asked.

"They had misdemeanor arrests for minor stuff. There's probably booking photos."

"What was his roommate's name?" Josie asked.

"His landlady said it was Jimmy Johnston. The apartment was actually rented by Jimmy who seemed to have some independent income like a small trust or something."

"Jimmy Johnston?" Marge asked. "Are we talking about the James Johnston who owns Gaby's house?"

"It makes sense," Josie said. "Gaby, Trumbo and James were all in San Francisco at the same time. Gaby and Trumbo came to Los Angeles about a year ago. She gets a job with the league, and with Castro's help, Trumbo joins the police department. Do we know if James is still living in San Francisco?"

"He gave up the apartment about a year ago when Trumbo left, and we can't find a trace of him," Richards said. "But he does own that property in Manhattan Beach."

"Where Gaby's living . . . I'm beginning to wonder if Trumbo isn't the only fucking skeleton in her closet," Marge said.

"What are you talking about?" Behan asked.

Josie explained her suspicions about Gaby attacking Petroski and maybe killing Trumbo and said, "It's beginning to look like she might've killed James too since he's nowhere to be found and she's living in his house claiming it belongs to her."

"What do you want to do?" Richards asked Behan.

"Send a team of detectives to the union office and bring her in here. We need answers," Josie said.

"We'll go," Richards said. He and Behan were up and out the door before she could object. If they were tired, they weren't showing it any longer.

She called them back and wrote down the address of the beach house. "In case she's not at work, but be careful. I'm getting a really bad feeling about this woman."

Marge dropped onto the couch and Josie sat beside her. They were quiet for a minute.

"Fuck," Marge said, breaking the silence. "I am so fucking pissed off. How could I be that wrong about somebody?"

"Me too. Get a booking photo from San Francisco PD of James Johnston if they still have one, so we have a clue what this guy looks like. We can show it around Manhattan Beach, find out when's the last time the neighbors saw him at the house."

"Okay," Marge said, groaning as she got up.

Maki knocked on the open door and said, "Ma'am, that priest Father O'Reilly is on line one. He says it's important."

Marge waited as Josie picked up the phone.

"Good morning, Father, how are you?"

"Can you come to the church?" he whispered.

"Are you all right? Are you sick?"

"No, no," he said a little louder. "Something I need to show you."

"I can be there a little later this afternoon or tomorrow, if . . ." she said.

"It's very important that you come now," he said, interrupting her.

Josie put her hand over the phone for a second, said "shit," then took her hand away and said, "I'll be there in a few minutes," and hung up.

"What's the matter," Marge asked.

"The good father needs moral support again."

"Tell him to fuck off. You're busy."

"You're going to hell, Lieutenant Bailey," Josie said, attempting to sound serious.

"Face it, boss, we both got frequent flyer miles straight to the fiery pit and no fucked-up padre's gonna fix that."

"Get the booking photo. I'll do my captain thing, hold his hand for a few minutes, and be right back."

Josie didn't disagree with her friend about their place in the hereafter because she knew they'd both done some questionable stuff that wouldn't earn any Brownie points at the Pearly Gates, but what working cop hadn't walked a little close to the edge at times. There wasn't anything she regretted and if she had to live her life again, wouldn't change a thing, not even her disappointing marriage because something special, David, had come out of it.

Saint Margaret Mary's church was only a few minutes from the station, but Josie didn't really need this distraction now. The investigation into Henry Trumbo's murder had started to take shape. She could feel all the momentum moving toward Gaby Johnston, the way it always did when the prime suspect matched the evidence. Piece after piece was falling into place completing the puzzle, and eventually the proof would be insurmountable and impossible to deny.

Josie recognized Father O'Reilly as a tortured soul, and she felt sorry for him. She couldn't explain why it mattered to her, but the man was obviously damaged and not helping him felt like kicking a puppy or ignoring a hungry baby. Maybe it was her Catholic upbringing, but something inside her was pushing the guilt buttons, so she'd sit back and enjoy the car's air conditioning for as long as it took to get there and then waste a few precious minutes helping him deal with his latest spiritual bogeyman.

The church's front door was closed. Josie went around to the side entrance leading to the catechism room. That door was propped open. She went inside and called out to the priest but there was no answer. All the lights were on but she didn't see anyone inside. She pushed open the gate to the altar, genuflected and peeked into the sacristy.

"Captain," a high-pitched voice called from somewhere behind her, echoing in the cavernous space.

Josie walked out toward the altar again and looked around. The church was empty.

"Up here."

She looked up at the loft where the organ was and the choir would normally stand during Mass. It was every cop's Achilles heel. Why is it we never look up, she thought. Father O'Reilly was there, but he wasn't alone. A tall blond man stood beside him.

"What's going on, Father?" she asked.

"Actually, I invited you. I thought you should be here," the man said.

Josie knew that voice, but it took a moment for her mind to process the connections. It was Gaby. Her hair had been cut short. She wore a man's shirt and pants, but it was her. A chill crept down Josie's spine as the picture came into focus and everything suddenly made sense.

"Hello James or Gaby or whatever you're calling yourself these days," Josie said in a tone that sounded a lot more confident than she felt. Her shirt was sticking to her back and beads of sweat started trickling down her arms and neck. There was something crazy going on, and from this position, Josie didn't feel good about her chances of controlling it. "What are we doing here?" she asked.

"I knew you'd figure it out, you and Marge, two clever girls," Gaby said. Father O'Reilly moaned, and she slapped him hard across his face. "Shut up," she ordered in a deeper voice.

"Why don't you come down here where we can talk," Josie said, trying to sound calm. She wanted to run up there but wasn't sure what Gaby would do to the priest if she moved. She looked around for the door that led to the loft. It had to be in the vestibule on the other side of the inner doors and she'd never reach it without Gaby knowing and reacting, giving her too much time to do whatever it was she intended to do.

"Are you all right, Father?" Josie asked.

"He's fine for the moment. I don't think we'll come down though. By the way, did I mention I have a gun? Ironic really, it's one of Henry's, so I'd prefer if you didn't come up here."

"I know it was you who attacked those drag queens," Josie said, her hand resting on the butt of her .45 waiting for whatever might come next. She wanted to keep Gaby talking until she could figure out what to do or until somebody at the police station realized she'd been gone too long and came looking.

"You didn't buy that whole queen-killer scenario? Kind of figured you wouldn't . . . hmmm, maybe I should've killed one or two of them, but Henry was the only one I wanted dead . . . well, there was Castro . . . but that was a kind of mercy killing, don't you think?"

"Why?" Josie asked, moving as she talked to get a better view. There was no cover where she was standing but it was clear she wasn't the target of Gaby's anger . . . yet.

"Henry had a fickle side. I shared my tiny inheritance with him, practically gave him a briefcase full of the city's money, and he thanks me by fucking that insect sergeant and the Kessler boy's bovine wife behind my back. Anyway, if I hadn't killed Henry, Susan probably would've done it eventually. I mean look at what she did to poor Patrick."

"That's why you killed Trumbo, because he slept with Castro and Susan Kessler?"

"I know it sounds crazy when you say it that way. I sort of lost my temper. Henry said some hurtful things . . . I said some things. Before you know it, we're in bed naked and I'm trying to whack off his head with a rusty old butcher knife . . . I was sorry when I calmed down, even dressed him up in my lace panties, but dead's dead and resurrection isn't for the likes of us folk. Is it Father?" Gaby asked, slapping the priest on the back of his head. "Pay attention."

Father O'Reilly kept his eyes closed and pressed his lips together as if he expected another blow. He stood there frozen, looking too frightened to move or speak.

"I can understand why you might want to kill Henry and even Castro, but what's your problem with the priest? Why not let him come down here? You've still got the gun," Josie said. She could tell Father O'Reilly was practically catatonic and getting worse. His shoulders were hunched forward, hands clasped as he stood near the railing. From some fifteen feet below, she could see his thin body vibrating.

"I don't think so. I never told you Henry and I grew up in this neighborhood," she said, her voice suddenly light and happy again. "Santa Monica Boulevard bun boys," she boasted, pacing behind the priest. "We were in love and ran away from home to live on Hollywood streets paved with gold stars. Sounded so romantic . . . wasn't. If the Regency Arms could talk, what stories it would tell. Isn't that right Father? These men of God took care of us," she said, indicating the church around her. "Nurtured our bodies and souls . . . mostly our firm teenage bodies."

"I don't know you," Father O'Reilly whined in a quivering voice. "I've been here less than a year."

Gaby shoved him hard, nearly causing the unsteady man to fall over the railing. "What's the difference? You're all alike . . . you, or something just like you, made us mis- fits . . . monsters," Gaby said, holding her arms out, gun in one hand, and turning around like a runway model. She stopped and put the muzzle near the tip of the priest's nose and said, "We all know what monsters do to their creators."

"Why did you want me here?" Josie shouted, hoping to take the attention off Father O'Reilly. Gaby was growing progressively more agitated and irrational.

"Game's over, needed to tell someone my sins . . . not this old pervert. Church seemed like the perfect place and you, well you're not the sort to get all emotionally involved, are you?"

"So talk to me, Gaby," Josie said, as she watched one of the doors in front of her and directly under the loft open slowly. Marge stood there staring at her from the vesti- bule. She had her .45 semiauto in one hand and, with the other, pointed at the loft indicating she was going up. "But put that gun away, it's making me nervous," Josie added quickly and scratched her head with two fingers knowing Marge would understand there were two people up there. Marge nodded and gave her a thumbs-up before carefully, quietly letting the door close.

"No, I think I'll be James for a while," Gaby said, strad- dling the rail with her back partly to Josie. "Henry pre- ferred James . . . but then Henry was a shit, so who cares." She laughed and punched Father O'Reilly on the shoulder. "That's funny old man."

With Gaby turned slightly away from her, Josie finally saw an opportunity to draw her weapon, and maybe if she acted quickly enough prevent a deadly confrontation between Gaby and Marge. It would be tricky from this awk- ward angle to shoot up into the loft and hit her target, but there was no doubt in Josie's mind that Gaby was on the verge of killing or seriously harming the priest. She drew her .45, pointed it at Gaby's long torso, but had barely touched the trigger when an object crossed her sights.

It happened so quickly, she wasn't certain if Father O'Reilly jumped or Gaby had pushed him, but he was hanging onto the other side of the rail desperately trying not to fall and Gaby was out of Josie's sight. The priest's feet were kicking wildly attempting to find something solid to hold his weight, but his fingers were slipping and in seconds he fell with a sickening thud onto the tile floor below. He landed on his back motionless just a few feet from Josie, and she'd heard what sounded like bones cracking when he hit.

She didn't stop to check on him but ran out the door into the vestibule and up the flight of stairs to the loft. Before she reached the top landing, a shot rang out, echoing in the empty church like the retort from a cannon.

When she got there, the door to the loft was open. She stopped, holstered her gun again and finally took a deep breath. Marge was standing over Gaby's lifeless body lying on the floor in a fetal position, her head engulfed by an expanding pool of blood. Her right temple had a dirty star-shaped hole with ragged torn edges. The skin around the wound had charring of the tissue caused by the heat of a revolver's muzzle blast pressed against her head. The nauseous odor of lead mixed with burning flesh hung over the body. The gun was several feet away, probably kicked away by Marge, but there was no chance Gaby would ever be a danger to anyone again.

"You okay?" Josie asked and noticed there were spots of splattered blood on Marge's clothes and bare arms. For an instant, the question of who had pulled the trigger entered Josie's mind, but she dismissed it, not willing to even consider her friend capable of such an act. Besides, gunshot residue didn't lie and Marge wasn't that stupid.

"Killed herself," Marge said, as if she'd read Josie's thoughts. She shook her head and turned away. "Fucking waste, I'll call for an ambulance and backup." She took a few steps, stopped, and handed Josie a piece of paper from the back pocket of her jeans. "This is what I came to show you," she said.

It was a copy of a booking photo from the San Francisco PD. The picture was a younger James Johnston, but it was unmistakably Gaby too, her hair cut short, looking the way she did today.

Josie could hear the wail of sirens in the distance before she got back downstairs where Father O'Reilly was lying unconscious on the tile floor, but he was breathing and had a weak pulse. She pulled a cloth trimmed with crochet from under a statue of the Virgin Mary and pressed it on the back of his head to stop the bleeding until the paramedics arrived. Even though she knew Father O'Reilly couldn't be held accountable for the acts of other priests, Josie's feelings toward the fragile man had changed; she felt less empathetic after witnessing Gaby's mental collapse. She doubted any priest was entirely responsible for the James-to-Gaby deterioration and certainly no one but Gaby should be answerable for her criminal actions, but Josie wondered what a person would have to endure to get that screwed up.

She was a cop not a psychiatrist, but even Josie recognized full-blown, ready-for-the-asylum insanity when she saw it and her experience told her James Johnston didn't get that way entirely on his own.

EIGHTEEN

Behan and Richards were on their way back from Manhattan Beach when Marge radioed for an ambulance and assistance. Martin was the first to arrive at the church, and she sent a team of detectives to the hospital with Father O'Reilly before making all the necessary calls and starting the crime scene investigation. The SID photographer had nearly finished his job by the time the coroner's investigator arrived, and when Behan got there a few minutes later, his partner had everything under control.

It took awhile for Marge to answer all Behan's questions and fill in gaps for the homicide supervisor, but he listened intently as she told him the background on James Johnston who had fooled all of them pretending to be a woman. Behan was relieved they had their killer and asked if Gaby had said anything to Marge before she killed herself. Marge shook her head, but Josie noticed her friend seemed uncomfortable.

"It's hard to believe she was a man," Behan said, standing over Gaby's body, and then turning to Martin, asked, "Did you check to be sure he was a man?"

Josie and the coroner exchanged looks. Here we go again, she thought.

"No," Martin said, moving closer to Behan. "Who gives a shit? Investigation's closed, suspect's deceased. We clean up the mess, do the reports, and let God judge the miserable asshole," she said, expressionless, repeating one of his favorite maxims.

He shook his head and walked away without a word, but Josie was relieved that it was beginning to look as if they might actually be able to work together. Unfortunately, Martin was gradually morphing into a short sober version of the grumpy redhead.

She expected a sarcastic remark or two from Marge, but her friend seemed preoccupied and not ready to engage. Marge waited until the coroner took the body before going back to the station. On her way out of the church, she'd made a half-hearted remark to Behan about a cross-dresser being prettier than her. Josie figured she was having a difficult time accepting the truth about someone she liked and trusted so much, but there was something else, and she wondered what had happened between Marge and Gaby during the few seconds it took her to climb those stairs and reach the loft.

A thorough crime scene investigation in the expansive church took technicians and detectives most of the day to complete. The team who'd accompanied Father O'Reilly to the hospital had been replaced by Richards, who called Behan at the station after dinner to tell him the priest was awake and intermittently alert enough to answer questions. Father O'Reilly was ready to talk to them, but he had specifically asked Josie to be there.

"You all right with this, boss?" Behan asked, after he told her what the priest had requested.

"Not really, but if it helps get to the truth, I'll go," Josie said.

She was tired and, like Marge, still uncertain how to deal with the way things turned out. There might not be anything sinister or unseemly about Father O'Reilly but Josie was done with him and the church for a while. She wanted to go home, take a cold shower, wash the dried sweat and smell of death off her body and then sleep for at least a day. Disappointment was a difficult emotion for her to deal with because she wasn't wired to regret anything or depend on other people. Nevertheless, for reasons she'd probably never understand, losing Gaby bothered her a lot.

RICHARDS MET them in the cafeteria at Cedars-Sinai hospital in Los Angeles. He wanted to brief them on the priest's condition before they sat down to talk with Father O'Reilly.

"The man's a mess," Richards said.

They were seated in a booth drinking coffee and sharing a bag of potato chips.

"That's no revelation," Behan said.

"He can't stop shaking and the fall gave him double vision but he insists he's okay to talk to us. I wanted to prepare you. The doctor says he might not make it through the night. His back and arm are broken and a lot of other vital parts I can't remember. He's got most of his head bandaged and it's in a heavy brace, not a pretty sight."

"Has he told you anything, yet?" Josie asked. She thought Kyle looked gaunt and very tired. His beard had a couple days' growth, and she knew he probably hadn't slept much for at least that long. "They've got decent food here," she said. "You want to grab a bite before we go up. The padre's not going anywhere."

"No, thanks, let's get this over with before he can't talk. He did tell me Gaby surprised him while he was praying at the altar, and forced him at gunpoint to call you. While they were waiting, he said Gaby rambled on blaming the church for his screwed-up life, said he'd been abused by them and sold his body on the boulevard because he felt worthless, blah, blah blah. You know the story. Ready to go?" he asked, sliding out of the booth.

She'd never seen Richards this impatient or fidgety. Maybe it was fatigue or perhaps, like her, he'd had his fill of these screwed-up people.

They were in the right tower, so they took the elevator up to the ICU and followed Richards to the priest's bed. It was an isolated space away from other patients where Richards had assigned a uniformed officer to keep watch and let him know if the priest's condition changed.

The curtains were closed, concealing the bed. Josie pulled them back and saw O'Reilly, or a battered version of him, in bed in a full body cast, his bandaged head held steady in a stainless steel frame that appeared to be screwed onto his body. A single sheet covered him and his face was swollen with a rainbow of colors, mostly purple.

Josie let Behan take the lead. He could ask the questions and conduct the interview. She was content to be a bystander this time.

"Father, did you know James Johnston, also known as Gaby Johnston, before today?" Behan asked.

"No," Father O'Reilly whispered, blinking his eyes with a nervous tic.

Behan asked him to repeat in his own words what Gaby had told him. It was obvious the priest didn't have the stamina to go through a prolonged interrogation. After taking a sip of water with Josie's assistance, he told them what he knew.

"He told me he ran away at fifteen with another boy . . . his parents disinherited him, but his sister left him everything when she died," he said, haltingly but without a trace of stutter. "He got a law degree in San Francisco and a job here pretending to be a woman."

"Did he say anything about a man called Henry Trumbo?" Richards asked.

"Was that his lover?" the priest asked. Richards nodded and Father O'Reilly said, "Yes, he felt guilty, wanted him back, but kept saying it wasn't his fault. He screamed at me that Henry was a slut . . . a selfish cheater. He deserved to die. It was horrible," the priest said, and his whole body seemed to tremble.

"Did he talk about Sergeant Castro?" Behan asked.

"No, but he said he should've killed the lawyer."

"What lawyer?" Richards asked.

"I don't know," Father O'Reilly whispered and grimaced in pain. His eyes closed for a few seconds before he struggled to open them again. "Captain Corsino, you have to believe me. I could never do what that man accused me of. God knows I'm an unworthy priest in many ways, but I'm not evil."

She got up, touched his hand and said, "Get some sleep, Father," and as she left the room, thought, if you did, I hope you're on that midnight express straight to hell with the rest of the child molesters and burn there for eternity.

She waited for Richards and Behan in the visitors' lounge where they joined her a few minutes later.

"Anything?" she asked.

"No," Behan said. "He's comatose. Wonder which lawyer he meant."

"Marvin Beaumont," Josie said. "It has to be. He was at the Regency the night Gaby killed Trumbo. I'm betting he saw a lot more than he's telling us."

"Let's pick him up and ask," Richards said.

"How about you two pick him up, and I'll take Red's car back to Hollywood," Josie said. "I've still got a station to run."

She could've gone with them, but she'd had her fill of this case, one disillusionment after another. Nothing was what it seemed to be or should have been—a double dose of animal life in the Hollywood zoo.

In less than an hour, they had Beaumont back in the station. Josie was working in her office, but curiosity got the better of her and she joined them in the interrogation room. She could tell immediately the lawyer was no match for the redhead and Richards. They never mentioned Gaby had killed herself earlier, but Behan did say Gaby confessed to Trumbo's murder and hinted she'd seen Beaumont at the Regency Arms.

"I couldn't say anything, honestly," Beaumont whined. "She swore she'd kill me if I did. You saw what she did to Henry. I was terrified, and then she put his gun in my office. She was telling me she could frame me for his murder. You must see I wasn't in any position to do or say anything."

"What exactly did you see that night?" Richards asked.

"Nothing, I saw her leave the room. I recognized her immediately. I knew she was Henry's lover . . . well, one of them. She warned me if she ever got arrested she'd tell the police everything she knew."

"Knew about what?" Behan asked.

Beaumont hesitated, looked up at the ceiling for a second and mumbled, "She didn't tell you, did she?" He sighed and said, "Oh, what's the difference? Trumbo told her what he did for me . . . special techniques we used to get bigger settlements."

"Special techniques, that's an interesting concept," Richards said. "How did Trumbo know Patrick Kessler?"

"I drew up the legal documents and made the arrangements for all Patrick's upcoming hormone treatments and surgeries. Henry Trumbo was my employee. He was supposed to pick up the initial payment from Patrick in front of that trashy hotel where Susan killed him. Susan didn't have the money, so I know Henry took it."

"Okay, so Patrick's dead and Trumbo has your money and you're trying to tell us you were going to a party with him that night," Richards said.

"I lied. I went to the hotel to demand my money, but Trumbo was dead, and Gaby Johnston killed him. She has my money."

"Actually, it's the city of LA's money, but there's more bad news. Gaby was a man; he's dead, and you're under arrest," Behan said.

"For what? I'm the victim here," Beaumont said and got very quiet. His brow wrinkled as he tried to comprehend what Behan had just told him.

"For interfering with a murder investigation for starters, but I'm sure if I think a minute I can come up with more charges."

"Captain," Beaumont pleaded, looking at her as if she held the last life preserver on his sinking ship.

"Sorry counselor, can't help you," she said and left the room.

She went back to her office and called Commander Perry to fill him in on what had happened, giving him every detail and explaining how the three homicide investigations had been closed. He seemed irritated that she had called in the middle of the night, but thanked her for the "good work" and told her to be certain to put all the details in her morning report. She did and threw the report in the out-basket for Maki to distribute in the morning.

The couch looked inviting, but Josie wasn't going to sleep there. She took her purse and briefcase, locked the wardrobe, waved at the watch commander and walked out the front door. There was only one place she wanted to be tonight and that's where she was going.

NINETEEN

Josie drove straight to Pasadena and pulled into the garage. She went in through the kitchen door, turned on all the lights and opened every window in the three-story house. A cool night breeze filled the rooms. The heat wave had broken and she felt a surge of energy in the chilly draft of air.

After a cold shower, she sat in the den in her favorite lounger, wearing a shabby bathrobe, with a towel around her wet hair, drinking a glass of brandy. Every superficial trace of a stressful day had been washed away, and she felt revived, ready to begin anew. She always understood it took a certain kind of person to do police work for as many years as she had without damaging not only her family, but her mind and soul. Her objective had always been to retire with her psyche and loved ones intact, but these last two homicides together with what was happening in her personal life had tested that resolve.

But, here she was still willing to be in the game . . . alone, but strong enough to know she'd be back at work in the morning and her relationship with her son would endure despite the divorce and his tiny, irritating companion. Thinking about Jake made her unhappy. Her marriage was a failure and she didn't tolerate failure well, but loving Kyle allowed her to believe she might get another shot at making marriage work.

The doorbell rang and she pushed the chair into a sitting position. The clock on the shelf over the bar said it was three A.M. She took the revolver she kept in the desk drawer and went down to the first floor as the bell rang again.

She turned up the outside light and looked through the bay window curtain hoping to see Richards, but Marge was standing on her porch holding up a bottle of wine.

Josie opened the door and as Marge brushed past her asked, "Did you lose Red again?"

"Nope, he's still with Martin finishing the paperwork," Marge said, walking straight to the dining room and rummaging in the credenza to find a corkscrew.

"You worried there's something going on there?" she asked, knowing Behan had a wandering eye, but the dour plain Martin was certainly no match for Marge.

Marge laughed as she poured wine into two glasses, "No, danger there, Corsino. She'd be more interested in you than Red, but Miss Ann's significant other at the moment is Nancy Springer on your burglary table. Is Kyle here?" she asked, handing Josie a glass.

"Not yet, he's probably still at the station with Behan," Josie said, shaking her head. She'd never had a clue about Martin. "I'm not good at this gender bending thing. I don't really care, but it's confusing the hell out of me."

"Like I've always told you, Corsino, you think too much. Life's complicated. Go with the fucking flow."

"Did the flow bring you to my front door at three in the morning?" Josie asked. She could sense Marge wanted to talk about something, but she was having a hard time saying it.

"The sonnofabitch thanked me."

"Who?"

"Gaby or James or whatever the hell his name was. Before he blew his fucking brains out and probably destroyed years of hormone treatments, he thanked me for being the only real friend he'd ever had and told me it was never about the money. He said I'd find it, every penny, in the briefcase on his kitchen table in Manhattan Beach. Don't worry. I already booked it with all the ledgers Patrick kept . . . a gigantic nail in Sergeant Miller's legal coffin."

"That's great," Josie said. "So what's the problem?"

"I don't know. He was as crazy as a schizophrenic chimpanzee on steroids, and I was ready to blow his confused ass away if I had to, so why do I feel bad?"

"Because in your other life you were Mother Teresa and you hate to see people suffer," Josie said, knowing she didn't have a serious answer, and if she did, it wouldn't help.

"Yeah, that's probably it . . . thanks, asshole."

Like her, Marge instinctively had to understand that dwelling on or acknowledging a sense of loss or emotional attachment in any investigation was deadly. If they wanted to survive in this business, those feelings got buried and forgotten.

"We're gonna be okay," Josie said, and she was pretty sure that was the truth.